Matthew Horace Hayes

Indian racing reminiscences

Matthew Horace Hayes

Indian racing reminiscences

ISBN/EAN: 9783337304966

Printed in Europe, USA, Canada, Australia, Japan

Cover: Foto ©Andreas Hilbeck / pixelio.de

More available books at **www.hansebooks.com**

BY

M. HORACE HAYES

(Late Captain " The Buffs ")

AUTHOR OF " RIDING ON THE FLAT AND ACROSS COUNTRY," "VETERINARY NOTES
FOR HORSE-OWNERS," "TRAINING AND HORSE MANAGEMENT
IN INDIA," ETC.

ILLUSTRATED BY J. K. FERGUSON.

London :

W. THACKER & CO., 87, NEWGATE STREET.

CALCUTTA : THACKER, SPINK & CO.

BOMBAY : THACKER & CO., LIMITED.

1883.

PREFACE.

———◦◦◦———

AFTER leaving India in 1880, I contributed to the Calcutta *Englishman* several articles under the title of "Indian Racing Reminiscences." These papers were so well received by the Indian Press and Public, that I determined to produce them in book form. The proprietor of the Calcutta journal, on the staff of which I have been for some years, generously waived his part-claim to their copyright. On rearranging the material I had by me, I found so much to add and revise, that more than two-thirds of the present book now appears for the first time.

After going to press, I received letters from the well-known Indian jockeys, Oscar Dignum and poor Tom Cozens, both grand horsemen, who enclosed accounts of the chief incidents of their lives for this book. I regret extremely that these communications came too late. Dignum, who thoroughly deserves his good luck, still continues his successful engagement as trainer to H.H. the Rajah of Paikpara. This native Prince is a beau-ideal sportsman : he keeps a large stable of horses, spares no expense in their purchase and management, never bets a penny, and races entirely for sport.

I am much indebted to my friend Mr. J. K. Ferguson for his trouble in illustrating this book.

M. H. HAYES.

Junior Army and Navy Club,
    St. James's Street, London, S.W.
  21st March, 1883.

T. Comyns Cole, Esq.

Page IX

THACKER, SPINK & C? CALCUTTA.

DEDICATION.

—◦◇◦—

JUNIOR ARMY AND NAVY CLUB,

ST. JAMES'S ST., S.W.

21st March, 1883.

DEAR COLE,—Long before I had the pleasure of meeting you and the honour of gaining your friendship, I, in common with every old Indian I have ever met who was fond of racing, regarded you almost as a personal friend, for you used to bring yourself very near to us by your charming letters in the Allahabad journal on Sport in England. By dedicating this small book to you, I venture to act as the spokesman of our Indian racing public, in expressing our gratitude and kindly feelings towards *Asmodeus* of the *Pioneer*, whose graphic descriptions of stirring scenes in the old country have brightened many hours we might have otherwise wearily spent bewailing our exile.

Believe me,

Yours sincerely,

M. H. HAYES.

To J. Comyns Cole, Esq.,
The Beefsteak Club,
King William Street, W.C.

CONTENTS.

CHAPTER I.

	PAGE
Round the Cape to India	1
Meean Meer	5

CHAPTER II.

	PAGE
Indian Racing	11
Breeding Horses in India	13
Walers and Arabs	15
Lotteries	17
An Indian Race Card	19

CHAPTER III.

	PAGE
The Seventh Hussars	21
The Umballa Meeting of 1868	23
Highlander	25
English Arabs	27
Caliph	28
Tartar and Countess	31

CHAPTER IV.

PAGE

The 7th Hussars at Meean Meer   .   34

Sir Lepel Griffin   34

CHAPTER V.

The 5th Fusiliers   38

The Gordon Highlanders   .   .   39

Cœur-de-lion and Ranelagh at Sealkote   .   43

The Jullundur Meeting of 1869 .   45

A Game at Pyramids   48

CHAPTER VI.

Captain Dudley   50

CHAPTER VII.

The 77th Regiment .   .   57

The 35th Native Infantry   .   58

The Adjutant's Horse   58

Our Colonel   ,   .   .   59

Objection   63

My First Attempts at Racing and Training   .   64

The Time Test .   .   65

Jack Tobin   .   .   68

Sir John Astley .   .   .   72

Sealkote Races, 1870 .   .   73

CHAPTER VIII.

PAGE

The Meerut Spring Meeting of 1871 .   .   77

CHAPTER IX.

Dehra Doon   82

The Dehra Races of 1871 .   .   .   83

Aboo Janoub and Abdool Rahman   .   86

Gooch and Dignum   .   .   89

Ranelagh and Karpos   .   .   .   92

Williams   .   .   96

CHAPTER X.

"Bricky" Collins   .   .   99

Vanderdecken   100

Jaffir and Roe   .   103

CHAPTER XI.

Cawnpore   107

Jack O'Connor .   .   .   109

Aligurh   111

Lucknow Races, 1872   .   113

Hawkestone   .   .   114

Cawnpore Races, 1872   .   120

Lucknow Races, 1873   .   .   127

Mr. William Thacker   .   .   .   131

CHAPTER XII.

		PAGE
Lurline		133
The Constable Cup		136
Gamester		138
War Eagle		141
Cawnpore Races, 1874		144
Daybreak and Bowman		145

CHAPTER XIII.

		PAGE
The Three Districts		151
The Planters		151
Mr. Laurence Crowdy		152
The Studds		153
Life in Tirhoot		155
Charlie Webb		156
Bob Crowdy		158
Dawk Driving		161
Mr. Abbott		162
Racing		163
The Behar Mounted Rifles		164
Polo		164
Jimmy Macleod		167
Rowly Hudson		168

CHAPTER XIV.

PAGE

Rebecca 172

Big Fences . 174

Mr. Short . . 178

Captain Papillon . . 178

CHAPTER XV.

General " Monty " Turnbull . . 180

CHAPTER XVI.

Lord Ulick Browne . . 193

CHAPTER XVII.

Red Gauntlet and Fairymount . . . 202

Cawnpore 206

Mr. Frank Johnson 210

Mr. Short 211

Congestion of the Liver . 213

Sikundur 215

Coomassie . . . 219

W. F. . . . 220

Jovial and Raven . 221

Hermit and the Sweep . . . 222

CHAPTER XVIII.

PAGE

Cachar	231
Tea Planters	232
Horses in Eastern Bengal	235
Exile of Erin	237
Munipuri Polo Players	242
Nagas	245
Indian Jails	246

CHAPTER XIX.

Dehra in 1878	248
Allahabad	251
"Roaring"	253
The 22nd Regiment	254
Vesper	255
Dolly Varden	257
Shoeing	259
Lucknow in 1879	261
Fisherman	262

CHAPTER XX.

The Staff Corps	266
"The Buffs"	266
Meerut	267
Reformation	271

CONTENTS.

		PAGE.
Mr. MacDougall	. .	276
Bismillah . .	. .	277
Mr. Anderson's Horses	.	280
Speechless	. .	284
Rampore Beauleah Races, 1879 .	. .	287

LIST OF PORTRAITS.

Captain M. H. Hayes . . . *Frontispiece*
J. Comyns Cole, Esq. . . . . *Dedication*
Captain Joy, 7th Hussars . . . . *p.* 21
Colonel Dudley Sampson 51
Captain Franks, "The Buffs " 93
J. Anderson, Esq., V.S., R.H.A. . . . 123
D'Arcy Thuillier, Esq., "The Cameronians" . 125
Harry Bowen 145
J. J. Macleod, Esq. ("Mr. John") . 151
R. Crowdy, Esq. ("Mr. Bob") . . . 159
H. E. Abbott, Esq. 163
Rowland Hudson, Esq. 169
General Turnbull . . . 181
Bill Brewty . . . 189
Lord Ulick Browne 193
Bertie Short, Esq. 211
Major Kinchant, 11th Hussars . . . 217
Lord William Beresford . . . 249
Captain Charsley Thomas . . . 271
D. D. MacDougall, Esq., 13th Hussars . . . 277
H. H. Coomar Indra Singh of Paikpara . . 289

INDIAN RACING REMINISCENCES.

CHAPTER I.

ROUND THE CAPE TO INDIA—MEEAN MEER.

FTER a Voyage from Gravesend round the Cape of a hundred and thirty-seven days in the good ship *Dilbhur*, we arrived at Kurrachee in the month of March, 1868. We had about five hundred men on board belonging to detachments of the Royal Regiment, 5th Fusiliers, 109th Regiment, and of the Horse Artillery, which I commanded. Our navigation was regulated by the old maxim of slow but sure, for our skipper's wife, who was on board, did not approve of carrying on sail to any great extent, and her worthy and obliging husband dutifully obeyed her orders on all occasions. Our commanding officer was an old colonel with a young wife, so he left the rest of us very much to our own devices. We accordingly got on well together, and had not an unhappy time of it. My detachment of about a hundred and fifty were almost all recruits, who violently resented any interference from the infantry non-commissioned officers: the consequence being that there were frequent courts-martial on my gunners and drivers, with, now and then, a flogging parade. I got on well with my men as I was fond of athletics, and used to encourage sparring and other sports among them to while away the tedium of the voyage. When they came into collision with the infantry non-commissioned officers they used to collect *en masse* and openly defy authority. On these occasions I was obliged to volunteer to go forward to the forecastle and secure the ringleaders, as they would allow no one else to interfere with them, although they cheerfully submitted to any order I gave. Whenever one of my men was to be "tied up," my soldier servant always came to me the first thing in the morning, and asked me to give him a bottle of gin, as "he felt very queer inside." Before being flogged, the prisoner always begged to be allowed a drink of water, which was invariably supplied to him by my batman out of a capacious pannikin. It would have rejoiced the heart of a Blue Ribbon Army man, had one been present, to have seen the exhilarating effect that water had on the culprit, who used to take his fifty with the utmost fortitude for the honour of his corps, and with evident satisfaction at the prospect of finishing the remainder of the contents of the friendly can, which, strange to say, smelt strongly of Old Tom on one occasion when I found it in my cabin after having been used for the sufferer's benefit.

Despite these occasional outbreaks of insubordination, we were a fairly contented party on board, and, as most of us were young, we were happy on the slightest provocation. We had immense resources in whist, *écarté*, ship's quoits, shooting at bottles, angling for Cape pigeons, trying to catch sharks, or boarding some vessel near at hand when becalmed, boxing, playing high cockalorum, and follow my leader up the rigging, getting up private theatricals, and writing for our manuscript newspaper ; while we had always the serious business of eating and drinking before our eyes. Life on board ship is a sadly tedious affair for passengers who have no congenial spirits, nor any all-sufficing pursuit of their own. I remember once coming from

Madras round the Cape in a crazy old hulk with only four or five passengers who were not lively. I was little more than a boy then, so fretted for amusement. Like a convict who spends the leisure of years in carving rings and imitation books out of stone with a rusty nail, I seized with enthusiasm the idea, suggested by one of the sailors, of cutting a chain and anchor out of a piece of wood. This industry of idleness kept me occupied for the greater part of the hundred and fifty-three days of our voyage, for, the wood being brittle, the links would often break. As my *magnum opus* approached completion, I used, in thinking of the triumph I would secure in exhibiting it, to overlook the petty miseries of life; forget that we had run short of milk and sugar for our tea; that we were reduced to "hard tack" and "salt tack," without even "soup and bully" as a change; and that a month sweltering in the "doldrums" had made me spend all my spare cash on claret and sparkling wines, so that by the time we were off Madeira and had bade good-bye to the trade-winds, I had hardly enough to buy a bottle of ship's rum. As soon as we got into the Channel and had picked up our pilot, I chucked the once precious chain and anchor to the only child on board, who promptly broke it to test its utility. Since then I have had many chains and anchors of various forms and materials. The last one I remember was what I then thought poetry, but now know to have been very poor doggerel, which I made during a month when snowed up once in the Himalayas. It shared the fate of its many predecessors.

After a tedious journey up the Indus I arrived with my detachment at Meean Meer, which is a large military station within four miles of Lahore, the capital of the Punjab. I have never been able to find out from man or book the reason why this site was chosen for a cantonment. The Sikhs had, in former days, made of it a resting-place for their dead. The entire surface of the ground is covered by a stratum, several feet thick, of *kunkur*, which is a deposit of the drift period, formed of nodules composed of lime, silica, and alumina. This makes the soil so barren that hardly a blade of grass, let alone a shrub, will grow on it without special cultivation. Various attempts at planting trees met with failure, until at last some ingenious person conceived the idea of boring holes right through the *kunkur*, and planting in them. The residents of this station were yearly impaled on the horns of a dilemma, for if they left nature to herself, the heat from the white plain was beyond all endurance in the hot weather ; while if they allowed the land to be cultivated by irrigation from the branches of the canal, fever and ague smote them down.

As Meean Meer is north of the latitude of the regular rains, the hot weather continues from March well into October.   Words fail to describe the heat of that blast-furnacelike season.   My first experience of it was that the thermometer in my room rarely stood under 98° F. for the greater part of the day, although the house was kept shut from sunrise till long after sunset.   As there was no steady wind, as in the North-West Provinces, we were unable to use the grateful *khus khus tatties*, which are made of bamboo screens covered with a thick layer of a kind of fragrant grass. When a dry, hot wind blows, they are placed to windward in front of an open door-way and kept wet with water, the result being that the air rushing through is rendered delightfully cool.   We, of course, employed *punkahs*, but they do not lower the temperature, although they make it more bearable. Sometimes, towards the evenings of these hot days, we had a remission.   The fiery sky suddenly became over-cast ; the troops of crows which had sat on the branches of the stunted trees for hours before, gasping between

life and death, with their beaks wide open, now flew
hither and thither in wild dismay and uttering cries of
alarm ; while far away in the southern horizon rose a
black band of cloud, which came dust-laden from the
Rajpootana desert, to wreak its fury on us. In a few
moments all was darkness, and then the storm of wind
and sand beat against our houses till they shook them
to their very foundations. Generally within half an hour
the tempest had spent its force, perhaps with an ac-
companiment of thunder and lightning and a few drops
of rain. And then we opened our doors, got into our
baths to wash off the thick coating of dust that enveloped
us, reclothed ourselves in cotton garments which still
glowed from the former heat, made our servants dust
off the sand that lay on every table and chair, and
issued out to find the air cool and bracing, and to enjoy
the delightful prospect of getting a good night's rest,
which cannot be obtained under ordinary conditions
during the hot weather at Meean Meer. While a dust-
storm lasts there is often a marked rise in the temperature of the air. I remember noting once at this station
that, towards the end of one of these tempests, the
thermometer registered 109° Fahr. in the open air at
nine o'clock at night.

Such was the place at which commenced my experiences in racing and training.

The artillery at Meean Meer were, at that time, composed of a Horse Artillery battery, F F., commanded by Major Delane, brother of the then editor of *The Times;* F-19, the battery to which I belonged, and a couple of garrison batteries. Delane took great pride in his men and horses, spent lots of money on them, and had, as his reward, one of the smartest batteries I have ever seen on parade. We were at first not so lucky, for our captain was hard up, was married, had a large family, and economized his contract allowance : the result being that the men were not able to turn out the horses in proper style, as the animals' clothing and stable gear were of a wretchedly inadequate description. Happily for the service, Government have long since abolished this allowance, which "slack" and needy captains were, in those days, far too apt to regard as a perquisite for their own especial use. After some time, we got a new commanding officer in Major Fitzgerald, who came to us imbued with all the grand traditions of that glorious corps, the old Bengal Horse Artillery. He was a smart officer, brave soldier, and handsome fellow ; he was a kind and indulgent friend to every officer and man in his battery, and was loved by us all. Besides the Gunners, we had at this station the 85th K.L.I., two Native Infantry regiments, and the 9th Bengal Cavalry, commanded by Colonel Campbell, who was known throughout the Presidency as " Steady Chick," from his fondness of betting, when he " fancied " himself at billiards, a *chick* (four rupees), no more and no less. He was one of the many old Indians who have set themselves the task of serving thirty-eight years to obtain what was called their off-reckonings, and which consisted of a pension of £1100 a year, and, despite having patched themselves up by various trips to the Hills, have failed, by dying, to secure the coveted reward of this test of endurance. His adjutant, Dudley Sampson, to whom I shall allude further on, was one of the best gentleman riders we have ever had in India. The 85th were a good sporting lot, who, although they were not very well off, were always ready to lend a hand at anything in the way of sport that might be got up.

At this time the 7th Hussars were stationed at Sealkote, about seventy miles north of Meean Meer. The 5th Fusiliers were at Ferozepore, on the other side of the Sutlej, a little over forty miles south. The

Gordon Highlanders were about eighty miles to the east at Jullundur. The 106th were to the south-east at Umballa; while far away to the west, at Mooltan, Mr. Torkington of the Gunners and Mr. Tucker of the Police had a string of very fair horses. The Artillery were well to the fore with Mr. Swinton's Challenger, "Pop" Gill's Rememhan, and the Hon. Ralph Hare's Jurham and Jerry.

The generous though keen rivalry which existed between the stables that represented these different stations was the one redeeming feature of the Punjab, from a sporting point of view.

CHAPTER II.

INDIAN RACING—BREEDING HORSES IN INDIA—WALERS
AND ARABS— LOTTERIES—AN INDIAN RACE CARD.

THE system under which racing is carried on in India, differs so materially from that which is followed in England, that it may not be without interest if I here briefly describe its more salient peculiarities.

In India almost every one owns horses, as they cost little to keep in that country, while the exigencies of the climate render their employment all but imperative. The bulk of the European population are men more or less in the prime of life, who have a good deal of time on their hands, and are fairly well off as regards money. Hence, like all Englishmen under similar circumstances, their thoughts naturally turn to racing. As there are too few first, or even second class horses to admit of the sport being pursued as in England, animals are divided into various classes and grades, so as to ensure " fields " for the different events. Under these rules, English and Australian horses give Arabs 3 st., country-breds 2 st., and Capes 14 lbs. ; while there are, of course, allowances for age. I may add that even with these very liberal concessions, the sons of the Desert and Indian produce have not the slightest chance, at any distance, with English or Colonial stock. There are very few Cape horses now imported ; the only good ones which I remember having seen in India were Mr. Collins' Merryman, a fair second-rater, and Echo, who was a great horse in his day, but was long past mark of mouth when he first landed in the East. Country-bred horses, having a strong dash of thoroughbred English blood, are generally faster than Arabs for, say, six furlongs, but do not stay as well.

On the vexed subject of breeding in India I may here devote a short paragraph or two.

In many parts of India, where the climate is a hot, damp one, it is practically impossible to breed horses which would serve any useful purpose whatsoever, even with the best dams and sires the world could produce ; while in no district in India, without constant importations of fresh blood, can horses be bred fit for racing, or for the requirements of Horse Artillery or English

Cavalry, although they may do admirably as remounts for the light Native Cavalry. No journey is too long, no weather too hot, for a good country-bred, who is unapproachable as a hack or campaigner in the tropics, so long as he is not over-weighted. The question of producing a permanent breed of weight-carriers is one that the Indian studs and private speculators have tried in vain to solve. The stock must be of Eastern or thoroughbred English parentage if they be required to stand the Indian sun, for no horse of coarse blood is worth a feed of corn for all the work he can do on a tropical day; hence the difficulty of obtaining bone and substance.

Horses obey the universal law which ordains that animals introduced into, to them, a new country, tend, after a few generations, to conform to the type peculiar to their species which are natives of that soil. This fact as regards men is fully admitted by human biologists: and so it is with horses. Thoroughbred English dams and sires will produce in India a foal that will be, to a certainty, unmistakable as a country-bred; while the second or third generation will possess but few European characteristics. I cannot help thinking that of all insane ideas, the maddest is the one which some enthusiasts have of permanently improving English race-horses by an admixture of Arab blood, as if the differences between the various breeds of horses were not the results of the effects of climate, selection, stable management, work, and training. I make bold to say that if one thousand Arab mares and fifty Arab horses of the purest Desert breed were imported into England, bred from strictly among themselves, and managed after our style, that the sixth generation would be undistinguishable from ordinary English animals.

The English and Australian horses which run in India are about the same class as the somewhat non-descript animals that run for hunters' races on the flat in England. As a rule, the colonials more than hold their own, as they are better able to stand the climate, and have sounder feet and legs than their English cousins.

It is an undoubted fact that the drier the country in which horses are foaled and brought up, the sounder and stronger are their hoofs. I am convinced from experience, though it is difficult to prove the case to demonstration, that the same rule holds good with respect to bone, tendon, and ligament. The conformation of the fore-legs of well-bred Walers, though not to the same extent as those of Desert-bred Arabs, is, generally, well calculated to resist the effects of concussion ; as their pasterns are, usually, fairly long, strong, and sloping. We seldom see among them the short, upright pasterns which disfigure so many English race-horses, and which indicate but too surely an early break-down. Not having such pure blood, they rarely show the brilliant dash of speed at a finish which is so characteristic of our thoroughbreds.

Persons unacquainted with the East find some difficulty in understanding the admiration with which many Anglo-Indians regard Arabs as race-horses. From an English point of view, they cannot gallop, to use a common expression, fast enough to keep themselves warm. Yet for all that there is a great deal to be said in their favour as high-metalled racers. They are, as a rule, game, honest, and grand stayers ; so sound that an inexperienced owner may take all sorts of liberties with them in their training, without breaking them down; docile and easy to ride; and, above all, the best among them show so little marked superiority to others of their own class, that in a two-mile weight for age race, with ten or twelve Arabs, we would be right, three times out of four, in predicting that the proverbial tablecloth would cover the field up to the distance post, and that the verdict would be in doubt up to the last stride. Again, Arabs, more than other horses, "gallop in all shapes," and have such a knack of improving with age and good treatment, that the owner of one which moves in anything like good form need never despair of winning a race with him: as witness the grey horse, Valentine, who belonged to Captain Davison of the 15th Hussars, beginning a fairly successful racing career at the mature age of thirteen years ; and Colonel Monty Turnbull's great horse, Rufus, who would have ended his days as a hack, had not Mrs. Turnbull discovered his capabilities during an *impromptu* spin with a sporting parson.

Speculation on Indian races is usually carried on by means of lotteries, which are managed as follows. There are generally a hundred chances at ten rupees each, the rupee being at present worth one shilling and eightpence, though formerly it represented two shillings.

The chances, like in an ordinary raffle, are numbered from 1 to 100, and are taken either separately by those who wish to invest, or are tossed for with dice. If A tosses B for, say, five tickets and loses, he has, naturally, to pay fifty rupees into the pool, but will share equally with B if any of their five tickets be so lucky as to draw one or more horses. Or, a few sportsmen may go in for a "sweep" of one ticket each ; in which case the highest thrower is entitled to half of whatever any of the numbers in the sweep may draw. Of course he has to pay for the chance he took, but if that draws a horse he will secure for himself the entire profit accruing from it. When the chances are all taken, gun wads or ivory counters, having corresponding numbers on them, are placed in a bag and well shaken up. The names of the horses running in the race are written on separate slips of paper, which are folded up and put into another bag. The drawing is commenced by one of the race officials, or any selected person, taking out of the bag one of the slips of paper, and after that, a wad, to the corresponding number of which, on the lottery paper, is written the name of the horse drawn ; and so on. After the drawing is finished, the chances of the horses, in the order they were taken out, are put up to auction. The purchaser of any chance has to pay into the pool the sum he bid, and also a similar amount to its drawer. The total sum realized by the sale of the chances should, theoretically, equal the value of the tickets, though it usually does not do so. Let us suppose, for simplicity's sake, that a lottery was held on a race for which three horses started, and that they were purchased, respectively, by A, B, and C, for Rs. 100, Rs. 400, and Rs. 500. In this case, A would stand to win (1000+400+500—100) Rs. 1800 and to lose Rs. 200; in fact, he would be taking 9 to 1 ; while A would get 1200 to 800, and B would have 1000 even. Backers, contrary to the rule in "the ring," have, generally, "the best of it" in lotteries, as the amount realized from the sale of the chances of the horses rarely equals the price of the tickets. A deduction of five per cent, which I have not reckoned in the foregoing calculations, is made for the benefit of the race fund.

In India there are no two or three year-old races, as owners are almost entirely dependent on imported stock, the majority of which are four or five years old when they land. Hence races for maidens of the season are substituted for the more orthodox events.

In India, race meetings are held at the various stations, so as to suit, as far as possible, the convenience of owners. Thus, in Bengal, the principal fixtures follow something like this order:—Dehra Doon in the early part of October; then Umballa, Meerut, Allahabad, Sonepore, Calcutta at Christmas time ; Dacca, Mozufferpore, Lucknow, and perhaps Meerut or Umballa, Spring Meeting; with the Lucknow Monsoon Races to break the monotony of the wet weather.

" Sky Races " is the term used, in India, for a meeting confined to horses or ponies belonging to residents of a certain station or district.

Australian horses are, in India, called " Walers," as, in the early days of the Colonies, animals were chiefly exported from New South Wales.

The following may be taken as an average programme for a good three days' Indian meeting :—

FIRST DAY.

1. For ponies 13 hands and under, ½ mile. Rs. 100 added.

2. For all maidens, 1 mile. Rs. 300 added.

3. For maiden Arabs and country-breds, 1½ miles. Rs. 500 added.

4. For ponies 13.2 and under, ¾ mile. Rs. 200 added.

5. Steeplechase for all maidens, 3 miles. Rs. 500 added.

6. Galloway Chase, 14 hands and under, 2 miles. Rs. 250 added.

SECOND DAY.

1. For ponies 13.2 and under, ¾ mile. Rs. 150 added.

2. Steeplechase for all Arabs and country-breds, 3 miles. Rs. 350 added.

3. For all Arabs, 2 miles. Rs. 500 added.

4. Steeplechase for all horses, 3½ miles. Rs. 700 added.

5. For all horses, 1½ miles. Rs. 500 added.

6. For all Galloways 14 hands and under, 1 mile. Rs. 250 added.

7. Selling Race, ½ mile. Rs. 200 added.

There would be various allowances for class, height, (4 lbs. the half inch), for not having previously won, &c. ; and penalties for winning.

The last day would of course be devoted, more or less, to handicaps.

CAPTAIN JOY, 7th Hussars.

Page 21.

CHAPTER III.

THE SEVENTH HUSSARS—THE UMBALLA MEETING OF
1868—HIGHLANDER — ENGLISH ARABS — CALIPH—
TARTAR AND COUNTESS.

WHEN the 7th Hussars were stationed at Scalkote they
were, without exception, the most sporting regiment
I have ever seen.   Lord Marcus Beresford and Captain
Joy, who raced under the name of "The Queen's Own,"
had, among many others, the Waler Cœur de Lion, the
Arab Dervish, the country-bred Eruption, and the ponies
Sweet William and Dutchman ; the Hon. Walter Harbord owned Milliner and Brigand ; Captain Powell had
the useful Whalebone ; Baby Blake belonged to Mr.
Hunt ; Mr. Beville possessed the clever chasing pony
Claribel ; while Captain Bayly, who was the finest rider
in the regiment, ran Polly Perkins and Rapid.   They
were always ready to back their opinion against that of

all comers, though I am afraid their luck on many occasions was not equal to their courage.

They had several good meetings at Scalkote, one of the best being that held in the spring of 1868, at which the Rajah of Jummoo presented a Cashmere cup of fine gold and exquisite workmanship, weighing two hundred and fifty sovereigns, for a race for all horses, distance one mile. The entries included Milliner, Baby Blake, Brigand, Whalebone, and Mr. Tucker's Samson, ridden by Captain Hawkesley Barber. There was a false start at the first attempt to get away, on account of which Mr. Soames, of the 4th Hussars, broke a stirrup leather and was unable to hold Whalebone, who bolted round the course and took Brigand along with him. Mr. Papillon, of the 92nd Highlanders, broke both stirrup leathers, tumbled off, and allowed Baby Blake, who had been heavily backed, to gallop home to her stable. All this time little Milliner remained at the post an emblem of docility. When the flag fell, Dr. Tippetts, of the 5th Fusiliers, who rode the mare, got off well with her and won easily. Captain Harbord presented this magnificent gold cup to his regiment.

Most of us who have, during late years, sojourned at

that delightful hill station, Mussooric, for the hot months
are acquainted with Mr. Quajjoo, the prosperous and
obliging livery-stable keeper, who hires out sure-footed
ponies at the rate of four rupees a day. When I first
knew him he was spare and dapper, as he had not given
himself up to the delights of sweetmeats and clarified
butter, as is the custom of the well-to-do Aryan. Lord
Marcus Beresford had not then taken to steeplechase
riding, for that was long before the Chimney Sweep
days. Captain Joy, although he had been initiated into
Indian racing at Secunderabad, when he was in the
18th Royal Irish, had not acquired that deep insight
into training which he subsequently obtained at French
Furze on the Curragh, so did not despise the assistance
of the ex-shoeing-smith Quajjoo, who rode and helped
to train the many horses belonging to "The Queen's
Own."

I was so much knocked up by the first hot weather
I spent at Meean Meer that I had to get three months'
sick leave to recruit my health in the hills. On my way
to Mussoorie I stayed at Umballa to see the October
Meeting of 1868, at which Lord Huntly, Captain Joy,
Colonel Trench, the Hon. Walter Harbord, Captains
Papillon, Maxwell, Soames, and Newbolt, Mr. Har-

greave, Mr. Darley, "The Bird," "Mr. Holdfast," "Captain Dudley," Mr. Saunders, of the Horse Gunners, and many other good sportsmen, were met to run their horses and back their fancies.

"Sweet George," as his friends—and they were many—were wont to call the owner of that matchless pony Sweet William, presided at the lotteries. His frank smile, winning ways, and cheery words preserved harmony among the elements of discord which were present. And yet his humorous chaff, while raising a hearty laugh, not unfrequently left a sharp sting in the minds of those whom he wished to scourge. In those days, the owner could make no claim to a quarter of his horse's chance in a lottery, though such a request was seldom refused. On one of the lottery nights of that Umballa Meeting, a certain captain insisted that a certain stud colonel, who had bought his horse, should give him a share of it. As the stud officer refused to "part," the owner threatened that if he did not do so, the horse should not win. The justly exasperated colonel thereupon appealed to the room, and expressed himself to the effect that this threat was the most disgraceful utterance he had ever heard at a lottery table. "Don't mind what he is saying," Captain Joy called out, "for many a true word is spoken in jest." The roar of laughter which followed this apparently innocently intended speech stopped the unpleasantness. The gallant hussar's coolness was sorely tested by the result of the race (about two miles) between Highlander and Caliph, two of the best Arabs of their respective classes we have ever had in India. The former belonged to Captain Harbord, while the latter was backed by Captain Joy. The bay, "having a leg," was short of work; while the grey Galloway was very fit and well. "The Bird" (Captain Massingberd, 5th Lancers) was given orders to make the pace hot for Dignum and Highlander. Instead of doing this, he started at a quiet canter, despite the shrieks of "go on" from the stand, and went no faster for the first half of the journey, while the jockey, Dignum, kept at an equally slow pace behind. When it came to racing, Highlander had of course "the foot" of Caliph, and won cleverly amid shouts of "Well rode, Dignum." This fine horseman had to do an immense amount of work in order to keep himself down to 8 st. 10 lbs., as his proper weight was about eleven stone.

Highlander had the reputation of being one of three English horses that were said to have been sent as

Arabs to India. The story, which is more *ben trovato* than *vero*, goes that the trio were consigned to a so-called gentleman owner, who was a confederate of a Bombay Arab dealer, who had not been let into the secret of the animals' nationality. In the first race for which any of these horses ran, the one entered was winning in a walk, being about a hundred yards ahead at the distance post, when, by an extraordinary accident, he broke his leg and lost the race. The unfortunate native part-owner was loud in his expressions of grief and mortification at having lost, as he said, a horse which could have given at least three stone to any other Arab that was ever foaled. At last, in order to soothe him, his English confederate took him aside and told him that he might well be comforted, for either of the two remaining horses could have given the broken legged one 28 lbs., and that they all three were small thoroughbred English racehorses. The Arab sportsman, instead of accepting his position, as many might have done, indignantly repudiated his connection with his European *confrère*, and said that he only raced with horses which were bred in his own country. One of the two animals was killed, taken out into the Bombay harbour and thrown overboard, while the other, Highlander, was smuggled up country. This grand Arab was gifted with extraordinary speed, and moved very much in the style Colonel McBean's Dhaman used to do : fore-legs shot out to the front without any apparent bending of the knee, while the hind-legs were brought well under the body, and were worked backwards and forwards with the quickness and precision of the piston of a locomotive. I may observe that the fatal trick of bending the knees spoils a horse's style of moving just as much as it does that of a ballet dancer.

An English traveller—Major Upton, I believe—said that he saw Highlander, when he was a colt, along with one of the Bedouin tribes in the desert.

This tale about English horses being sent out to India to run as Arabs, was told for many years with strange persistence, and, naturally, with variations. The Bombay gossip-mongers seemed agreed, however, that two of the animals in question were thoroughbreds, called Chateau Lafitte and The Pony, while the third was unnamed. Some asserted that the mighty Raby was one or other of the first two, and advanced the arguments of his vast superiority to the typical Arab racer ; of the fact that his antecedents in the desert could not be traced ; and of his suffering, just like many English horses in India, from bad feet during the whole time he was in training. I remember Raby, 8 st. 12 lbs., winning the Forbes Stakes, two miles, at the Bombay Races, February, 1866, in a canter in 3 min. 51 sec.

Caliph had a long and successful racing career. He first belonged to Sir Seymour Blanc, who helped to bring Jousiffe, who now trains at the Seven Barrows, Lambourne, into prominence as a jockey. The Arab Galloway then passed into the hands of Mr. Depuis, who exchanged him for War Eagle (late Coventry) with the Gordon Highlanders, the reason for doing so being as follows : On one occasion, when Caliph was suffering from indigestion, Mr. Depuis had him examined by a veterinary surgeon, who, finding that his pulse did not beat regularly, pronounced that he had heart disease, and advised his owner to get rid of him as soon as possible. Mr. Depuis acted on this counsel, and lost one of the best Galloways India has ever known. This was a good instance of the proverbial danger of a little knowledge. Thanks to the advance of veterinary knowledge, all now know, as some did then, that an intermittent pulse may be caused by some trifling indisposition, and is not necessarily associated with organic or functional derangement of the heart.

I may remark that Jousiffe, whose name I have just mentioned, was, thirteen or fourteen years ago, an excellent jockey, possessing a firm seat, good hands, and a clear head ; and could then ride 8 st. 7 lbs., although he now turns the scale at about double that weight. He was also a careful and successful trainer. Seven or eight years ago he was racing in India along with Dignum, and owned Toujours Prêt, Little John, Risk, and other good horses. Since then, he has settled down near Lambourne, and has trained for the Marquis of Huntly ("Mr. Bird"), Lord Kesteven, Mr. Robert Peck, and many others.

The first important race which Caliph won was the Ticaree Cup, at the Sonepore Meeting of 1867, in which he was ridden by Lowe, and carried 7 st. 11 lbs. This event was a handicap for country-breds and Arabs, R.C. Half a mile from home Mr. J. Collins' gr. a. h. Prince Alfred, 10 st. 7 lbs., who was one of the best of his class that ever faced the starter, was leading, with Dignum in the saddle, while George Gooch, on Colonel Robart's Diamond, 8 st. 7 lbs., Khoob Lab on the famous Growler, 8 st., Jaffir on the speedy country-bred mare Eruption, 8 st. 1 lb., and Livesay, steering the country-bred gelding (not the chaser) War Eagle, 7 st. 12 lbs., were close behind.   At this point, Lowe, who had been bustling Caliph along in order to keep within hail of the leaders, felt the grey Galloway going so badly that he ceased riding him, and let him go at his own pace for the next furlong.   He then, suddenly, of his own accord, took hold of his snaffle, ran through his field, who had all been in front of him, and won a most exciting race by a length, with War Eagle and Eruption second and third.

Seven or eight years after that I often saw the handsome Prince Alfred at Cawnpore, being tooled about in a trap by Mr. Petman, who was an assistant to Mr. Collins, and to whom "Bricky" had given him.   The grand old horse always appeared to my eyes, as he passed me during my evening ride on the Mall, as a dream of beauty, despite the crazy vehicle that rattled behind him.   The last time I saw Growler, who, ridden by Gooch, won the Calcutta Derby in 1867, he was doing duty at the stud up in the Punjab.   I believe his stock has turned out well.   The name of these two, horse and man, were like those of Anarchy and Ryder, in that they were long identified together in many stirring scenes on the Indian turf.

The great event of the meeting was the steeplechase

which was won by Countess, who was subsequently disqualified, and the race awarded to Tartar, who ran second, on account of the mare not having carried a penalty for a previous win in Australia. Her owner, I believe, was well aware of her colonial performances, but he was a non-racing man, never betted, had won Countess in a raffle, was very fond of her, didn't see why she should be penalized for her former win, didn't see why her back should be broken by carrying the top burden, so, without meaning ill, or wishing to defraud any one, but with the strange wrong-headed-ness of the non-sporting mind when it turns its attention to racing matters, innocently did that for which you or I, my racing reader, might have been warned off for a couple of years. The Gordon Highlanders had come in force from Jullundur to back Tartar, who was ridden by Major Eustace Hill of the Police. This bold Peeler was supposed to be the most cast-iron man in India; and he well need have been, for the handsome grey gelding, who was then in the heyday of his power, was as strong-necked a specimen of a puller as I have ever seen. The lion-hearted major let him "rip." The brave horse knocked down three or four walls, shivered the strong post and rails, and tore through half a mile of plough before he settled down into his stride. He was then—they had gone about a mile and a half—fully two hundred yards ahead of Countess, who was leading the remainder of the field, seven or eight in number. All that time "Steenie" had not moved on his mare, but let her gallop and take her fences at her own sweet will ; and right well did she accomplish her task, for a more perfect jumper has never looked through a bridle, on an Indian "flagged course," than the bay Countess. The mare rapidly drew up on Tartar, who was now in difficulties, and won by fifty lengths. How the remainder of the spread-eagled field fared I really do not remember. I only recollect that Thunderbum carefully deposited his rider, Captain Papillon, before they had gone half a mile. Captain "David," who was then the ruling spirit of the Gordon Highlanders, did not, I should think, concern himself much on account of being involuntarily made a field officer, for he was the chief winner over Tartar, who was after that named Objection.

A very inexperienced person might think that the lesson Objection got against the sunbaked mud walls and strong post and rails might have cured him of running away. Nothing of the sort : in fact, he pulled just as bad as ever, till the native jockey Kairoo was put up to steer him in a chase. Kairoo, who was naturally a fine horseman, rode on Allen McDonough's principle—namely, "don't pull your horse and he won't pull you"—though I am quite certain that he had never even heard of the great chase rider and trainer who used to live at Fairymount. Kairoo rode the grey in a snaffle and solved the mystery of his pulling. Not long ago I read an article in a London sporting paper, in which the writer advocated the practice of allowing a horse to run away as a cure for hard pulling! Strange to say the writer was not of the Haymarket or Criterion style of sportsman, but one who ought to have known better. People who write like this have probably never heard that a horse has got such things as suspensory ligaments and back tendons.

Mr. Hargreave followed his luck (as far as honour and glory went) in winning on Countess, by securing the Galloway chase on Adèle for the Horse Gunners. He was an uncommonly hard man over a country, though he lacked some of the finish and elegancies of the art of race riding, so well illustrated by poor Mr. W. Thacker, "Captain Dudley," and Mr. Rowland Hudson.

CHAPTER IV.

THE 7TH HUSSARS AT MEEAN MEER—SIR LEPEL GRIFFIN.

IN January, 1869, the 7th Hussars marched down from Scalkote, and camped near Meean Meer, at which place I was stationed with my battery, F-19. We had, while they were with us, races, billiard matches—for which I had the honour to successfully represent the Gunners on two occasions—and theatricals. In acting they were particularly strong, and gave us an admirable performance in aid of the fund for the Famine which at that time was raging. Owing to the dearth of ladies at this station, the female characters were taken by young subalterns of the regiment; while the epilogue was composed and recited by the since famous diplomatist, Sir Lepel Griffin, who at that time was a junior in the Indian Civil Service. The lines are so happily and brightly written that I take the opportunity of bringing them

to the notice of my readers, who, I am confident, will
appreciate them.   They are as follows :—

" I do not come before the lamps to-night
　To speak the prologue that I did not write.
　A place is paved with things that I've intended ;
　I crave your pardon—least said, soonest mended—
　But this last night, when, for a time uncertain,
　These gifted actors pass behind the curtain,
　I cannot speak what all must wish expressed,
　Our praise, our gratitude, and—all the rest.
　When loved friends part, when gleaming eyes are wet,
　It may be vain to say, in phrases set,
　Our happiness is dead, our hearts are broken ;
　The truest, fondest thoughts are never spoken.
　But we, whose hearts are somewhat hard, may tell
　Our friends how loth we are to say farewell
　To those to whom our warmest thanks are due,
　And these I offer on behalf of you.
　Myself an actor in the corps, ere age
　And failing memory forced me from the stage,
　I claim a right to plead the. actors' cause,
　And ask from you their crown of just applause.
　The actresses require no words of mine
　To praise the charms which heaven has made divine.
　Miss Lydiard, *piquante*, beautiful, and young
　As any goddess poets ever sung ;
　Miss Beresford,¹ whose eyes no hearts resist,
　The sweetest maid that ever yet was kissed :
　And darling Esmeralda, who need never
　Ask Art to make her ' beautiful for ever.'

---

¹ Lord Marcus.

You'd never guess these angels go to 'stables,'
And smoke cigars and sit on billiard-tables,
Nor yet believe that they are ever seen
Walking about without a crinoline.
They well have learnt the fascinating arts
Which women use to snare unwary hearts;
The sweet face flushing with a feigned surprise,
The slow, shy raising of half-opened eyes,
The backward glances as they gain the door,
The glove—the flower—dropp'd upon the floor,
The thousand chains with which their hands endeavour
To bind us to their chariot wheels for ever.
Then come the men—but, though I wish to flatter,
The praising men is quite a different matter
From praising women—neither may be true,
But I prefer the latter of the two.
You never praise a man but you repent it;
But with a woman—why—perhaps you meant it.
Here's Powell, on the stage as cool a hand
As you will see him in Tod Heatly's Stand,
Laying the odds, and safe to win, of course,
Like Dudley Sampson on a losing horse;
And Denison, whom fate, had she been sager,
Had made an actor, not a Sergeant-Major;
And Childs, who shines alike in every part,
Whose art is natural but still is Art;
Then the great master, whose enchantment seems
To call from heaven the music of our dreams,
Whose skill can draw from out the charmèd air
All love, all grief, all passion, all despair.
And lastly, Barron, who, with brush in hand,
Transforms a desert into fairy-land.
Then, ladies, you whose smiles decree our laws,
Confirm my praises with your sweet applause;

> The noblest aims prompt all our actors do,
> The love of charity and love of you,
> Which is the greater power, which the less,
> I've no idea, but you yourselves must guess."

In September, 1869, Lord Marcus Beresford and Captain Joy ran at Poonah the bay Waler mare, Milliner, with bad luck, as she was defeated three times by Hungarian, and once by Captain Dent's Pioneer: a result which was very galling after bringing the mare all the way from Sealkote in the Punjab. It was not Milliner's fault, for she was good and honest enough; but the 7th Hussar jockey, Auckland, did not look after her properly in her training. Like many young, strong, and wise men, both before and since, he succumbed to the insidious flutterings of a bit of muslin, and proved an unprofitable servant.

A funny thing about Hungarian is that, although he was bred in the country from which he took his name, he appears to have run at the previous Bombay meeting as a colonial! His owner was evidently not a swell at geography.

CHAPTER V.

THE 5th Fusiliers, who were stationed at Ferozepore,
were at the time of which I am writing one of the best
regiments in the service. Dr. Tippetts was their great
flat-race and training authority, while Messrs. Hargreave,
Darley, and Gall were ever ready to steer a horse, no
matter how unschooled, across country. "Jack" Darley
was then the smartest of adjutants, except when laid up
with broken bones from accidents in steeplechasing,
which was often. His good-natured colonel at last
could stand the usual excuse no longer, when, on one
occasion, to his order of "Send for the adjutant," the
orderly-room clerk replied, " Please, sir, Mr. Darley
has met with an accident." " Damnation !" shouted

he, springing from his seat ; " bring me an adjutant who doesn't jump."   Next day Jack turned up repentant in splints and bandages, and promised to sin no more. Barring an occasional fall, which Dr. Tippetts considerately entered as " intermittent fever," he kept pretty straight up to his promotion, which he got after about seventeen years' service ; for the 5th Fusiliers was one of those grand old regiments into which, if a man of the right sort once got, he made it his home and his world for the best years of his life.

In 1869 the Gordon Highlanders, who were stationed at Jullundur, had a strong stable, presided over by Captains Maxwell, Papillon, and McGregor.   They owned the aptly named Ranelagh—out of Princess by Peeping Tom—Caliph, Objection, the Black Waler chaser, Gamecock, Hooshiari Pissoo, Crazy Jane, Jesuit, and others.   Captain Papillon was the Captain Machell of the confederacy, although he sometimes made a mistake.   He was a good and determined performer both on the flat and across country.

Crazy Jane was a smart country-bred pony of the whipcord and fiddle-string type.   One evening, after a cricket match at Umballa, when Captain Papillon, Mr. Beadon, and several others who were fond of racing were present, the conversation turned on ponies. The Gordon Highlander was anxious to match Crazy Jane, whose galloping fame, he thought, had not reached so far south. After an innocent question or two from the owner of Seagull as to the capabilities of the mare, and an equally innocent reply or two as to her not being of much account, Mr. Beadon expressed his general unbelief in Jullundur and her ponies, and said that he wouldn't mind backing a certain chestnut "tat," which was standing under a tree, tied up by a piece of frayed rope, against the reputed flyer. After a careful inspection of the chestnut, who stood with drooping head and humble demeanour under that shady tree, Captain Papillon, inwardly chuckling at the disparagement which had been heaped on his Crazy Jane, closed with the match, and got on as much as he could afford to " plank down." That mean-looking thirteen-hand "tat" was the mighty Orion, who with a feather weight up could do half a mile in fifty-five seconds. Needless to say the Gordon Highlanders suffered an easy defeat.

Captain Papillon was also unfortunate in a match he made with Crazy Jane against that sweet pony Minuet, which was the property of Dr. Tippetts of the 5th

Fusiliers. He was a grey Arab of the purest Nejd breed, and was as good as, if not better, than Gazelle. If there be a doubt, ask my friend Jack Irving, the well-known jockey. At that time Minuet was fourteen or fifteen years old. Captain Papillon did not believe in the stories of the *laudatores temporis acti*, and knew not how greatly superior, as a rule, Arab ponies are to country-bred ones; the result being that his pony was beaten in a common canter.

The Hooshiari Pissoo (*Anglicè*, Clever Flea) commenced his career as a baggage pony in the Cashmere hills. He was bought by Captain Papillon and turned out a very successful chasing Galloway; for, although he was incapable of doing a mile under three minutes, he was an extraordinary fencer, and fortifications were the order of the day, at that time, "between the flags." It was a standing joke of the Highlanders to profess ignorance of the position the Pissoo ought to occupy among the *equidæ*, for his ears were long, and his general appearance asinine. They generally entered him as "Captain Papillon's brown mule or pony."

Captain Maxwell tells me the native jockey Quajjoo appeared one day, during the rains at Jullundur, with several horses which he was bringing up country, and took them to the Gordon Highlanders' stables to be put up for the night. Captain Papillon and his friends, of course, made a careful inspection of the new arrivals, their attention being particularly attracted to a great slashing chestnut. "What's that horse, Quajjoo?" they asked. "That's Captain Joy's new maiden," replied the ready-witted Mahommedan. The answer did little to calm their alarm, for they could not help asking themselves what chance Ranelagh, who was then the best in the Punjab, could have against such a galloping-looking customer as the chestnut? Not long after Quajjoo had left with his string for the North, the Highlanders received a letter from the 7th Hussars, inviting them up to their meeting at Sealkote, where they and Ranelagh were promised a "good time of it." They accepted the hospitable offer, and appeared in due course on the scene, eager for the fray and ready to carry off the collected gold back with them to Jullundur. When, however, the entries appeared for the big race of the meeting, in October, 1869, they were thunderstruck to see the name of the great horse Cœur-de-lion, who had run so well at Secunderabad, and had proved himself not much inferior to the mighty Vanderdecken, the Australian Kingcraft of that time. They rushed off to

Captain Joy, and complained bitterly that they were done out of their expected benefit. He soothed their fears as Irishmen will do, and they returned to their quarters well assured that the morrow was to be "their day out," and that Cœur-de-lion was to enjoy an "airing" for the down country handicaps. That evening they went to the lotteries, backed Ranelagh for a hatful of money for the Trial Stakes, one mile, and came away delighted with themselves ; especially as the buyer in the lotteries and backer of the big chestnut was an officer of the 7th Hussars, who was entirely unconnected with Captain Joy's stable. The morning brought reflection, and then arose the burning question in their minds: why should a man whom they never knew before to have bet a rupee on a horse-race, have backed Cœur-de-lion for so much money ? The thought was intolerable, so off they went to Captain Joy and asked that the meaning of this parable might be expounded unto them. "Faith, Ranelagh will have to gallop to win, and that's the long and short of it," replied the genial Irishman. "You may beat us, but you won't break us," was all they said, and then they returned to their stable to prepare to bravely face the sore defeat they felt sure was in store for them. That accomplished horseman, good at need, Captain

Dudley Sampson, rode the hope of the Gordon clan, while little Quajjoo was perched on the big, raking Cœur-de-lion. The race up to the turn home looked like a contest between a pony and a horse, for the chestnut kept "lollopping" along at his ease, a length in front of Ranelagh, who had to do all he knew to keep near his rival. When they came into the straight, Captain Dudley caught Ranelagh "by the head," sat down into his saddle, and drove the gallant son of Peeping Tom alongside the big chestnut, who was well able to quit his opponent without an effort at any moment. But he saw the crowd on each side of him ; he heard their shouting, and the rattle of Ranelagh's hoofs ; and then, for the first time in his life, he put his ears back, "dug his toes in the ground," slackened his speed, despite the determined efforts of his jockey, and allowed Ranelagh to beat him on the post. They met again in the Stewards' Handicap, ¾ mile, but with the same result. I do not know what happened to Cœur-de-lion after that.

And then the Gordon Highlanders invited the Hussars down to Jullundur to their November meeting. I was marching through with my battery (F-19, R. A., they have changed the numbering now), for I was then in the Gunners, and saw some of the racing. Coventry,

who, as War Eagle, subsequently distinguished himself in so many chases, won for Captain Maxwell his
maiden race—the Gordon Highlanders' Cup. Captain
Ralph Hare's Arab pony Jerry, in receipt of 12 lbs.,
beat Sweet William for half a mile. Dr. Tippetts'
English mare, Grace, late Wild Duck, defeated Captain
Joy's Arab, Jurham, in the charger race; while Caliph
beat Captain Joy's black country-bred gelding Rupee
(who was a "caster" and had been bought for sixteen
annas), and Colonel Bolton's Arab Galloway, Ruby, who
broke a blood-vessel, in the race for the Arab and
country-bred stakes. What a row there was over the
last mentioned event! Captain Papillon lodged an
objection against Caliph for carrying wrong weight, the
terms of the race being: weights to be raised 10 lbs.
over weight for age and class. A short time before
that, the Calcutta stewards had made a rule that when
Arabs and country-breds met, the scale was to be
raised a certain amount. Caliph's jockey seems to have
thought that the 10 lbs. mentioned in the terms of the
race included the weight to be raised according to the
C. T. C. rule. He was of course wrong, as it was exclu-
sive of it; and the race was awarded to Rupee. That
was the commencement of the row which followed; for

the wrong people, in this instance, backed the right horse. In a straight-away race it would have been absurd to have supposed that the Hussars could have deemed Rupee capable of defeating Caliph, of whose speed and staying power they were well aware.

In the Arab handicap, Captain Papillon on Captain Joy's Jurham could only get a moderate third to Caliph, ridden by Captain Dudley. This was such a startling reversal of public form that the Queen's Own challenged the Highlanders to a match between the two horses. The 7th Hussars were obliged to put up Dr. Tippetts, who was much inferior as a horseman to Captain Papillon. Yet for all that, Jurham would have won comfortably enough, had not Caliph's rider "bustled" (not jostled) him all down the straight. The doctor picked up his whip, but finding Caliph too close to use it in the proper manner, got excited, and hit the Scalkote horse with it wherever he could get an opening. After a desperate finish, and by magnificent riding, Captain Papillon managed to win by a head, and thus to confirm the running of the previous day. The scene which followed between the rival parties in the weighing tent was indescribable. One Hussar, whose family has always been as ready to give a blow as a gift, and a gift as a blow, rushed at the man whom he thought to be the author of all their sorrow. A good-natured captain of his regiment stopped him midway in order to prevent a quarrel, and got knocked down, for his peaceably intended pains, into an empty champagne-case, which stood in the corner of the tent; while his "pal," vowing that he would never come back to Jullundur again, left the course, got into his post-cart, and went straight off to Scalkote.

Speaking of Jullundur puts me in mind of an incident which once happened to me when I was passing through that station. At the time in question my battery was at Mecan Meer. One evening, on which there was a large station ball, I happened to ask Captain Maxwell to dinner at our mess, after which, neither of us being dancing men, we spent the evening playing billiards and pyramid pool all by ourselves until the small hours. When the Gordon Highlander returned to his regiment, he was asked at mess how he had got on at Mecan Meer. "Capitally," he replied, in chaff; " Hayes asked me to dinner, gave me the very best of everything, and then, in a casual manner, invited me to play pyramid pool. I agreed to the stakes he proposed, and after he had let me win the first few games, I said I was tired, would play no more, pocketed the money, and here I am." I may observe that we did not bet at all, and that he was only poking fun at me. The story, as stories do in dull Indian stations, "took" immensely in the regiment, and Mr. Brooke, one of the subalterns, was so tickled with it that he vowed he'd play me the same game on the first opportunity.

As luck would have it, I called on the 92nd mess when returning from Umballa shortly after this. I met Mr. Brooke in the ante-room, and he asked me to have lunch with him. The weather being sultry and my host pressing, I did ample justice to the excellent fare, and to more than one bottle of Christopher's Perrier Jouet. After lunch, Mr. Brooke proposed a game of pyramid pool. I replied that nothing would delight me more. He asked me what stakes I would play for, and I expressed my willingness to gamble for anything he chose to name. We finally agreed to play for stakes which were quite high enough for my pocket, although I knew that, bar some extraordinary accident, I was certain to win, as I was then much the best player in the Punjab. I was in grand form that day, "went out" for everything "possible," and made it. My opponent didn't mind losing the first game, but when he lost the second and then the third by many balls, he could not conceal his astonishment, while I was still more bewildered at his infatuation in continuing a game at which he had not a 100 to 1 chance. At last my post-horses were ready, and I had to proceed northward, so I bade good-bye to my hospitable entertainer, pocketed my winnings, and tumbled into my ramshackle post-cart— called in Hindustanne a *dawk garee*—on most excellent terms with myself. The proceedings of that pleasant afternoon which I spent at Jullundur, were for a long time a puzzle to me, until Captain Maxwell explained what fun they had out of Mr. Brooke for his virtuous attempt to teach me a lesson for my supposed sharpness. I must add, in justice to Mr. Brooke, that he was a grand sportsman and generous fellow, without a particle of guile in his composition, which fact made the story all the more ridiculous.

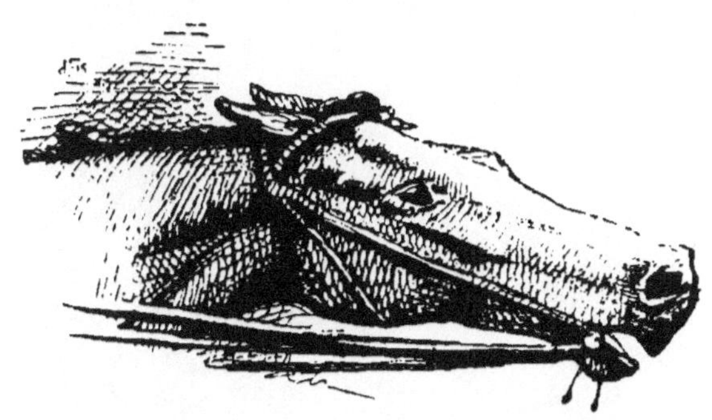

CHAPTER VI.

CAPTAIN DUDLEY.

THAT grand horseman, Captain Dudley Sampson, to whom I have casually alluded, is worthy of more than passing mention, although now, alas! he pulls the scale at eleven stone, and his silk and satin know him no more. As we belong to the same club, the Junior Army and Navy, in St. James' Street, we often meet and have a talk over bygone scenes which we have witnessed in the sunny East. It is nearly twenty-five years ago since he began his racing career in India. He commenced riding, with a good share of luck, at Benares, and went on to Faizabad, Gonda, Gorakpur, and Lucknow. The experience he gained was, luckily, sufficient to convince him how much he had to learn; so, when he went home on leave, he put himself under George Fordham's old master, poor Drewitt of Lewes, and got a thorough

COLONEL DUDLEY SAMPSON.

Page 51.

schooling into all the mysteries of professional horse-manship. He then learned to regard race riding as a fine art, which requires nerve, brain, strength, hand, seat, and, above all things, sympathy with the horse—that sort of feeling which comes through your knees and tells you what pressure he is working at. That great Arab Galloway, Caliph, whom I trained for many victories, completed the riding education of "Captain Dudley," who won on him seventeen races in one year, at all sorts of burdens, for he taught the then adjutant of the 9th Bengal Cavalry how to wait. This matchless grey knew, as I have said before, more about racing than many professionals, and could judge the right moment to "come," in a close thing, far better than most men who had ridden him. Captain Dudley found out that he dared not commence riding him when coming home until the horse gave the invariable signal, a long lung-filling breath, and then he could sit down on him and finish with the fullest confidence that the little Arab would respond to his call with unflinching gameness.

Captain Dudley had a most successful season in 1869–70, winning out of fifty-six mounts, forty-two races, running second ten times, being third three times, and unplaced only once ! Some of these wins, such as when Whalebone beat Cœur-de-lion, Toprail, Eruption, &c., at Sealkote, were on extreme outsiders. I have previously mentioned his clever win at that station on Ranelagh. A still more meritorious one was when he defeated Arnutt on Fermoy, the Body Guard's horse, by a short head at Dehra Doon on the son of Peeping Tom and Princess. This winning bracket to Ranelagh's name was altogether due to a judicious pull, which had to be made almost on the post.

The incidents connected with the race for the Jhind Cup, won by Captain Dudley at Umballa in 1868, are worthy of mention. He and "Pop" Gyll took Remenham and some other horses down from Meean Meer to the Sirhind meeting. They came to great grief the first day over the Derby; for Remenham, who was an exceedingly nervous horse, became so excited at hearing the band and seeing the crowd, that he was beaten before he had gone half a mile. At the lotteries on the next day's races, they had to bear a good deal of chaff about coach horses and cocktails. Indeed, it seemed any odds against "Old Remnants," as the unrighteous called him, for he had to meet the Calcutta cracks, Tomboy, Baby Blake, Colloby, &c. Early on the morning of the race they took the horse to a half ruined house which stood just opposite to the mile-post, put him into the cook-room, barricaded the doors and the windows, and left him in peace until Captain Dudley had weighed out, and the field were coming slowly across to start. The saddle was then slipped on Remenham, and before he had time to think, he was down to the post and the flag lowered. Though anything but a cur, he was one of those horses which run better in front than behind, so Captain Dudley slipped off at a good pace, knowing that his only chance was to take a lead and keep it, if possible. Meanwhile, the cracks were all comfortably looking after one another, and paying but little attention to the despised outsider, who, their riders thought, was sure to "come back" to them. But when two-thirds of the journey had been completed, and they saw that Remenham was as far ahead as ever, they began to think that he might require a little catching after all. Then ensued an exciting and almost laughable scene. "Ben" Roberts on Colloby was the first to sound the alarm, and was followed by the riders of the great Tomboy and the Calcutta mare. But all to no avail; for, after a tremendous "set to" between the four, Captain Dudley just managed to squeeze in Remenham a winner by a short head. There was a good deal of money lost and won over this race, and never did a rider, on an Indian course, receive a heartier or better-merited greeting than Captain Dudley did on returning to scale.

During one of the days of the Lahore Spring Meeting of 1868, Captain Dudley, who had won the first two events, was glad to have the chance of " standing down " for the third, as he was engaged for the last two ; there being altogether five races on the card. The brief and acceptable respite which he was taking on this sultry Indian afternoon was abruptly shortened by a racing friend of his coming up to him and begging, by all things sporting, that he would ride his mare, Vivandière ; for he was unable to do so himself, as he had that morning, when schooling a raw Waler over a country, fallen and sprained his wrists. Though Captain Dudley pleaded fatigue, thirst, the shocking bad chance the mare really possessed, and many other valid reasons, remonstance proved useless, for to each excuse the reply was, " So awfully obliged if you would." As the saddling bell had ceased ringing, he soon found himself, much against his wish, cantering down the course, in the blue and white of his Artillery friend, to join a large field of horses at the post for the Stand

Plate. His annoyance was quickly changed into dismay, when it suddenly flashed on him that this was the identical race for which he had backed—a most unusual occurrence with him—in the lotteries over night, a certain horse which he considered had an excellent chance of winning if his gentleman rider would only sit still ; and here he was come to do battle against his own selection. The flag fell, and the field streamed away together. As they rounded the turn for home, Captain Dudley began to appreciate the situation in all its horror. The stewards of the meeting, for some mysterious purpose of their own, had had about five yards of the course next the rails ploughed up, on which heavy ground the two favourites were now racing against each other, whilst he was sailing along comfortably on the hard ground outside. He "felt" the leaders with Vivandière, and then knew but too well that he had only to sit down and ride her home to beat the others, including his own selection. True to his principles of right and sportsmanlike feeling, he gradually brought the game mare level with her opponents, and then, just at the proper moment, he came with a rush and won by half a length ; thereby losing fourteen hundred rupees, as his own " fancy " was second. The moral of this is that a man should "stand down" when he is backing other people's horses ; for if he rides and wins, he loses ; while, if he loses, he will win everything but golden opinions behind his back, however "straight" he may be.

At this meeting, out of nine mounts, Captain Dudley won seven.

Towards the end of his riding career Captain Dudley rode principally for the Jullundur stable of the Gordon Highlanders, although in no way personally interested in it.

CHAPTER VII.

THE 77TH REGIMENT—THE 35TH NATIVE INFANTRY—
THE ADJUTANT'S HORSE—OUR COLONEL—OBJEC-
TION — MY FIRST ATTEMPTS AT RACING AND
TRAINING — THE TIME TEST—JACK TOBIN—SIR
JOHN ASTLEY—SEALKOTE RACES, 1870.

I ARRIVED along with my battery, in course of relief, at
Agra towards the end of 1869, after a six weeks' march
from Meean Meer, to which burnt-up station I had
shortly to return, as I was appointed a probationer to
the Bengal Staff Corps, to do duty with the 35th Native
Infantry, which was stationed there. I enjoyed my four
or five weeks at the city of the Taj, as we had an
excellent club at the place, and were honorary members
of that "smart" and most hospitable regiment, the 77th,
which was then commanded by Colonel Kent. They
treated their guests in fine old style. Whatever a man
craved to drink was set before him in a full bottle, not
passed round by mess waiters, as is the degenerate

custom now-a-days. As soon as the bottle was empty it was promptly replaced by a full one.

Not long after I joined the 35th Native Infantry, our adjutant, Captain Bunbury, died. Among other effects his charger, a smart bay stud-bred gelding, of mature age, was put up to auction and fell to my bid of £6 10s. I bought him for some sky races which were got up at Umritzur by Captain Maxwell and a few of the local talent. My new purchase was an animal which had enlisted my sympathies on various occasions, for the extremely rough time he had during and after almost every parade to which he went. The syce—as grooms of every nationality will do—always put the regulation bit so high up in the horse's mouth, that whenever the Adjutant touched the curb reins—which was often—the pain inflicted by the chain on the sharp edges of the animal's lower jaw was so severe, that the poor horse threw his head about and evinced his discomfort, with the result of incurring abuse, digs of the spurs, raps over the head with the flat of the sword, and, after parade, an hour's punishment drill for "unsteadiness in the ranks!" It was no use my interfering on behalf of the more intelligent animal of the two, by a gentle remonstrance and an offer to put the bridle right; for in those days I had written no book about horses, and no one would have heeded what I might have said.

"Ours" was an odd regiment at that time. It was commanded by Colonel Blackwood, who was a son of the original old man whose portrait adorns the cover of the monthly magazine of that ilk, published in George Street, Edinburgh. He had a sleeping interest in the concern, and right royally did he spend his private income and his pay. The old man had a passion for backing his luck at games with those fatal bits of pasteboard. I never knew him refuse a bet at cards, and can well believe the story told of him when playing whist at the Agra club one evening. His two opponents happened to be a couple of very distinguished English tourists, who had come for the cold weather to see India. One remarked to the other that India was a stupid place, and that it was impossible to back one's opinion there; while if he was at his club in London, he could have a "monkey" on the rubber if he liked. "Sir," cried the old Colonel, as he put his glass in his eye with a delighted chuckle, "you express my own feelings, so let us have a 'monkey' on each rubber for the rest of the evening : or," said he, pausing, as he observed the boaster's face lengthen, "let us have a 'monkey' on each odd trick." It took a long time to make him understand that his opponent did not mean as big as he talked, and then his disgust knew no bounds. He was a good loser and never but once, so the story goes, showed that he "felt the needle." On the occasion in question he backed No. 11 for the maximum at one of the German gambling - tables for ten successive times. He then stopped, and had the mortification to see No. 11 come up the very next time. Had he but ventured once more than he had done he would have won an enormous stake. I do not know if the facts happened exactly as I have told the tale, but the very mention of No. 11 was certain to send him away from the place in which he had heard it named. He had a fine old Indian way of keeping men steady on parade. If he observed any sepoy of his regiment looking about in the ranks, he rode up to him and whacked him on top of his head, where the folds of the turban are thin, with a little stick which he carried, and which had a convenient crutch handle. The old man was hospitable, and liked to drink in company, so he always asked, by turns, one of us— there were only three dining members—at mess to help him through his champagne. We appreciated the kindness, as we were thirsty subalterns.

I found that my sixty-five-rupee horse, after I had given him a few feeds of corn, could gallop a bit, so I engaged "Missy" Knox of the 85th K.L.I. to ride him at the coming Umritzur sky races, which were certainly for the benefit of the local sportsmen, of which Captain Maxwell was the great representative; for the rule was catch weights for all races, while he had two native boys, Tilka and Buddul, who could ride at that time about 6 st. each. Besides these feathers he had that fine horseman, Captain Dudley Sampson, to ride for him. Mr. Knox and I went to Umritzur with our country-bred "gee," which won the two chief races, although he was giving away quite three stone to all the other horses entered, the result being that we won what little money had been speculated. As the Rawul Pindi races were to come off about three weeks after this sky affair, Captain Maxwell sent Ranelagh and Caliph to run there. The sporting division of Lahore and Meean Meer, hearing of the departure of the two cracks, got up a sky meeting for their own benefit, to come off at the same time as the Rawul Pindi fixture. Captain Maxwell hearing of this, and anxious that they should not have all the fun and profit to themselves, called on me, proposed that I should run his other horses at Lahore,

and offered that we should go share and share alike.   I
accepted the terms, and the next day he sent me Objection, a country-bred mare called Grace Darling, and the
pony Quaker. The first named had a terribly bad splint
on his near fore-leg and was very lame, so it was with
grave misgivings that I accepted the mount on him for
the two hurdle races.   I kept my secret so well that no
one knew of the arrival of the horses until the entries
were read out at noon the day before the first day's
racing.   When the local owners heard the name of
Objection, late Tartar, they went as one man to the
racecourse, summoned coolies, and made the hurdles,
by means of thick logs and deeply fixed posts, as
unbreakable as turnpike gates, for they knew what a
determined runaway the big grey was, and how much
he liked "chancing" his obstacles.   For this little
attention I had to thank my quondam partner, Mr.
Knox, as he had a mount in the hurdle races on
Gamecock, a black Cape horse, which I had sold to
Captain Cockburn of my regiment, and accordingly
lent his aid to the heartless plot of breaking my neck.
When the first hurdle-race came off, I found myself
alongside Mr. Knox on Gamecock, "Tiger" Burns (the
doctor of the 85th) on Crazy Jane, and two or three

others on animals of sorts. As Objection had not had a gallop for a month he was fit to jump out of his skin, so I thought it best to wait with him, for if he ran away and hit his "game" leg, both of us would have been slain to a certainty over the palisades which acted as hurdles. "The Tiger" tried to cross me at the first obstacle, but the big horse knocked him aside and should have brought him down had the old mare been less clever than she was. On coming to the next hurdle, I heard the doctor shouting to Mr. Knox not to let me pass, and as "Missy" endeavoured to obey the warning by attempting to pull Gamecock across my line, I raced Objection past the black and took Gamecock along so fast that he had no time to rise, so struck the hurdle and "turned turtle." Objection now settled down into his stride and won as he liked. Next day I won another hurdle-race and a flat race on the old chaser. Quaker won his races, and so did Grace Darling, except a handicap, in which she ran second to Crazy Jane, admirably ridden by "the Tiger." We won at this small meeting something over two thousand rupees, and so pleased was Captain Maxwell, that he made me a present of Objection to ride as a charger, and sent me his horses to train. I bought

Captain Sampson's half-share of Quaker. Captain Maxwell had the other half.

My first efforts at training were attended by some difficulties; as the Lahore racecourse, which was the only place fit to gallop on within reach, was more than three miles distant from our " lines," while I had to be back by sunrise every morning to be in time for parade. Even had I had more leisure, it would not have mattered much, for the weather was so hot that the horses would have had to return, all the same, before the sun was well up. Exercise in the evening, beyond an hour's walk, was quite out of the question, for the parched plain, when once heated, took many hours to cool down again. I was always up before four o'clock in the morning, saw the horses have a few go-downs of water and a double handful of corn, and then we started for the racecourse so as to arrive just as the day was breaking. As soon as the work was finished, and I saw the horses were all right, and had been scraped and wisped over, I got on my charger, for I took care to be in uniform, and cantered back in time to " fall in " on parade.

It is a noteworthy fact that horses thrive well during the months of extreme heat in the Punjab and North-West, where, in the afternoon, the thermometer will often register considerably over 100°F. inside the stable; provided always that there is a thick roof overhead, to ward off the direct rays of the sun, and a free current of air through the stalls. As long as these two conditions are attended to, and proper stable management is observed, it matters little how hot the air may be if it be but dry. At Mecan Meer, Meerut, Cawnpore, Allahabad, and Lucknow, I always found my horses "do" quite as well, if not better, during the hot months than in the cold weather, while the opposite was the case to a marked degree in Bengal, the atmosphere of which during the great heat is laden with moisture. The experience of private breeders, and of the officers of the Indian studs, also, conclusively proves that it is a hopeless task to endeavour to breed good horses in a warm, damp climate. The only drawback to breeding in a hot, dry climate is the difficulty in obtaining suitable forage.

In India and the colonies much importance is attached to the "time test," as the majority of racecourses in those countries are very similar to each other, being "dead" level and light "going." In England, however, this criterion of speed is regarded as being valueless, on account of the great variety in the different courses and in the nature of the weather from day to day, so that it would be as futile to judge the powers of a horse on an English track by the watch, as it would be to estimate the capabilities of a sculler by sending him a trial against time from Putney to Mortlake, in which journey it would be impossible to make due allowance for the effect of the tide. Yet on still water, or on a level cinder path, the stop-watch is an admirable guide for the oarsman, swimmer, or a pedestrian. We are, of course, aware of its great use in match-trotting. Any calculations based on time performances of horses up or down hill, or through heavy ground, should be disregarded, as a slight incline would make a difference of three or four seconds in a mile, while a steady fall of rain might protract the gallop to double or treble that extent. Take, for instance, the race for this year's Goodwood Stakes, two and a half miles, which was won by Fortissimo, one of the best stayers we have in England, carrying 8 st. 3 lbs. in 5 min. 18 secs. after a desperate struggle with that good horse Reveller at even weights: Fordham and Osborne up. The "going," however, was very deep. On an ordinary Indian racecourse a first-class Arab would, with the burden carried by the Goodwood winner, do the same distance in nearly half a minute faster ; although I am convinced that Fortissimo at even weights for two and a half miles could give two or three furlongs start and a beating to the fleetest son of the desert ever foaled. Again, horses vary so much in their respective powers of going up or down hill, that timing them on an ascent or descent would furnish no reliable data by which to measure their speed on the flat. They also, sad to say, often run differently in public to what they have done in private. It is no use trying a horse against the watch without having previously satisfied one's self that he is thoroughly " game."

Although I had been accustomed to horses as a boy in Ireland, and had learned all about their management, from a military point of view, in D-20 and F-19 Royal Artillery, still I knew nothing practically about getting them fit for racing. I had, however, some knowledge of training for rowing and pedestrianism ; for I had been taught to " catch the first of it " by Jack Grant, Tom Mackinney, Clasper, and Tom Pocock when I was in the Cork Harbour crew on the river Lea at Glenbrook ; while, as a cadet at the Royal Military Academy, Woolwich, I won many foot races, in which I was much aided by the advice of the ex-champions Jack Levitt and Jim Pudney. My last experience in pedestrianism was when I was home in Ireland on sick leave from India in 1867. It happened thus.

One day I went to Queenstown to see some foot races at which four or five men of the 65th Regiment were running. As that battalion had several "fleet of foot," I watched the 100 yds. open race with interest. A large field, which was dispatched in one heat, faced the starter. On the word being given, a sergeant of the 65th, who was their speediest man, went to the front and seemed to be winning easily, as the other runners, from their numbers, were impeding each other, when suddenly, on an opening occurring, a country lad who was running, dashed through his men as if they were standing still, and beat the sergeant on the post, although he was fully five yards behind him, ten strides from the tape. I was so astounded by this performance that I could hardly speak when I went up to the young winner, John Tobin. I took him aside and asked him if he would come and stay with me for a short time, and that I would get on a good match for him. To this he readily assented. Tobin was then about twenty-two; he stood just six feet, and was built on the "lines" of a Waterloo Cup winner, being all steel and whipcord. The first time I tried him, he did his 100 yds. in 10¼ secs..

That was "good enough" for me, so on the next occasion I met the officers of the 65th, I introduced the subject of the Queenstown foot race, and praised the young countryman's running. To this Mr. Marryat, one of the subalterns, replied that they had a man in the regiment who could beat Tobin. We thereupon made a match for £100 for 110 yards. When the paper was signed, Mr. Marryat named himself. He at that time, and as I knew, was one of the fastest gentlemen sprinters in England, and, at his best, could do 100 yards in the same time as my raw country lad, running barefoot, did his trial in, or perhaps a yard better. During the month or so in which I had to train Tobin, I took care to keep him strong and fresh. He used to have a quiet walk for a couple of miles before breakfast. Two hours after that he had a smart walk for five or six miles, and after being rubbed down I sent him a spin for something under his distance, or a couple for 50 yards, or practised him at starting. Some time after dinner he had another walk in the country. As he carried no superfluous flesh, I allowed him to eat whatever wholesome food he liked, and did not even grumble when, on Fridays, he, being a good Catholic, "fasted" on fish. I used to arrange the start which he had to give the man that ran with him, so as to enable Tobin to win cleverly, for he was one of the sort, just like many a horse, that, though thoroughly "game," gets discouraged by defeat. Whenever I found, as I timed him in his spins, that he was making no improvement on his last essay, I used to promptly give him a couple of days' rest. As soon as he learned to move in proper spiked running shoes, the watch showed, as I had expected, that he was capable of beating "even time." Being an old ped., I know what a bold assertion this is, yet I make it with absolute confidence in its correctness. The man who used to lead him in his gallops was the best runner in Cork, and could do his 100 yards comfortably in 11 secs., yet Tobin, giving him 11 yards start, could always defeat him by a yard or two. Had I had Tobin for a year, I believe he would have turned out a second Harry Hutchens.

At the time I was training my young countryman, I belonged to the Cork City Club, at which there was a good deal of high play. As most of the officers of the garrison were members, and as they "fancied" Mr. Marryat's chance immensely, there was some very heavy wagering between them and my friends, whom I "put on" this very "good thing." Before the race, our party had over £3,000 on it. On the day it came off, the

Englishmen brought so much money to back Mr. Marryat that he started favourite at 30 to 20. The national rivalry broke out so strongly that in the City of Cork most of the shops were shut, while the people came down in thousands to the New Wall to see the race. As the Corporation had granted their permission for it to come off on their public esplanade, and also lent their assistance in keeping order, the arrangements were perfect. The course was roped in, while ropes also divided the respective tracks. A capital start was effected on the signal being given by Major Burnside, but my man quitted his opponent in the first few strides, and won with the greatest ease by five or six yards. The excitement of that vast multitude was simply indescribable. Nobody did any work that day, while every one, after yelling themselves hoarse, went and got more or less drunk.

A few days after the match I had to embark for India, so lost the chance of winning a fortune with Tobin, who, subsequently, did nothing, as he could get no one to train him properly.

I have found that the broad principles of training, whether man or horse, are always the same : their application, of course, varies.

Writing of Cork and pedestrianism reminds me of the great match which took place at "the beautiful city" in 1859, between Sir John Astley and Mr. John Taylor, a local celebrity, who had defeated Captain Machell and many other good men. Sir John, four or five years previously, had proved himself to be the fastest sprinter in the British Army when in the Crimea, and had also done some great performances in England. The match in question came off in the Cork Barrack Square, and on a cold winter's day. As Mr. Taylor lived some distance off, and had no one to look after him from a training point of view, he drove up, lightly clad, on an outside jaunting car, and was, when he arrived, to use an Irish expression, "perished with the cold." Sir John, on the contrary, came out, wrapped in a fur coat, from his quarters which looked on to the Square, and kept his opponent waiting some time as he went up and down the course booking every bet he could get against himself, until at last, even at odds, there was no response to his challenge: "Who'll back the Irishman?" If I remember right, Jimmy Patterson, "the flying tailor," trained the stalwart Guardsman. Although Jack Taylor was naturally as fleet a man as ever faced the starter, he could not, shivering with cold and running in his stockings, prevail against such a flyer as Sir John, who just managed to defeat him after a desperate race. I need hardly say that when Cork had her revenge over the sporting Sassenach with Jack Tobin, no Sheffield "gaffer" could have tended his "tryer" more carefully than I did my Lismore boy.

By the beginning of the cold weather of 1870 I had the horses fairly fit. As we had determined to try our luck at Sealkote, where the 5th Lancers were stationed, and as Captain Maxwell could not get leave of absence at the time, I started with Ranelagh, Caliph, the pony Quaker, and a chestnut Arab, belonging to the Hon. Ralph Hare, of the Horse Gunners. This son of the desert showed fair speed, but could not stay. Added to his inability to travel a distance, he had an unfortunate knack of kicking, which he practised the moment he started to gallop, and did not leave off until he had gone a couple of hundred yards. Needless to say, he did not pay his hay and corn bill. The only horse worth mention that Ranelagh had to meet, was Toprail, and that Caliph had to oppose, was the grey Arab Salar, both belonging to Charlie Bailey of the 20th Hussars. This fine horseman had also that brute Prince Rupert, late Pill Garlic. Our trio won ten or eleven races—in fact, all I asked them to do—and were well ridden by Vincent Wing, R.H.A., who also won the steeplechase on his chestnut mare, Destiny. The only race which fell to the local talent, as far as I can remember, was the buggy stakes won by that smart country-bred, Jack o' Lantern. The Rajah of the place gave a pretty Cashmere-worked gold cup, which fell to Ranelagh's share. On the last day of the races, the Honorary Secretary, after an excellent lunch, put this piece of plate into one of the very capacious pockets of his shooting coat, which was long in the skirt and antiquated in build. He then mounted his pony, and cantered gaily down to the Grand Stand to present the cup to me. When it was produced it was flat as a pancake, as he had done John Gilpin on it all the way down. Although we were unable to drink champagne out of it, we did out of less costly vessels— and the Perrier Joüet tasted quite as well.

There was a five-year-old Arab at this meeting called Morning Star, which ran and showed some slight promise of form. As he was in miserable condition, Captain Maxwell and myself thought we might do something with him, so my Gordon Highlander friend bought him and sent him to me. I brought him back to Meean Meer, gave him nice quiet work, the best of oats, and then asked him the most moderate question ever put to a supposed racehorse : it was to bring the Galloway Caliph home for the last half mile of a four-mile sweat. The little grey "lost" our new acquaintance, although he was giving him at least 28 lbs. in the shape of hoods and rugs. As men will do, we comforted ourselves with that fine old racing adage, "The form is too bad to be true." "A darn sight too bad," we should have said. We eased him in his work. We watched him with the solicitude exhibited by a hen towards her only duckling, and were rewarded, when we tried him again with Caliph at a difference of two stone on the Dehra course, the following season, for a mile, to see him tumble down at the turn home, being evidently appalled at the look of the hill in front of him. My friend sold him as a charger, for which character he was well suited, as he was a fairly handsome peacock.

After Sealkote, I returned to Meean Meer, got more leave of absence, and then went to Ferozepore, where we won most of the races, but not much money, as the regiment there at the time did not go in for sport.

I had a mount at that meeting on Mr. Bailey's Toprail, whom he had sent along with Captain Maxwell's horses in my charge. At the last moment I was disappointed about a rider for the race for which he was entered, so had to get up myself. As soon as I was in the 2 lbs. saddle which I had to use to "get the weight," I found that the stirrup irons were of the very smallest size and far too tight for my feet, especially as I had on rather stout top-boots. There was nothing for it but to proceed, as the remainder of the field were waiting for me, so I took the stirrups up and cantered down to the post. Toprail had much the worst of the handicap on public form, and was, besides that, in a bad temper ; while I, of course, thought there was no chance without stirrups, so I let him go at his own pace—which was a slow one. When we had gone half a mile, our horses were quite 150 yards in front of us. Toprail suddenly, out of, probably, pure contrariety, took the snaffle between his teeth, laid himself down to gallop, and would actually have won, had he not twisted a racing-plate at the turn home and lamed himself for the time being. "What a proof," I mused to myself, "of the advisability of letting rogues make their own running."

CHAPTER VIII.

THE next meeting for which we entered the horses was the Meerut Spring fixture of 1871. Owing to an inspection or some other unavoidable circumstance, we were unable to go down with our animals, so sent them to that best of Horse Gunners, Mr. Barry Domville, to whom the descendant of the Earls of Nithsdale and now owner of Terregles sent a commission to back Caliph in every lottery, although the little Galloway—he was 13.3 easy—had to meet such good Arabs as Mr. Solano's Rising Star, Captain Phillips' Arab Chief, and Captain Kington's Tredegar, for he was a sanguine and impulsive Scotchman, who brooked no interference with his plans. Drawers of horses being as keen to detect a fixed determination to buy, as bookmakers are to scent out a "safe 'un," my friend had naturally to pay a very long price for his property in the second and third lottery, though he got him fairly cheap in the first one.   I felt sick at heart on learning the state of affairs when I arrived at Meerut, a couple of days after the horses.   The jockey whom we had engaged to ride Caliph was a very promising Australian lad, by name Cook.   Caliph was a peculiar horse to steer, and had a natural and, perhaps, not very uncommon idiosyncrasy which I subsequently understood, though I was utterly ignorant of it when he first came into my hands. He was one of the gamest and most generous horses that ever breathed if he was allowed to make his own running ; but if his jockey interfered with him, and wanted to make him adopt tactics which were not after Caliph's own heart, he would stop galloping ; not from sulkiness, but simply because he had no other means of saying to the stupid man on his back, "I know better than you how to play my own game, and if you don't let me play it my own way I won't play at all." When the race came off Cook caught Caliph "by the head," and began to bustle him along, as the Galloway was a slow starter.   He thereupon began to charge his leg, went slower and slower, and finally shut up like the proverbial scissors.   His running was so bad that he got favourably weighted in the next day's handicap, for which John Irving steered him, and after a fine race made a dead heat with Mr. Raphael's Sultan, ridden by Kairoo. Donaldson rode Sultan in the deciding beat and won easily. For the third day's handicap we put Mr. Hoyes of the 109th Regiment on Caliph, and manfully dashed our pieces down, as we knew our horse was of the improving sort. Irving was on Mr. Solano's Rising Star, Donaldson rode Arab Chief, Kurreem piloted Mr. Sewell's Kyber, while there were some other horses whose names I have forgotten. Mr. Hoyes sat still and left Caliph to his own devices. The grey Galloway took matters very leisurely at first, and was several lengths behind at the turn into the straight. Coming up to the quarter of a mile post, he began to improve his position, and had his field " settled " at the distance, when Arab Chief interfered with him in the most palpable manner. Mr. Hoyes thereupon pulled up to let Captain Phillips' horse pass him on the inside, as he knew he could have him disqualified for jostling. While, however, our G. R. was looking to his off side, and, probably, meditating the precise wording of his intended objection, Kurreem came up on the outside and cleverly beat Arab Chief on the post before Mr. Hoyes could set our

Galloway going again. The agony of that moment was something quite too terrible to bear. We fled the course and hid ourselves in our rooms at Gee's Hotel, where we strove to quench with strong waters the burning thoughts that consumed us. Towards midnight my friend arose, seized me by the arm and said, " We'll make a match." We tumbled into a *ticca garee* and drove off to the 4th Hussar mess to find the owner of the hated Arab Chief. We got into the compound just in time to hear the last bars of the National Anthem played by the band. The astonished Hussars met us with hospitable offers of refreshments ; but we abruptly told them that Caliph must be revenged, and that we'd match him against the bay Arab at the handicap weights ; in fact, we'd gladly give him 5 lbs. just to show what we thought of things in general. Our impulsive challenge was gladly accepted ; we had more drink, and departed to our respective beds entirely satisfied with ourselves, as we had a right to be ; for next day, Caliph, ridden by Jack Irving beat Arab Chief with consummate ease for Rs.500 a side. Jack won at this meeting the half-mile handicap for us on Ranelagh against Mr. Collins' Lucknow and some others. This was one of the best ridden races

I have ever seen. Irving knowing what a game horse the handsome son of Peeping Tom was, began to ride him at the quarter of a mile post, as, carrying top weight, he had to do all he knew to keep alongside Lucknow, to whom he was giving a lot of weight. Although Mr. Collins' horse had drawn clear of Ranelagh a hundred yards from home, Jack took a pull for a few strides, then sat down, and with a couple of cuts of his whip, which sounded like two pistol shots, landed him a winner by a short head. Never have I seen a grander horseman then Jack Irving when at his best. Before he went out to India, many years ago, he was one of the best light weights in John Scott's stable.

Some months after that Meerut meeting, Cook accidentally shot himself. He was a quiet, unassuming lad, and would have made, had he lived, a good name for himself, as he could ride a big horse well.

CHAPTER IX.

THE rains of 1871 fell so heavily in the Punjab that when I started with Ranelagh, Caliph, Hawkestone, and Spavin, about the beginning of August, for Dehra Doon, we had to march the whole distance, as the heavy rain which had fallen had rendered the railway unserviceable.

Although the time has long since passed, I well remember the first time I saw the lovely Doon. A six-mile walk through a wooded and winding mountain road took us over the Siwalik range, and then, suddenly, at a turn of the road, the green expanse of plain and valley, covered here and there with the grey mists of morning, burst on our view. Ten miles beyond where we stood, the dark Himalayas rose abruptly from the plain, which stretched far away to the right to meet the Ganges, and to the left to touch the Jumna.

Captain Maxwell and myself had taken two months' leave to spend at Dehra Doon, and had a good house near the course with lots of stabling. Poor "Bricky" Collins was also there with the Arabs Granby and Neville, the Cape horse Merryman, the Waler Pitsford, and others. He had a jockey in the shape of Rowe, who amused himself by composing what he was pleased to call poetry on his fine old master, and on the once mighty Vanderdecken, that Eden Allan gelding which poor Rimmer loved so well. Captain Phillips, of the 4th Hussars, had Arab Chief, Tredegar, Kussdom, and the steeple-chaser Challenger, with Donaldson as his jockey; and a right clever one he was in those days. Colonel (now General) Sir H. T. Macpherson, V.C., who commanded the Indian contingent in Egypt, looked after his lucky Malabar, and had Mr. Hoyes of the 109th to ride him in his gallops. Captain Franks brought Brown Duchess to run. Mr. Collins of Meerut had Navarino, an Arab whose name I have forgotten, and Pavarino for selling races, with Kurreem and a couple of other native boys to send them along. These three lads had a real good time of it. They wore resplendent gold lace caps; they smoked the biggest of hubble-bubbles; they rejoiced in trousers whose tightness precluded the idea of removal at night or at other times; and they wore "Coachwans" of the darkest type. As they did not trouble themselves to get up very early, we were always in time to see them arrive on the course arrayed in all their bravery, and mounted each on his respective steed, as doubtless the tightness of their *pyjamas* prevented them from walking the half mile which intervenes between the Victoria Hotel and the racecourse. No sooner had these three little negro boys, as Captain Franks used to call them, arrived on the galloping track, than they amused themselves by racing round with their cap tassels flying over their horses' tails and their toes stuck out well in front of their animals' noses. And then they cantered home to their breakfasts and their *hukkas.* No wonder that Navarino gave us in the Derby of that year no taste of the excellence which he subsequently displayed under improved management. And Kurreem, how changed is he since those salad days of his hot youth! The schooling he had in the King-craft stable under Kelly, Kurreem Beg, and Ramchurn screwed his head a bit tighter on; lowered his fists a good deal; brought his toes a little back—not much; and taught him to have the best "hands" I have ever seen with a native jockey.

We were early risers in those days; had our work done before the sun was up; our horses rubbed down in our own sheds, which were on the inside of the course, and jealously protected by bamboo screens in front; and had our cup of coffee and cheroot at the stand before proceeding homewards. This coffee-shop institution used to be established nearly a couple of months before the races came off. After work on the course, we generally retired to Bricky Collins' hospitable quarters, where he usually had many tender beefsteaks, bunches of watercress, hot rolls, and Guinness's XXX. to give us an appetite for breakfast. Jaffir was always by the old man's side, and helped, with many a quaint saying, to while away the time pleasantly. When our visit to Mr. Collins was over, we either got up lotteries on the forthcoming Derby, amused ourselves through the listless day, or drove up to Rajpore and rode up to Mussoorie. I liked to go there to cool my eyes with a sight of the distant peaks of the Snowy Range, and to feel that strange exhilaration of spirits all but the dullest experience on first coming up to the Hills from the plains. The event of our evenings was seeing the Arab Malabar doing his gallops with Mr. Hoyes in the saddle. Colonel Macpherson, watch in hand, directed his horse's work ; while Mrs. Macpherson usually looked on from her carriage, with heartfelt interest in the gallant grey's doings. I adore (I speak in general terms, *bien entendu*) a woman who loves a horse, and recall with pleasure the lady's happy smile when she heard that Malabar had done his work well. I am glad to say that their trouble was rewarded by Malabar winning the Derby and the Arab Handicap. In the former he beat a good field, including Kussdom, second, Aboo Janoub, third, Star of Cashmere, Granby, and others, in the good time—for the Dehra course—of 2 min. 29 secs. for the 1¼ miles.

A week or so before the races came off, Mr. Lethorne, who had at that time a very large stable, arrived from Poonah with Karpos, the Arabs Aboo Janoub, Star of Cashmere, and Abdool Rahman, late Little Hercules, and brought Dignum and Gooch to train and ride them. The Star was one of those supposed pearls of great price whose former owner sold all that he had to keep this gem of horse-flesh. What this animal could do when untrained and unfit surpassed anything done in

public by the fleetest of Arabs, even when favoured
by the fastest of stop watches, which are often sad
flatterers. As a natural consequence, when the Star
was fit and well and had something speedier than the
rails alongside of him, he proved a miserable failure.
The Gordon Highlanders got him afterwards, but
could do nothing with him, so sold him to one of the
4th Hussars as a charger. Aboo Janoub was a big,
strong grey with a coarse head. He showed little
quality, though he was said to be of very high caste.
He never ran very well, and had more than the usual
number of excuses made for him. His owner backed
him heavily for the Calcutta Derby that year, and has,
I think, hardly yet done wondering how he lost. Some
evil-inclined person was supposed to have mixed datura
seeds in his corn prior to the big event, and thus made
him "safe." Instead of framing excuses for horses,
how seldom do we hear an owner say that the reason
his horse lost was because he did not gallop fast enough !
I saw Aboo Janoub, after the Calcutta Derby, at Lucknow and Benares, and beat him with Caliph each time
they met. The excuse then was that he had not got
over the effects of the datura. I believe the horse was
a good one, but unsound.

Among the many speedy animals which were assembled at Dehra, none was more worthy of notice than Mr. Lethorn's Arab pony Abdool Rahman, late Little Hercules. He was a dark bay with black points, standing 13.2 easy, and was the incarnation of quality and beauty. He had, about three weeks before, won a 1½ mile handicap up the hill at Poonah in 2 min. 55 sec., carrying 8 st. 10 lbs! and was to oppose Caliph in the mile Galloway race. We backed, with the enthusiasm of young hands, our matchless grey, and heeded not the pleased looks and ill-concealed elation of those who, having received the straight tip from Poonah, laid against us as if it was all over, bar shouting. To us Caliph was a religion, a god—at least he often proved a saviour from ruin when, beguiled by the hope that tells a flattering tale, we backed the wrong horse. Caliph on these occasions came forward and did some great performance which filled our emptied pockets. Mr. Lethorn's pony and Caliph were to meet in the one-mile Galloway race at Dehra. George Gooch steered the former, while Williams, our jockey, rode the latter. The race may be quickly described. Our grey Arab jumped off with the lead along with King David, was caught by Gooch, who had got a bad start, half way up the hill, and, having always the best of it, won cleverly at the finish. The result was a heavy blow to Mr. Lethorn and Dignum, who reproached old George for unwonted sleepiness at the post to which I went down, for Caliph wanted some one at his head, at times, to get him under way. Had I not been there to have given Williams a hand, the result might have been different, for the old horse was inclined to be as fractious as Abdool Rahman, who was a little too much for Gooch.

George Gooch was one of the few men we meet with in a lifetime who are real geniuses. He learned to ride in an English training stable, and came out to India more than thirty years ago. The first big race he won in the East was the Calcutta Derby of 1853, on Nero. As he was always able to ride 7 st. 10 lbs. without wasting, and was a consummate judge of pace, he had as many mounts as he cared to take. At the commencement of his career he made a lot of money, and was at one time a partner in a large Calcutta commission and livery stable. He married, but was unhappy in his domestic arrangements; and then everything went wrong with him. Poor George, being confiding in his disposition and free with his rupees, found companions who led him astray, and with whom he sought consolation to drown his cares. He soon lost every penny he had, and, for the last fifteen years or so, has lived from "hand to mouth," quite contented if, after a spree, he can scrape together a few coppers a day on which to live. Yet, in all his want and misery, old George, when well enough to ride, is still the cool, finished jockey, and has always been the same "straight," honest fellow in his calling that he was when he left the old country, over thirty years ago.

Shortly before this Dehra meeting, Dignum, who was training Mr. Lethorn's horses, picked Gooch up and gave him employment under himself: an arrangement at which the old boy somewhat chafed, as in former days their positions, in Colonel Robarts' great stable, were just the reverse. Dignum, being somewhat too heavy himself, got Gooch to ride most of the training gallops. As old George's seat on horseback was not quite to his employer's liking, Dignum used to "check" him, as soldiers call it, for bumping in the saddle. This slur on his riding rankled in the mind of the Yorkshireman, especially as it was made by an Australian who had never been on the Newmarket Heath, let alone the Doncaster Town Moor. Then, again, Gooch's win on Ranelagh did not, perhaps, improve matters. After the Dehra Meeting was over, Mr. Lethorn's horses went in due course to the Meerut races, in one of which both Abdool Rahman and Aboo Janoub were entered. Mr. Lethorn backed the former to win a large stake, and gave the mount to Dignum, while he put Gooch on the latter. Now it happened that two or three sportsmen, thinking that the grey was the better horse of the two, purchased him in the lotteries, and put old George on fifty pounds to nothing. When the race came off, Mr. Lethorn's pair led their field to the distance post, and then Gooch drew away in front of his stable companion, bumping up and down in the most ridiculous manner, and turning round to shout out, " Do I bump in the saddle, Mr. Dignum ? "   I am afraid that the owner and trainer did not join very heartily in the uproarious bursts of laughter which greeted this absurd attempt to pay off an old score.

I must add that both Mr. Lethorn and Dignum undoubtedly thought, from the Dehra form, that Abdool Rahman was the better of the two. They, however, overlooked the fact that the grey was rapidly " coming on," while the bay was susceptible of no further improvement.

One of the most important events of that meeting was the 1¾ mile all horse handicap. Karpos, 10 st., Merryman, 8 st. 2 lbs., Ida, 6 st. 10 lbs., and Ranelagh, 7 st. 9 lbs., were entered for it. Our horse got pricked in shoeing five or six days before running, so we called in Mayhew the farrier to treat him. Mayhew cut with a drawing knife boldly down on the offending nail from the outside, put the foot in a poultice, which was kept on all night, and applied a bar shoe, with the result that the son of Peeping Tom and Princess was out next day sound as a bell. Luckily no one else saw him go sound, so we profited by the report of his lameness ; gave him a couple of gallops by moonlight ; bought him in the lotteries ; backed him besides ; engaged Gooch, to whom we promised a hundred rupees and his winning mount, to ride ; and had the satisfaction of seeing him canter in the easiest of winners ; with Karpos, ridden by Dignum, second. The much fancied Ida and Merryman were beaten off. When Gooch got into the scales to weigh in, he could not, to our horror, pull the weight, even with the assistance of the bridle. I could have shrieked with laughter had not that moment been too serious for mirth, at seeing old George almost burst himself, while his eyes were starting out of their sockets, in the frantic

CAPTAIN FRANKS, "_The Buffs._"

Page 93.

efforts he made to draw in his breath to make himself heavier, and thereby bring the beam down ; but it was all in vain. As I knew we had quite a pound in hand, I insisted on the weights being overhauled, and then found that a mistake had been made in computing the native weight, a *mun*—the clerk of the scales being short of half hundredweights—as 80 lbs. instead of 82 lbs.

Ranelagh furnished a good exemplification of the rule that a horse with high action performs best on a hill, for he was very moderate on the flat.

The steeplechase was won in brilliant style by Captain Franks on Brown Duchess, with Challenger second, ridden by Captain Phillips. After the race Captain Maxwell and I bought the mare between us for Rs.1600. I subsequently purchased my friend's share.

Karpos, late Detrimental, though a game, fine stayer, and possessed of fair speed, was a very unlucky horse. At the end of the preceding year, 1870, he had a great chance of winning the Viceroy's Cup, which was presented by the late Lord Mayo, at the Calcutta races, the distance being two miles. As this event furnished a good instance of the evil resulting from the too hasty exhibition of virtuous indignation, it may be worth describing. The following is the detail of the race :—

Mr. W. W.'s Favourite, 9 st. 7 lbs.	Dignum	1
Mr. W. W.'s Longden, 9 st. 7 lbs.	Hackney	2
Mr. C. Herberte's Detrimental, 9 st. 7 lbs.	Donaldson	3
Mr. Sheardale's Melbourne, 9 st. 7 lbs. ...	Williamson	0
Mr. Seventank's Miss Trelawny, 9 st. 7 lbs.	Wheal	0

On entering into the straight, Favourite was leading, with Detrimental right behind her. Hackney then closed up alongside Donaldson, and "nursed" him so carefully that he could not get through. Melbourne finished fourth, and the English mare, Miss Trelawny, last. The stewards disqualified Longden on the plea that the "nursing" constituted jostling, and fined Hackney eighty rupees. They also disqualified Favourite because she belonged to the same owner as did Longden. The objection to Mr. W. W.'s horses was made on behalf of Detrimental by Messrs. Lethorn, C. Herbert, and C. W. Wilson, who quite forgot that by proclaiming a joint ownership they revealed an undeclared confederacy, which was against the Calcutta Turf Club rules. Detrimental was, thereupon, promptly disqualified ; and as only three horses had been placed, and as they all had been disqualified, the race was declared null and void. Melbourne's jockey, not having weighed in, had, of course, no claim. The case was sent up to the stewards of the Jockey Club, who naturally decided that Favourite ought to have been declared the winner ; for, if a jockey chooses to attempt to get through on the inside, he has only himself to thank if the other riders refuse to pull out for him. The stewards of the Calcutta Turf Club and Indian Sporting Press had previously arisen as one man and denounced Hackney for his supposed foul riding. How very silly they must have felt afterwards ! As regards Miss Trelawny's claim, Lord Ulick Browne, who is justly regarded as our Indian Admiral Rous, although he was wrong about the " nursing," still he clearly demonstrated that had the three placed horses been rightly disqualified, the English mare ought to have got the cup, by citing the case of the Claret Stakes at New-market in 1831, which was as follows :—By the terms of the race the second horse was to save his stake. When the race came off, only two horses were placed, while none of the remaining four obtained a " situation." The first horse was disqualified for a cross, and the second declared the winner. The question then was mooted, what horse's stake was to be saved ? The stewards of the Jockey Club decided that the disputed stake should be divided among the owners of all the unplaced horses. This decision clearly defines the position of unplaced horses ; namely, that they are not disqualified by the mere fact of their not being placed.

As a wind up to this very successful Dehra Doon meeting, we had a match with Caliph against a fifteen-hand Arab, called the Sheik, who belonged to Mr. Minto, the tea planter. The distance was about six furlongs, and we had to give away some weight. The evening before the match I found Caliph so stiff all round that he could hardly walk. I kept him standing in buckets of warm water all night, had him out for an hour in the morning previous to running, rubbed his fetlocks, knees, and hocks well with laudanum, gave him a quarter of a pint of spirits in water, and had him trotted and cantered up and down. The stiffness wore off, and he won very easily. I had not alone to doctor the horses, but also to prescribe for our jockey Williams. He was a typical specimen of an old and, I trust, now extinct species of Indian jockey. He had been a soldier in some line regiment, but finding that he could ride a little, and that the services of any one who could "stick on" and scale less than 9 st. were in great request in those days in the Punjab, he purchased his discharge, and entered upon his new life with a pair of boots and breeches and an unquenchable thirst for ardent spirits.

Though Williams was not much better than a good amateur, still he was well able to take his own part among the company he usually met, for do we not all know that in the kingdom of the blind the one-eyed is king? Having served with many masters, he came at last to me in dire poverty. As I could get no one better, I engaged him on the distinct understanding that he was to "go on the strike" as regards all fermented liquors ; and right loyally did he keep his promise for a time. The old boy pulled himself together, lived in our house, got strong and well, and rode very fairly indeed. Whether it was the unaccustomed regular hours and wholesome food affected him, I cannot say, but his nose turned purple and looked as if it was likely to tumble off. As I could not stand the idea of Caliph being ridden by a noseless man, I gave Williams some simple medicine, which cooled him down and made him all right. Far from thanking me for restoring him to his former good looks, he declared that the physic which I had administered, gave him such an intolerable thirst that he no longer considered his total abstinence promise binding on him, so he took the four or five hundred rupees which were owing to him, went down to Meerut, fell into gay society, and ended his career by falling or being thrown out of the top window of some slummy house.

As the Dehra Doon races were followed, after an interval of a few days, by those at Umballa, we sent Ranelagh in charge of Mr. Knox to run there, as we had to return to our respective regiments in the north. The son of Peeping Tom, after winning the All Horse Handicap, came back to my stable.

CHAPTER X.

MR. J. P. COLLINS, to whom I alluded in the last chapter, commenced life as a working brickmaker. Being a man of powerful *physique*, strong will, and great natural shrewdness, he soon rose among his fellows, and during the Russian war became an overseer to a gang of navvies in the Crimea. Some time after the fall of Sebastopol, he went out to India, where he soon made himself known as the best brickmaker in the country, and got large contracts in that line of business. He once told me that in his early days he was whip to a pack of Irish fox-hounds, of which Lord Howth, if I remember right, was master. Perhaps it was in that capacity he gained the fine knowledge of horse-flesh which he possessed. As soon as he got on in the world, he commencd racing, and formed a confederacy with Dr. Rimmer, who had been brought up to the sport, and could have "held his own" "on the flat" in any company. They purchased a bay Australian gelding, called Eden Allan, by Dolo out of Madcap by Ransom (imported), out of Medora by Peter Fuin (imported), and bred by Mr. L. Hunter in 1858. This gelding stood 15 hands 3 inches, was a three-cornered looking customer, had a Roman nose, curby hocks, and appeared singularly devoid of racing points. He had been imported by a Mr. Williamson, who sent him to a large Calcutta racing stable, the trainer of which, after trying him, returned him as being too slow for racing. Old Jim Collins and Dr. Rimmer looked the horse over, and bought him for, I believe, about Rs. 1800. With them he began his racing career as Vanderdecken.

In the season of 1863–64, he won his first race at Umballa and his second at Allahabad; but at the latter meeting was beaten in the Welter Handicap by the Arab, Rajah, 9 st. 12 lbs. He won at Lucknow; but, carrying 8 st. 6 lbs., was beaten by Captain Baumgarten's great horse, Lord of Clyde, 10 st. 9 lbs.

The next season he started thirty-one times, and won twenty-five races, beating the best horses in India at all weights and distances. Vanderdecken continued his victorious career for about five years, and won such an extraordinary number of races that his name in India has passed into a proverb. He was a wonderful stayer, and could carry any weight. The old horse continued running, though but a shadow of his former self, until he was about fifteen years of age, and then found rest in harness. Despite Vanderdecken's fame, there was little to choose between him and Colonel Robarts' Australian gelding Rocket, who was running at the same time, and who did not possess even a "salt water" pedigree. One of their fastest races was that for the Merchants' Cup, two miles, at Calcutta, January, 1868, when Rocket, 9 st. 9 lbs. beat Vanderdecken, 9 st. 4 lbs., in 3 min. 44 secs. Colonel Robart's bonny Waler mare Favourite—or Jenny, as her jockey, Jack Irving used to call her—was about as good as either of these geldings; while in later days, Ali Abdoolah's Satellite and Mr. Maitland's Kingcraft were, perhaps, 10 lbs. better. Satellite was an extraordinary good horse, but from an unfortunate habit he had of over-reaching, did not fulfil the promise of his youth. At Sonepore, 1873, carrying 10 st. 8 lbs., he is stated to have gone out the first mile in the Ticcaree cup in 1 min. 44 sec. Perhaps the best average of a large number of races in one season in India was that of Lord of Clyde, in 1863–64, when, out of thirty-eight times he started, he won thirty-two.

At the time Vanderdecken commenced running "Captain Charles" (Colonel Smith, better known as "Smith of Asia") owned a thoroughbred English mare called Morning Star, who, for a mile, was 2 st. better than the Waler, and 21 lbs. his superior for 1½ miles, as the old man told me, and as her performances testify. At Calcutta, December, 1865, in the Trial Stakes, one mile, carrying 10 st. 1 lb., she defeated Vanderdecken, 9 st. 4 lbs., in a common canter in 1 min. 47 sec.! She was, perhaps, the fastest miler we have ever had in India. As Mr. Collins could not beat her, he bought her. He told me that he once tried her, with 8 st. up, to do a mile in 1 min. 41 sec. She was an unlucky purchase for Mr. Collins, as she was not long in his possession before she died of some internal complaint. Death also removed poor Dr. Rimmer. From that time, Mr. Collins raced and trained his own horses with considerable success, as far as wins went, though without profit from a pecuniary point of view, as, being illiterate, he kept no accounts himself, and was frequently deceived by persons in whom he rashly put confidence. The old man was a great "character," and possessed a large fund of ready, though very rough humour. He used to attend every race meeting within reach, much to the detriment of his business, and was never so happy as when surrounded by a lot of racing men, with whom he used to drink, chaff, and exchange stories. Although he knew every one from the Viceroy downwards, and often dined at the different messes, he never affected any other character than that of a bluff, honest English navvy.

After Dr. Rimmer's death, Mr. Collins took into his employment the native jockey Jaffir, who served his old master, through all his ups and downs, with unwavering fidelity. Jaffir was then able to ride about 6 st., and although he was rather too fond of "making the running," and of having his stirrups at extreme *haute école* length, still he was a good horseman, and "had a head on his shoulders." He was extremely quick-witted, and was even a keen critic of newspaper reporting. He once feelingly complained to me that whenever he lost a race, he was returned as "Jaffir" in the account of the meeting ; but when he won, he was sure to see himself described as "a native." On one occasion, at the Sonepore races, he gravely asked a half-caste jockey if he was not going to claim half the 3 lbs. allowance they gave to native jockeys!

Among Mr. Collins' many *protégés* was the Australian lad Roe, to whom I alluded in the foregoing chapter. He was a slight, respectable-looking young fellow, who had lots to say for himself. Jim Collins' genial heart "warmed" to the lad, as he thought he had seen better days, and as he was fairly educated. His efforts at prose and poetry were regarded with the most profound veneration by the old man, who could barely spell through them. Roe had "a very good time of it"; he lived with his master, had to ride only two or three training gallops in the mornings, and was never short of money. His poetical compositions were quite unfit for publication: not because they would raise the proverbial blush, but they had neither sense, rhyme, nor rhythm. In prose he was more successful, as he was amusing and almost graphic, although probably not in the way he had intended, as the following extract from a report of his of the Cawnpore races, 1869, in which Colonel Robarts' two mares, Favourite and Bellona, and the Hon. Walter Harbord's Milliner, competed, may show.

"They are off! Away they fly past the post, Bellona

leading, Milliner close by her side, and Favourite hanging back from outside place to press in afterwards for inner running. Cunning Dignum, splendid Favourite! Yet Dignum was no young enthusiast, so would not give in to the cravings of the spirited mare. But now they're coming! The whip home is dreadful. All is breathless silence and agonizing expectancy. No man can say which of these handsome and splendid conditioned mares lead. They're at the straight struggle for the post, head to head. Now the mare with most mettle must answer kindly to the whip, and now for the jockey's nerve and judgment! They're upon us. The Favourite is victorious over Bellona, and Milliner is by Bellona's flank." In describing the steeplechase he said, "Not one of the horses shyed or fainted at the jumps."

Roe did not seem to appreciate Mr. Collins' kindness, for he was missing one morning not long after the Dehra meeting, and has not been since heard of.

In 1879, at Meerut, when Mr. Collins was driving home one night, his trap upset, and he was thrown out and killed. He left a comfortable sum to his faithful henchman Jaffir, who has now a racing stable of his own.

CHAPTER XI.

CAWNPORE — JACK O'CONNOR — ALIGURH — LUCKNOW
RACES, 1872 — HAWKESTONE — CAWNPORE RACES,
1872 — LUCKNOW RACES, 1873 — MR. WILLIAM
THACKER.

SHORTLY after my return to Meean Meer, I had to
"fall in" with my regiment and proceed to the Camp of
Exercise at Delhi. Foreseeing this contingency, I got
Mr. Knox to kindly look after Ranelagh, Caliph,
and Hawkestone, while I took Objection and Brown
Duchess with me. I had rather a pleasant time of it,
as General Payne, in whose brigade we were, frequently
got me to do galloper for him.

When our mimic warfare under the gallant Tombs
was over, I sent for the three horses which were at
Umballa, packed up my luggage, and saw the animals
made comfortable in their boxes in the train. I re-

member well the cold morning we arrived in Cawnpore cantonments, which looked, in the grey light, like a city of the dead rather than a place to live and be merry in ; and yet I have spent many a pleasant hour on the racecourse ; many a brave day at Sumbulpore and across the river with the Tent Club under the skilful leadership of Mr. Maxwell, of the Elgin Mills ; many an afternoon larking on Brown Duchess, Rebecca, and others, over fences natural and artificial, on the light sandy soil on the Oude side ; and many jolly evenings at the club by the church, and at our Mess House by the river.

Having seen that my fellow-passengers Caliph, Ranelagh, Brown Duchess, and Hawkestone were watered, fed, and bedded down, I went to the race-course and found its track almost obliterated and the ground as hard as any metalled road ; while the stand, which has since been pulled down, stood as a melancholy memorial of the days when old Jem Collins used to camp hard by in the Sevada Kothee at the brickfields, with his large string of horses, led by Vanderdecken, and trained by the trusty Jaffir. The course was soon put into galloping order, for Cawnpore then possessed a number of ladies who were fond of riding, and had no other place than it on which to "tittup." I represented to them that conversation with their escorts, when riding, could not be easily carried on amid the clatter of the horses' hoofs on the hard ground, and I also pointed out to their husbands and fathers that the softer the "going," the longer would the horses' legs and feet stand ; the result being that a good and lengthy list of subscriptions to the racecourse fund came in, and we got a mile and a half of the finest tan gallop I have ever seen.

About three weeks after our arrival in Cawnpore I went to Lucknow to run our horses at the Spring Meeting of February, 1872, which had to be postponed for a fortnight ; for the day previous to its commencement the sad news of the assassination of Lord Mayo was telegraphed. As the Aligurh races were to come off in the interval, I put the horses into the train and started off with Donaldson, who was then one of the most successful jockeys in India, and a very Archer for getting the best of a start. Mr. "Joe" Anderson also journeyed up from Lucknow with poor Jack O'Connor, the pony Wooloomooloo, and Bohomahondai, that horse of many names, who began life as Nadir Shah in Bombay, from whence he went to run in

Ceylon, where he distinguished himself. Jousiffe bought
and then lent him on racing terms to the popular and
genial veterinary surgeon of the Horse Gunners, who
baptized him Cast Off. In those days some persons
had a way of changing horses' names at almost every
meeting to which they went. The five gold mohur
penalty for so doing, which is now enacted by the
Calcutta Turf Club rules, has, happily, limited the
practice. Cast Off finally figured at Meerut as Redan,
and was the cause, as well as I can recollect, of some unpleasantness between the 15th Hussars and Mr. Maitland.
Jack O'Connor was born in New Zealand, where
Mr. Anderson knew him. He was a light weight, could
ride about 7 st. 7 lbs., had no style or finish about him,
but was one of the bravest lads I have ever seen over
a country. No horse was too uncertain, no fence too
big, for the lion-hearted boy. He was not quite a
model in other respects; but *de mortuis*, &c. He
met his death in a strange way. In the days when
honorary secretaries to race meetings made steeple-chase
courses as if they were in the wilds of Ireland, and
had been commissioned to provide a corpse or two
for the "diversion" of the "boys," the Meerut racing
authorities constructed a course the like of which

was never seen before, and will, I hope, never be again. Instead of a "double bank," they made a fortification, which was high enough to effectually conceal the view of the country in front from any approaching horseman. It, of course, stopped all the field except Jack O'Connor, who was mounted on the runaway Antelope. The harebrained pair charged it at racing speed; with one mighty bound the mare sprang on the top, and was off again with the quickness of thought. Seeming to exult in her "deed of derring-do," she broke from the lad's control. Poor Jack had been ill from fever for some days previous to the chase, and was unable to guide the mad mare. At last, being quite exhausted, it appears that he tried to throw himself off, and came in a sitting position on the ground. Some bystanders helped him up. He said a word or two, tried to drink some water, lay down and died. The poor fellow had ruptured one of the blood-vessels in his brain.

The only horse worth mentioning that Caliph, Hawkestone, and Cast Off had to meet in the Arab and country-bred race at Aligurh was the grey Arab Fluck, belonging to Captain Napier, of the 3rd Hussars, and lent by him on racing terms to Mr. Robarts, an Aligurh planter. This horse was a rank bad one, but was supposed to be something very first-class. I backed Caliph in the lotteries, and did not touch Hawkestone, as he had been recently suffering from catarrh. Caliph romped in a winner, and Cast Off, with Jack O'Connor up, displayed a form that was quite too bad to be true. I could judge by the whispers and looks of the local talent that our grey Galloway would have a heavy impost assigned to him in the last day's handicap. As I had nothing to thank the good people for, I humoured their evil intentions and gave full vent to my admiration for Caliph. The Aligurh sportsmen being delighted with the temper in which they found me, asked my advice as to the handicap, and suggested 12 st. for Caliph. I assented, and put their maiden down at about 3 st. less. They were so pleased at this flattery, that they turned the remainder loose, among which was the dark Cast Off, of whom they knew nothing, and who was probably quite as good that day as Caliph for the mile they had to travel. Mr. Anderson and I bought in Cast Off in the lottery, and allowed the Aligurh division, after running up Caliph to spite me, as they imagined, to have him all to themselves. I gave them a good run for their money, as I put up Mr. Reilly, a veterinary surgeon of the Royal Artillery ; but good as the little horse was, the weight was too crushing, and Cast Off won in an exercise canter.

I should have done well at that meeting had I refrained—but what man can refrain?—from leaving my money in the air; I mean backing a horse in the "lep" race. Donaldson had brought Captain Phillip's Challenger to run in the hurdle race, for which I had entered Brown Duchess. There were three or four other runners, among the rest a country-bred "tat" about 13.2, called Doddles. This animal, though as slow as a man, was an undeniable jumper. Captain Knox, of the 85th K.L.I., rode my mare, who got well away at the start, jumped so big at the first hurdle that she broke one of "Missy's" stirrup leathers, and raced at the next hurdle with all her wonted impetuosity. But "Missy" was on her way to England on leave, he thought—well, he hadn't much time for thinking—for not liking the pace with only one stirrup leather, he pulled the mare round, and before he could get her into a collected canter, the despised Doddles had cleared all the obstacles and won the race, for which I had backed the mare for all the money I could get on. Challenger, being in an uncertain mood, would have nothing to say to the hurdles.

That fine old sportsman, Mr. Rainsford, was the chief

winner at Aligurh. He did good business with a grey country-bred Galloway, Charlie, and another, in the local events, for which the animals had to be the *bonâ fide* property of residents at Aligurh, or, as it appeared to me, of their friends not more than hundred miles away.

The judge at Aligurh very kindly gave me stabling for the horses, the honorary secretary treated me to one *chhoti haziri* (early morning breakfast). *Voilà tout.* I wrote an account of the meeting in the *Oriental Sporting Magazine.* I praised their unbounded hospitality, said they were jolly good fellows, and all that. Unfortunately my Parthian shafts glanced off their thick hides, for when they read my account, they sent for many copies of the magazine to circulate among their friends, to show that one at least appreciated them. Since then I have given up sarcasm.

On my return to Lucknow with the horses, I found a strong muster of racing men intent on the all-absorbing business of trying to get three to two the best of their neighbours. Jousiffe had little John, who was called Marathon by Mr. Collins, of Meerut, and Royal by that good sportsman, Mr. Doyne, of the 13th Hussars, and the English horse, Toujours Prêt, who expended himself by jumping out of a train on some line on the Madras side. Royal subsequently had something to do with breaking that excellent rider, singer, and pedestrian, Mr. Johnson, at *the* big Umballa meeting ; for the dark bay gelding proved somewhat "reluctant," as we used to say in Muskery long ago. John Wheal, the well-known "Stumps" of Indian journalistic fame, had brought to the capital of Oude, "Mr. Seventank's" (Babu Shama Churn Mullick's) horses, Gipsy, Acrobat, Syrian, and some others. Dignum and Mr. Lethorn had Aboo Janoub, Abdool Rahman, the country-bred Verbies, who had beaten Hawkestone and the ever-green hero Shamrock at Deyrah, and two or three more ; while there were many other owners and horses. We had entered Hawkestone for the Lucknow Derby, for which the black mare Gipsy, who had beaten the Earl and Silvertail at Calcutta, for a mile in 1 min. 52 secs., was running. I knew that our slashing country-bred, who was somewhat straight and heavy in front, would per- form very differently over the easy Lucknow mile, than he had done down the descent and up the ascent at Deyrah, so accordingly backed him. On the last occa- sion I saw poor Ralph Hare (Lord Listowel's brother), who had owned Hawkestone as a colt, he said to me, with almost tears in his eyes, " I'm seldom wrong about a horse, old fellow. I was right in sticking to Jurham, Jerry, and Whalebone. Do take the word of an old friend who has ridden and owned a few, that Hawke-stone is a racehorse." I believed him, and had a " flutter" over the Lucknow event. There was one difficulty; I didn't know the horse's age, for Ralph Hare had not given me a copy of the stud certificate. I went to the stewards of the meeting and requested them to age him. They sent the veterinary surgeon of the cavalry regiment which was then stationed at Luck-now to determine the point. The M.R.C.V.S. being somewhat timid of " gees," approached the brown horse cautiously. I opened the animal's mouth for him. He gave a hurried glance into it, and said, " Three years old." Thereupon I closed that mouth and sent the horse straight off to his stable, although John Wheal and others wanted to have their look too. Now Hawke-stone happened to have an old side and a young side to his mouth. The vet. inspected the latter only, and never looked at the former at all ! He also, probably, forgot that country-bred racehorses took their ages from January 1. It was then February—and no doubt considered he would be four on the following May 1—

according to the English calculation for half-bred animals. Of course it was not my place to set him right, for I had only my own unprofessional opinion, and had not the presumption to oppose it to his duly accredited one. John Wheal, however, took down the stud marks which were on the horse's back and telegraphed off to the stud authorities to find out his date of foaling. Government officials being somewhat tardy in their movements, the answer was despatched by post. In the meantime Hawkestone, carrying three-year-old weight, easily beat Gipsy and the others. So that was first blood to us. After it was all over, it turned out that the brown horse should have run as a four-year-old, he having been foaled in August. Moral.—In ageing a horse, look at both sides of his mouth, and also at his back teeth, in case of doubt.

Hawkestone followed up his success in the Lucknow Derby by winning the Talukdar's Plate, a race for all country-breds; while Caliph secured the Dilkoosha Stakes for Galloways, beating Abdool Rahman, Acrobat, &c. Up to this time, my friend Captain Maxwell had not arrived, as he could not get leave for the first two days' racing. When he came, he was overjoyed to find such a good amount to the credit side of our account, and resolved to have a gamble on the steeplechase, although I entreated him to "leave well alone." I allowed him to have his plunge on Brown Duchess all to himself, as he had asked me as a favour to give Mr. Wade, of the 26th Cameronians, the mount in order to save three or four lbs., as I could not get up lighter than 11 st. 7 lbs. Mr. Wade appeared on the day of the chase in an enormous turban, with racing jacket, boots, and breeches. He explained to me that the Oriental head gear was admirable for saving a man from concussion of the brain. Knowing what would happen when men talk thus before riding a chase on a horse that does not know how to fall, I felt too sick to take any further interest in the day's proceedings. Of course the mare— No, she didn't refuse—anyhow, she didn't jump, and the Aligurh *fiasco* was repeated. Next day I had to go back to Cawnpore to obtain some more leave, and as the Arab and Country-bred Handicap for one and a half miles had not been published, I told Captain Maxwell that Hawkestone could not get that distance with any weight, and that he must solely rely on Caliph, if the little horse was at all leniently treated. I did my day's "sentry go" and ate my dinner at our mess in Cawnpore, meditating the while on the lotteries that

were being held at Lucknow on the next day's events.
Immediately after parade on the following morning, I
started for Lucknow and found, to my horror, when I
arrived there, that, while I had been spending my
evening quietly in Cawnpore, my friend, having taken
the advice of some of the would-be-knowing ones,
had gone in recklessly to back Hawkestone, who had
fetched high prices in the lotteries. Besides that, he
had various other plunges on equally hopeless chances.
I managed to get a little on Caliph, but not enough to
save ourselves, and had the barren satisfaction of seeing
the justness of my opinion vindicated by the gallant
little Galloway, magnificently ridden by Dignum, winning
one of the finest races I have ever seen from John Wheal
on Acrobat ; while Hawkestone was beaten off quite fifty
yards.   I felt so " broke " that a meeting which ought to
have been a brilliant success had turned out a disaster
to us, that I sent off Captain Maxwell's horses to Dehra,
and thus ended my racing connection with him.   I had
further cause for remembering that meeting.   At the
settling, a man who owed me Rs. 750 over the races,
asked me to give him Rs. 250 as he was short of ready
cash, and that he would give me a cheque for the
Rs. 1000 on Calcutta.   I handed over the money and have

never seen a copper of it since. Finding that I could not get the cheque cashed, and hearing that the person in question had gone to Meerut, where a race meeting was being held, I went there, and found him playing the old game he had performed at Calcutta and Lucknow, of plunging in the lotteries. I stopped it pretty quick despite his showing me what "good things" he had on, and which were sure, so he said, to come off; but I didn't "tumble to it," to use a current London expression. We had him subsequently warned off, and since that time, whenever I go to Calcutta, I pay a visit to the Grand Stand on the racecourse and read his name on "the board," just to give me an appetite for breakfast.

As the hot weather was now coming on, and as I had only my own mare New Broom (late Brown Duchess) to look after, I thought I might with advantage enter myself for the High Proficiency Stakes in Hindi at Calcutta, with Rs. 1500 added by Government; and won easily, after a couple of months' training under our regimental pundit, and a month in Calcutta with that venerable old Bengali, Shiv Naryan, who, having since died, is now, probably, disporting himself on a lotus leaf in the sea of milk (*chhirsamundar*) with his namesake.

I must pick up now the thread of my narrative. On my return to Cawnpore from Calcutta during the rains in 1872, after having got the money for the High Proficiency prize in Hindi, I received a letter from Captain Maxwell asking me to lend him Brown Duchess, on racing terms. I assented to this, and despatched her off to Dehra Doon to him. She won, for the second year in succession, the Dehra Grand Annual Steeplechase, ridden by Captain Papillon, and beating War Eagle and some other good horses. That fine horseman, Charley Bailey, of the 20th Hussars, not satisfied with his defeat in the Doon, carefully schooled War Eagle over the Umballa course, and got him so fit and clever, that he beat his former double victress, after one of the finest races over a country ever witnessed in India.

When the mare came back to me, I found that the people of Cawnpore were willing to make an attempt to revive the glories of that old racing centre, so I asked some of the local swells to be stewards, sent round the hat, drew out a prospectus, and advertised the races to come off, just before the Sonepore fixture. We added five hundred rupees to the steeplechase, and got a large number of entries, though the flat events were not well patronised. "Bricky" Collins brought

Black Eagle, Mr. Lethorn arrived with the black horse Morialta, that good sportsman "Mr. John" came from Chumparun with the country-bred mare Lurline and the pale-faced Delphos, who ought to have won the big chase at Calcutta, over which so much ink was shed by Captain Phillips, of the 4th Hussars. Although Brown Duchess, after the Umballa *fiasco*, had won a flat race at Meerut, beating among others that excellent miler Prince Alfred, who had been brought over under the name of Coventry from Mauritius, along with Partisan, by Mr. Bradshaw, the stable of the Gordon Highlanders were not able to pay me my share of the mare's winnings, so sent me Caliph to run at Cawnpore, on the chance of his recouping me the money they owed me. The gallant grey easily accomplished his task, for he won the Arab and country-bred race and handicap, without giving a chance to Lurline, who was the only one that could get within hail of him. As all my time, before the races, was occupied in getting the flat course in order, I deputed a friend to look after the steeple-chase one, which was on the Oude side of the river. He was one of those big-minded heavy weights who think that chasers ought to be able to get over at racing pace, for three miles, any obstacle which a clever hunter might, if allowed to take his own time at it, and accordingly constructed a series of fortifications which were truly appalling to behold. Out of a large number of entries, only four faced the starter. There was Mr. Macleod on Delphos, Mr. Guise of "the Buffs" on Rufus, Mr. Oakeley of the 8th King's on Lady Jane, and myself on Brown Duchess. On being shown round the course, we managed to prevail on the stewards, who were present, to cut down a little some of the fences, the most of which, however, were too stiff to yield to mere hand work. When we were delivered over to the starter we found facing us an unbreakable hurdle nearer five than four feet high. Mr. Macleod and myself were the first over it, and we took, side by side, the second fence, a high mud wall, over which Lady Jane fell and parted from her rider. Brown Duchess jumped the next obstacle, a watercourse, very stickily, so I had to ride her, to keep by Delphos, going at the fourth fence, a post and rails, made of logs, and quite four feet high. The mare negotiated it with all her marvellous cleverness for timber, but Delphos struck it heavily and came down. After that I had a quiet ride over the course, as Rufus, the only other animal that got round, refused repeatedly at every fence.

J. ANDERSON, ESQ., V.S., R.H.A.

Page 123.

As the Benares races were to come off soon after those at Cawnpore, Mr. Anderson, the genial and kind-hearted veterinary surgeon of the R.H.A. who is so well known at Lucknow, sent me Jack O'Connor, the pony Wooloomooloo, and the syce Ooree, three as bright specimens of their kind as it was possible to find. Poor Jack I have already described. The pony was a dark iron-grey, standing 12 hands 1 inch, could do his half mile in 57 secs. with 7 st. up, and was one of the greatest rogues that ever looked through a bridle, though he could give no weight away in a contest of sharpness to Ooree, who had the gift of silence, which is as rare as the four-leafed shamrock. On one occasion, an inquisitive gentleman asked Ooree, who was leading Wooloomooloo, "What pony is that?" "Master's," he promptly replied. "What is his name?" continued the questioner. "I don't know," he unblushingly lied. "He seems in very good condition, what do you feed him on?" "Eight pounds of meat every day," said Ooree. "Who are you, then?" asked the gentleman. "I am a Brahmin," answered Ooree. "I do Puja so that he may win. Instead of the racecourse I take him every day to a temple to worship, and that's what makes him in such good condition." That gentleman, thinking the man mad, hastily broke off the conversation and departed.

There was never a man loved a mount in a chase, or who paid more dearly for his devotion to the sport, than did poor Bailey. He was a tall, fine young fellow, standing over six feet high, who ought, from his build, to have weighed quite 12 st. 7 lbs, although he used to ride his confederate Captain Studdy's black English horse Call, about whom the row was, 9 st. 10 lbs. He had a strange fancy for riding bad horses—brutes which would refuse, fall, or do anything rather than jump. His grey Australian gelding, Prince Rupert, late Pill Garlic, was one of that sort. In a steeplechase up Campbellpore way, the misnamed Prince fell bodily into a ditch with Mr. Bailey, and as he was struggling out of it, the gallant 20th Hussar man caught him by one of his hind legs, hung on till he was pulled out of the water, then managed to seize the bridle, mounted, and won his chase. His end was a sad one. He died either just before reaching England, or just after landing, I forget which, his constitution having been utterly broken down by overtraining. I mean no reflection on the many good riders at present in India by saying that Bailey, at his best, was the finest horseman over a country I have ever seen in the East.

D'ARCY THUILLIER, ESQ.
" The Cameronians," 1872.

Page 125.

I journeyed to Benares with Brown Duchess, Caliph, Wooloomooloo, and Jack O'Connor. The grey Arab met Aboo Janoub twice and defeated him, giving him, on the second occasion, 7 lbs. and a beating for a mile and a half, which he accomplished with 9 st. 7 lbs. in 2 min. 55 secs., an excellent performance for a Galloway only 13 hands 2½ inches. In the pony race, quarter of a mile heats, Wooloomooloo distinguished himself by romping in the winner of the first heat by three or four lengths; but he refused to try a yard in the subsequent ones, so we lost our money.

Although the Benares sportsmen had advertised a steeplechase, and had a chaser of sorts in the Waler mare Gipsy, they had no intention of giving Brown Duchess a try, for they made up no steeplechase course. It was quite as well for me that they did not do so, for my mare, on her arrival at Benares, got an attack of jaundice, and was not fit to quit her stable, let alone perform over a country. I represented to the local stewards the hardship of my bringing the mare all the way from Cawnpore without getting the chance of a run, and they accordingly gave me eighty rupees to defray her travelling expenses.

During the remainder of the racing season I did little

except to organise sky meetings, which were well patronised, as Cawnpore then boasted of a "Garrison class" under Captain Holmes.   Among the pupils was poor D'Arcy Thuillier, one of the best sportsmen and cheeriest comrades, whether in or out of luck, I have ever met; Pat Hughes and Mr. Jamieson, of the "Cameronians;" Mr. Brown, of the 10th Regiment, and some others who dearly loved a horse.

When that good horse Hawkestone left my stable, Captain Maxwell put him into training on the Dehra Doon racecourse, whose descents and ascents were ill suited to this heavy topped, somewhat straight-shouldered, and long-striding animal.   The jockey who gave him his gallops weighed close on 10 st. when out of training.   Then there was the saddle and the usual 21 lbs. of clothing, for he was a gross horse.   Small wonder that his not over-strong fore-legs gave way, though not without lots of warning; for break-downs, under this style of work, are, as I have frequently remarked, almost always a gradual process, with more or less an abrupt termination.

That cold weather, Captain Maxwell left for England. On his way down country he stayed with me at Cawn-pore.   I bought Hawkestone from him for Rs. 500 to ride on parade, as he was a strikingly handsome horse, though, in my opinion, too infirm to race. I took him over with me as a hack to the Lucknow Spring Races of 1873, and swapped him there with Mr. Macleod for the smart country-bred mare Lurline and Rs. 300. I had the best of the bargain, for the mare was sound, won me a good stake, and I sold her for Rs. 600 ; while Hawkestone, even in Mr. Macleod's able hands, failed to stand training. He was then tried for stud purposes, but would not fulfil his obligations, and was sold, I heard, for Rs. 20 at Mozufferpore. *Sic transit*, &c.

At this meeting of 1873, Karpos, who then belonged to Messrs. "Arthur" and "John" (Butler and Macleod), won in excellent form the Lucknow Cesarewitch, for which the black horse Morialta, who was trained by Dignum, was made a strong favourite on his down-country running. Prince Alfred, who had done some good performances in Mauritius, also started, as did Ranelagh, ridden by Mr. Thacker, and several others. Karpos was not fancied at all except by his owners, who trained him principally, I believe, by walking exercise, as he had a thickened back tendon. Our Chumparun friends, as usual, knew what they were about, and brought their horse to the post fit to run for a kingdom.   At the last moment I was so much impressed by his appearance as he went down to meet the starter, that I hurried off to the *pari mutuel* box and put sixty rupees on him.   The box was well patronised that day, and I was delighted to learn from the casual remarks of the many backers that my selection found no favour.   The flag fell, and up came the horses along the straight and past the stand with Karpos leading them by a couple of lengths, and going as strong as a steam-engine.   I turned with an exclamation of delight to an acquaintance who was just behind me, and caught him in the act of depositing a ticket.   I seized his arm and told him that the box should have been closed, and that he must not put any-thing in.   "It's only five rupees on Karpos," he said ; and with that he dropped the pasteboard into the box. I thought he lied, but as I wanted to see the race I let the matter be.   When the horses had reached the mile post on the far side of the course, and it was apparent to every one that Karpos could not help winning, unless he fell down at least a couple of times, I felt a man brush past me as he went in the direction of the *pari mutuel* table.   His hand, too, carried a ticket with the name of Karpos written on ; but I was too sharp for

him, and sent him off quicker than he came. I felt sad
to think that two men in good position, as these scamps
were, should have " tried on " such a shady trick ; but felt
far sadder to find, when the *pari mutuel* boxes were
opened, that the first man had put in ten times more
than he had told me, and that, had I been but firm in
maintaining right, I should have been the richer by four
hundred rupees.

Lurline was the most fidgetty and impetuous animal
I have ever known. She looked like a flashy two-year-
old, all fiddle-strings and whipcord, and was in striking
contrast with the ordinary coachy Waler we were accustomed to dignify with the name of " racehorse " in India.
She was the most unpleasant hack I have ever sat on
She would neither walk, trot, nor canter. She would
passage, shoulder-in, progress tail first, waltz, or go in
any mad style of her own, but travel as a rational hack
ought to do, she would not. On the racecourse she
would run away for five furlongs, and then speedy-cut
herself and be laid up for a couple of weeks. I cured
her, for the time being, of this failing, by lowering the
outside quarters of her hoofs more than the inner ones,
and then sent her to Mr. Hartwell at Lucknow. He
took great pains with her, and by patience and good

"hands," got her well and moderately quiet. I know no one whom I would sooner trust with a horse than Mr. Hartwell. At that time Dr. Deane of my regiment—the 35th Native Infantry — owned a slashing Waler gelding, called Cynic. The first time I saw this animal run was at Aligurh, where his rider did the wrong thing with him. He was very fast, and would have made a name for himself had he been properly managed, but as it was, he never fulfilled the expectation one might have formed on seeing his racing shape and fine action, and knowing his thorough gameness.

Some time before this meeting, Mr. D'Arcy Thuillier of "The Cameronians," and I bought between us the speedy pony Primrose for Rs. 600. Ridden by Mr. Thacker, she won for us the Tom Thumb Stakes, but "dropped" all we had acquired by losing the handicap. Cynic did remarkably well by winning the Selling Stakes, for which I ran Colonel Bolton's Solitaire, and defeated Delphos at even weights over hurdles. I may mention that, in an evil moment, I allowed Primrose to go without me to a couple of meetings, at which she was mismanaged, and, consequently, lost her form for the time being. I was so disgusted at my own foolishness that I persuaded Mr. Thuillier to sell her to that grand

sportsman, the late Mr. Gore Ouseley, for what we had
given for her. She recovered her form in his hands, and
won several good races.

Mr. Thacker, whose name I have just mentioned, was
the best gentleman rider on the flat I have ever beheld
either at home or abroad. He was a "rare plucked 'un."
On one occasion at Warwick, if I remember right, he
got a desperate fall, and smashed his nose almost into a
pulp. By way of breaking the news gently to his wife,
he telegraphed to her: "Nose knocked into a jelly,
what shape would you like it?" When he came out to
India he was over fifty years of age, and yet he was
always ready to ride any brute in a steeplechase out of
sheer love of the sport, till he was made by his friends
to promise that he would give up cross-country work.
When he donned silk, he looked a jockey all over;
while, without wasting, he was always able to ride
8 st. 10 lbs. I remember seeing him ride a horse at
Lucknow against some others which were steered by
gentlemen amateurs. At the distance post, riding began
to tell, when that good horseman Mr. Macleod, who was
looking on from the stand, shouted in the excitement of
the moment, "The professional wins." "You mistake,"
said a bystander, correcting him, "there are no profes-

sionals riding." "That's a jockey, anyhow, on the winner," replied the Chumparun man, pointing to Mr. Thacker, whom he had not seen before.

Poor Bill Thacker was a "hard" man, who cared little for falls, though much for horses. One dark night, when he was living at Simla, while riding on his pony along the edge of a treacherous precipice, in order to make a short cut to a friend's house where he was going to dine, the animal lost his footing and fell down thirty or forty feet with his rider. Some friends who heard the crash hurried to the spot, and pulled Thacker out from under the pony and *débris*. "Are you hurt?" they asked, as they set him on his legs. "Got a rib or two broken, and I can't lift my right arm. But never mind me, run and get a light," he gasped, "for I want to see if the gee has chipped his knees." Poor fellow, his cheery voice is now stilled for ever.

CHAPTER XII.

I SPENT the hot weather of 1873 in getting Lurline quiet and "fit," and in preparing Brown Duchess for the Constable Cup Steeplechase. Knowing what a wonder Lurline was for half a mile, and being aware that the public would have none of this cast-off of the clever Chumparun stable, I determined to "slip" the speedy daughter of Eastern Maid for the six furlong selling race. A day or two before it came off, Dr. Deane and myself tried Cynic with Mr. Hartwell up and Jaffir on Lurline. My orders were that they were to start at the mile post, finish at the quarter, and that the winner was to pull up and leave the loser to lead past the winning post. Lurline won very easily, and Cynic romped in past the stand in front of her, and in the sight of several racing men who had come early to see what work was going on. They were perfectly satisfied with the trial, and went away with the fixed determination to back Cynic.

A few days before that, Mr. Elphick, the veterinary surgeon of the battery which was at Bareilly, sent over to Mr. Anderson a chestnut gelding, called Pretender, who had an enlarged knee, to run for the selling race for which Lurline and Cynic were entered. Mr. Elphick wrote to Mr. Anderson to say that he only wanted the horse sold, so would let him go in case he won, which he felt certain to do, as he was a flyer for the distance ; that he did not want to back him in the lotteries, and that he was not coming over to the races. Such being his instructions, Mr. Anderson naturally thought that if it was really "good business," it would be a pity not to win something over him, so he came to me and asked for a trial with Lurline. Though I ridiculed the idea that he could beat my mare, still, to convince him, I consented, and we ran the trial while every one was comfortably at breakfast. Of course my brown mare, who was able to do her half-mile in about 50 secs., won with ease.

In the lotteries, Fanny, Cynic, Duchess, and some

others fetched good prices, while Lurline fell to my bid of Rs. 30. As I had entered her to be sold for Rs. 300 she carried a very light weight, so I put up Jaffir. The race was never in doubt, for Lurline and Cynic had it all to themselves, the former winning in a canter. When she was brought into the ring to be put up to auction, every one rushed to see the flying mare whom they had once held so cheaply. The condition of the sale was, that the owner of the second horse was to get all the surplus over selling price, so when the eager bidders had run her up to about double the amount for which she had been entered, it dawned on them that Dr. Deane, the owner of Cynic, whom I had helped to train, did not wish me to lose my mare, so gave up the bidding as a bad job, and she returned to my stable.

Mr. Elphick, I had almost forgotten to say, turned up on the racecourse a short time before the event was run, and seemed much annoyed at our having had a trial with his horse, Pretender, as his syce had told him all about it, and what a wonder Lurline was; but after the race he offered to "make friends" if I would sell him Lurline for Rs. 600. I agreed to this, as I did not want to be on bad terms with any one, and, besides that, I did not care to keep such a thoroughly exposed animal, one that " stayed " so badly, and was so difficult to train. Mr. Elphick, for some reason that I do not know, promptly sold her to Captain Papillon, who could do nothing with her. She never won a race after leaving me. I do not know what became of her.

The great event, in July, 1873, of the Lucknow Monsoon meeting, which has now become a regular fixture, was the Constable Cup ; a steeplechase for all horses, with a hundred sovereigns added, in a handsome purse of native manufacture, and worth over three hundred rupees. This substantial prize was given by Mr. Constable, on the occasion of his winning about forty thousand rupees in the Lucknow Derby sweep. Mr. Constable's very sporting gift naturally attracted the attention of owners and riders of steeplechase horses from far and near. For it, poor Captain Grant of the Horse Artillery rode his mare Sunbeam ; Captain Papillon steered his uncertain Duchess ; Mr. Short was on War Eagle ; Mr. Hartwell on Marquis ; Jack O'Connor on Hildegarde, late Premier's Daughter ; Fred Welcome had been sent for all the way from Calcutta to ride Mr. Bushman's unlucky Harkaway ; Captain Frank's piloted that mad horse Time, late Gamester, who had a story attached to his name ;

Crook was carried by that slow but safe conveyance, the Duke ; and I rode Brown Duchess. Sunbeam and Duchess were jades of the deepest dye. Harkaway had been spoiled by bullying and ignorance. Hildegarde, one of the lightly weighted ones, had a great chance, as Mr. Anderson, her owner, and myself had tried her over the steeplechase course with Brown Duchess a few days before, and found her good enough to win. The Duke, though sure, was very slow. War Eagle, though out of sorts, was such a quick fencer, and his rider such an undeniable man over a country, that the pair were worthy of every respect from plungers. My mare was so fit and well up to three o'clock in the afternoon of the day before the race, that, as I looked at her in her stall, I could not help stroking down her glossy brown neck and telling her how I longed for the morrow to show them the way. On my return to the stable in the evening, I found that the poor animal had been "nobbled." Some one had struck one of her fore-legs a heavy blow just above the knee, rendering the limb stiff and painful. I did not care for the pecuniary loss ; for £ s. d. had not then the hard practical significance they now bear to me. I was young and foolish enough in those days to value success for the praise from one's fellows it brings, and I was fond of the old brown mare.

I must give Time a couple of paragraphs all to himself. As Gamester, he belonged to Mr. Charlie Wilson of Calcutta, and was expected to do something great, but never succeeded in accomplishing it, if we may except a match he won against the very moderate Jerry, whom I once saw well ridden in a steeplechase at Lucknow by that brave man Mr. Germany, late of Cawnpore. Gamester was said to have come up to Lucknow to run in a steeplechase more than a year previous to the Constable Cup, but did not. It happened thus. That plucky horseman, Captain Franks of "The Buffs," who used to race under the name of "Mr. Norman," and is now in civil employ at Indore, had a fine cross-country horse called Kingcraft, whose excellence was only known to "Mr. Norman," Mr. Edward Beadon, Mr. Hartwell, and one or two more. Kingcraft was entered for a Lucknow steeplechase, for which, purely as a lark, Mr. Beadon entered the ch. w. g. Gamester : a description that tallied with that of Mr. Wilson's animal, but had no reference to him. There were some other horses running, which, however, have no connection with our story. Before the lotteries commenced, all those not in the secret, were anxious to gain information about the chesnut Gamester, and to know whether he was Mr. Wilson's reputed great horse. Either the denial was not believed, and backers rushed blindly on to their fate, or it was a bit qualified, for the Lucknow Gamester was far and away the favourite in the lotteries ; while the " real good business," Kingcraft, was allowed to go to his party very cheaply, except in the last lottery, for backers then were beginning to understand that no one "in the know" had bought Gamester in the previous ones. Colonel " Smith of Asia," who owned Morning Star in the days when Vanderdecken was in the zenith of his fame, was the first to sound the alarm, and to warn the assembled racing public not to trust in the assurance which Mr. Hartwell frankly gave, that the Gamester which was entered was not the real Simon Pure. Soon after the saddling bell for the race had been sounded, the backers of Gamester in the lotteries were put out of their misery, for Jack O'Connor appeared on a sorry chesnut " garran " which could hardly get out of a feeble amble, and which knew as little about fencing as he did of differential equations. And this was the supposed flyer ! The race was won by Captain Franks, who had

far from a pleasant mount on the impetuous Kingcraft,
while his party netted about Rs. 7000 over the transac-
tion.   So many morals might be drawn from this story,
that I refrain from giving any.

Some time after this, Captain Franks bought the real
Gamester, and brought him up to run for the steeplechase in the spring meeting at Lucknow in 1873. Mr.
Macleod, after riding a beautifully judged waiting race
on Delphos, defeated Captain Franks on Gamester
over the Meryaon course. Although the chesnut horse
received nearly three stone from the pale-faced one,
still the excuse was made for him that he was not fit,
while it was asserted that he could be improved more
than that difference.

In those days there dwelt in the North-West a well-
known plunger, who, from his exploits in the country
of the Celestials, was known to fame as "China Jim."
I could tell the wondrous story he related to me of his
looting the golden gods during the sacking of the
Summer Palace, but refrain, as it has nothing to do with
India or racing. As maidens for the Constable Cup
received, by its conditions, two stone from platers, Time,
late Gamester, was "spotted" as "the good thing" of
the meeting. That now eminent financier, China Jim,

having heard of the supposed certainty, hastened down to Lucknow and backed the horse in the lotteries, as if the race was "all over bar shouting." Captain Papillon and myself "went for" Duchess and Brown Duchess, while we "saved ourselves" on War Eagle. Both of us, and Mr. Short, knew that if the fearfully impetuous Time were allowed to go quietly over the first couple of fences, he would, after that, settle down, and, favoured by his light weight, almost to a certainty win. Hence we resolved to make the pace as hot as we could from the start, which, on that occasion, was quite a quarter of a mile from the first fence, a mud wall that was hardly broad enough for three horses abreast—such was the management in those days! When the flag was lowered we all went away as if we were doing a five-furlong scurry. The leading horses, Time, the two Duchesses, and War Eagle, were racing at each other when they came to the mud wall. The squeeze here of the large field was so tight, that Time, just on my right, struck it very hard, pecked badly on the other side, and disposed of his rider. Duchess rolled over Captain Papillon. Sunbeam tumbled down with Captain Grant. Hildegarde fell on her shoulder and injured herself for life, while Harkaway also came to grief.   War Eagle, who was half a length ahead of everything, Brown Duchess just behind him, with the Duke and Marquis in attendance, and two others, cleared the obstacle in their stride.   After jumping the water in front of the stand — an ugly straight-cut obstacle—I found my mare was going lame, so pulled her up after jumping the big wall on the far side.   War Eagle, sailing in front, struck the post and rails, which resembled in strength and height a railway crossing gate, so hard with one of his hind legs, that he fractured the top bar, and would have fallen had he been held together by a less powerful rider than Mr. Short.   The best man and the best horse (that day) continued to lead the now thinned field, and won " anyhow."

Some soldiers who were on the course seeing Captain Papillon lying on the ground insensible after his fall, hastened forward and picked him up.   They were so assiduous in undoing his necktie, and freeing him from anything that might impede his breathing, that they actually took off his brand-new, heavily plated racing spurs and quite forgot to return them.

About the time the Constable Cup was run, Caliph again came into my hands to be trained.   After the Benares meeting of the preceding year, Captain Maxwell wrote and asked me to have the grey Galloway raffled. I did so, and the lot fell to a lady in my regiment. She, at first, was delighted with her new horse, but as he got wofully out of condition and was, metaphorically, eating his head off, she offered him to me on racing terms. As Caliph was getting fit, Colonel Harris, of the 45th Sikhs, after the Constable Cup was run, begged me to send him to run at Moradabad, where he was organizing a meeting, and where he and Mr. Maitland had some enormous gambles together. The result to me was that I got the horse back.

On my way to Naini Tal on two months' leave, after the Lucknow Monsoon meeting, I stayed a day at Bareilly with Mr. Elphick, the Artillery veterinary surgeon, who showed me a very smart-looking country-bred colt, which looked a galloper all over, and offered to "trade" for Brown Duchess, whom he was confident he could make all right again. As I held a different opinion, we struck the following odd bargain. He got the mare and Rs. 32, while I took in exchange the c.b. colt, a country-bred pony, which I afterwards sold for Rs. 200, a brindle terrier which was never promoted beyond the name of "Pup," and a steeplechase saddle. I called the colt Fairy Mount, and had him quietly hacked about for the sixty days in the hills, and also through the following cold weather.

We got up some sky races at Naini Tal that year. We made a steeplechase course across the cricket-field, over the shingle, and down the hard road in front of the Assembly Rooms, which was buried by the landslip a couple of years ago. I recollect in one chase, which I won, my pony and myself got a fall at every fence, for the little animal had not the slightest idea of jumping.

The lotion, embrocation, vesicant, or whatever the stuff was with which Mr. Elphick hoped to patch up the old mare, was of no avail, for he was never able to bring her out fit to face the starter.

In 1874, being the honorary secretary for the Cawnpore Races, I arranged them to come off in February. They were well patronized. John Wheal brought Kilmore, Somerset, and Jessie. Messrs. Short and Elphick—they were then in partnership—came with the country-bred Mermaid, late Jessie, whom Jaffir afterwards called M. T. (Mail Train), the chaser Daybreak, and Chemisette, late Antelope. Mr. Tavenor had Robert and the black Waler, Recovery. Dignum brought Bowman, who had won shortly before at Ballygunge. Dr. Deane ran Cynic. Mr. Hartwell had Marquis to the fore. I had

HARRY BOWEN.

Page 145.

Caliph and the Arab, Talisman. Poor D'Arcy Thuillier looked after Scotsman. Mr. Maitland gave Crossbee a gallop ; while there were other owners and horses whose names I cannot call to mind. The country-bred Mermaid, who then belonged to a native at Mozufferpore, had shown extraordinary good form down country, and was brought to oppose Caliph in the Arab and country-bred Give and Take Stakes, in which she had to concede him two stone. Mr. Short and I tried them before running, with the result that the mare beat the horse in a common canter. Although I put money on Mermaid still I determined to give the backer of Caliph in the lotteries, Captain Charles Apperly, the best possible run for his money, so put up Donaldson, who had steered the Galloway for me in many races with signal success; and at that time was one of the best jockeys in India. When the flag was lowered, Donaldson jumped off with the lead, and whenever the mare came up, he rode at her and bustled her so much that, being a soft-hearted jade, she refused to try, despite Bowen's efforts, and Caliph just managed to win a fast race by a short neck. So much for trials ! I rode Cynic in the first-class selling race, which was won by Daybreak. Kilmore won the handicap. For the steeplechase, Daybreak, ridden by Mr. Short ; Bowman, steered by Dignum ; Marquis, piloted by Mr. Hartwell, and one or two others put in an appearance. Unfortunately for Dignum, there was a hurdle at one part of the course, which Bowman would not jump. Daybreak came down, and gave so much time to the slow but clever Marquis, that Mr. Short's horse did not catch him till within three-quarters of a mile from home. The race was naturally a mere procession, for the speedy Daybreak raced over the remaining fences, all but one, with the country-bred far behind him. As I had backed Mr. Short's mount, and had seen him miss out one of the obstacles, I rode up to him, as he was coming home into the straight, and told him of his mistake, and that he must go back. Strange to say, Mr. Hartwell, from watching his leader instead of taking his own line, had also missed out that particular fence. Mr. Short, in the hurry of the moment, after he had returned and jumped the left-out bank, quite forgot to come straight home, for he had already gone over the other fences, and took Daybreak over them again, while Mr. Hartwell, still following Mr. Short, lost the race for the second time by committing the very same error as his opponent had done.

Three or four days after this, the Lucknow Spring

Meeting came off. As Dignum did not fancy the mount on Bowman for the Lucknow steeplechase, he asked me to ride, to which I gladly consented, as I was only too delighted to have a chance of sporting silk. Mr. Short was on Daybreak, Mr. Hartwell on Marquis, Mr. Baker on the chaser Kingcraft, and some one on Nelly. That year they made the big wall on the far side of the course 4 ft. 9 in. high! This was done, I suppose, for the country-bred's benefit. A short time ago I met Mr. "Joe" Anderson, who had measured this unbreakable fortification, as he was one of the stewards. He assured me that it was within three inches of five feet. In my book on "Riding on the Flat and Across Country" I gave, when mentioning the incidents of this chase, the height of this wall as 4 ft 6 in.; for I was not quite sure of the measurement, and thought it best to err on the safe side. Before the race came off, I begged Mr. Anderson to have the wall cut down six inches, for I knew that Bowman would never clear it. Joe said he would, but didn't. He tells me now that he was not able to accede to my request, as the course had been passed by the stewards and could not be altered. What a bright lot they must have been! Marquis went so slow that, although Bowman and Daybreak refused a couple of times, I found myself leading at the end of the first mile. I endeavoured to get Mr. Hartwell to give me a lead over the big wall, but he, seeing what I wanted, kept behind, so I hardened my heart and sent Bowman at the masonry. He tried to "cut it," but I held him too straight and kept him going too fast to allow him to do so. He took off too soon, struck the wall with his chest, and rolled over with me on the other side. I was knocked insensible for a few moments, for there was a terrible lot of "bone" in the ground, as the bloodthirsty stewards had taken good care not to make "the falling" soft. When I came to myself I found I was sitting on the ground, and saw, as if in a dream, Daybreak with Mr. Short see-sawing on the wall, his head and fore legs on my side of it, his hind legs on the other, and his body wedged in the gap I had made. Mr. Short got over with a fall, but quickly re-mounted. Mr. Hartwell, however, had obtained such a long start that he won easily, despite Mr. Short's desperate stern chase. I was badly shaken, and was glad of a help back to the Stand from Mr. Charlie Mangles, who, having backed Daybreak, waited on the landing side of the big wall to get on the chestnut gelding, and finish the chase, in the event of Mr. Short being too much hurt to remount, for both of them were convinced that Daybreak could never get over without a tumble. I did not begrudge Mr. Hartwell his win, for he was a capital horseman, both on the flat and "between the flags," and had undeniable pluck. That fall I had seems to have shaken all the other incidents of the meeting out of my memory. I believe Caliph won the Dilkoosha Stakes.

Some time afterwards, as Bowman happened to go lame, one of his fore legs was examined by a veterinary surgeon, who found that he had firmly fixed in his frog a piece of wood, which must have been there for months, and which was quite sufficient to account for this once fine fencer turning out such a determined refuser. In this connection I may mention the fact of poor Kain's death (see page 227), caused by his riding a horse which had corns in a steeplechase. It is but too common for inexperienced horse owners to mistake symptoms of foot or leg sorenesss for vice, which is "hard lines" on the poor animal.

I spent the next hot weather in Mozufferpore, the capital of Tirhoot, in command of a detachment of sepoys who had to do escort and guard duty during the famine there. Being shut up in the house through the weary burning days, and having neither horses nor regimental work to occupy my time, I thought I might amuse myself by writing a book on "Training and Horse Management in India," with the off chance of its paying its expenses. In the first edition I expressed myself badly, but I had something new to tell. As the reading public was indulgent, I did better the next time. I went home to study at the New Veterinary College, and I have, I believe, committed to print almost every useful hint about horses I have ever acquired. Although that book I wrote in the Circuit Bungalow at Mozufferpore has now been before the public for eight years, it has, up to the present, been a steady income to me. I am glad to say that my other books have also turned out well.

J. J. MACLEOD, ESQ. ("Mr. John").

Page 151.

CHAPTER XIII.

THE THREE DISTRICTS — THE PLANTERS — MR. LAURENCE CROWDY — THE STUDDS — LIFE IN TIRHOOT—CHARLIE WEBB—BOB CROWDY—DAWK DRIVING—MR. ABBOTT — RACING — THE BEHAR MOUNTED RIFLES — POLO — JIMMY MACLEOD — ROWLEY HUDSON.

BEHAR, or "the three districts," as it is locally called, comprises Tirhoot, Chumparun, and Sarun, whose fertile plains are studded here and there with indigo factories, at intervals of from, say, four to twenty miles. The planters are as fine a set of fellows as have ever represented the "old country" in any clime. They are hospitable and generous to a fault; devoted to sport, especially on horseback; loyal to their Queen and country; and the "best company" in the world. They are true to the old, princely Indian traditions of bygone years, despite the fact that the present times are somewhat out of gear.   Take Mr. Laurence Crowdy, who manages the large factory of Munjoul, near Mou-ghyr, as an instance.   Whenever an assistant in the district loses "his berth" he, quite naturally, packs up his things, goes straight to Munjoul, and stays with Laurence, who takes it as a matter of course that he should provide for him until he can obtain another situation.   Laurence, like all the Behar planters, being a skilful and enthusiastic polo player, is fond of a game ; so, during the season, every hard - riding youngster, within a radius of ten or twelve miles, comes over to Munjoul, once a week or once a fortnight, as the fixture may be, to stay for a couple of days and play polo.   He is also a captain in that splendid corps, the Behar Mounted Rifles.   When his troop parades for training they of course "fall in" at Mun-joul, and horses and all "put up" with their gallant commanding officer, who has the rare knack of making his guests thoroughly "at home" and comfortable.

My readers who do not know the country may think, from what I am writing, that a planter's life is all "beer and skittles."   Such, indeed, is far from being the case, as they have, on the contrary, an immense amount of work and anxiety at certain times, especially during the *mahai*, as the manufacture of indigo is called ; while through the entire year there is a vast quantity of administrative or *kutcherry* work to be transacted with the native cultivators. This forms the midday occupation of the planter, who, unless when manufacturing, has the cool hours of the morning and afternoon in which to ride over the *dehat*, or outlying cultivation, and to amuse himself with his horses and dogs.

Although indigo has no direct connection with racing, it has had a sufficiently indirect one, as far as I and many of my friends are concerned, to warrant a brief digression about Tirhoot ; for did I not recruit from that land of the *leel* (*Anglicè* indigo) those good horses Rebecca, Vesper, Red Gauntlet, Dolly Varden, Exile of Erin, and others?

While I was at Mozufferpore I often went to stay with Mr. Edward Studd at Dhooly, and with his assistant, Mr. C. R. H. Webb, at Birowlee. The master of Dhooly and Mr. Henry Studd of Dhurriah are sons of the well-known " Salamander " Studd, who, in his early days, being an accomplished rider and good judge, made money in India with horses, and raised himself to opulence, later on, by speculations in indigo. He pursued the old game on his return to England, and effected one of the largest *coups* ever made " between the flags," when Salamander won the Grand National in 1866, after having been beaten a short time previously in a small selling race. When he became well stricken in years, he recognized the vanity of racing, and devoted himself to the gospel according to Messrs. Moody and Sankey. His two sons were as fine specimens of the athletic young Englishman as one might wish to meet, and were " bad to beat " at every manly game. The house at Dhooly, as well as that at Dhurriah, was one of those grand old *Leel Kothees* which were built in the days when planters were kings. "Polly," as Mr. Edward Studd was familiarly called, had a stable of about twenty horses, the majority of which were in a chronic state of being blistered or fired. Not that he over-rode or over-drove them ; quite the reverse ; but he had a mania for doctoring his animals. There were generally enough, however, to pigstick with, hunt jackals, or even wolves at times, and " lark " over the steeplechase course which he had constructed round the four hundred acre indigo field that was close to the house. " Polly " was a very early riser, and had us all out of bed before ever a streak of light was to be seen in the eastern horizon. We hastily swallowed a cup of tea, got on our riding "togs," and were down to mount our horses that were waiting for us in front of the house. A score or more of dogs of various breeds, from the greyhound to the nondescript pariah, were then let loose, and off we trotted to hunt any jackal, fox, hare, or wolf we might meet with in a two or three hour circuit. Unlike most parts of India, the "going" in Tirhoot is generally good, with a fair sprinkling of fences, without which a gallop is but tame fun. We were hardly ever without a few runs, and usually wound up by a "school" home. By the time we returned the air was all aglow with the fierce heat of the sun, and we were glad to get under shelter, drink an iced brandy and soda, take off our clothes, and have a comfortable bath. That being over, we got into our clean cotton and linen garments, had our *chhotee haziree*, or little breakfast, and trifled with tea or coffee, hot buttered toast and poached eggs, preserved tongues, tinned red mullet, herrings *à la sardine*, and other *hors d'œuvres*, which would not seriously interfere with the all-important tiffen. We read or answered our correspondence, looked through the papers, had a game or two of billiards, "bucked" about sport and our morning's adventures, and thus pleasantly whiled away the time till twelve or half-past, when tiffen was announced and then we did ample justice to the mulligatawny soup, rump steaks, chops, fish, curries, phillows, chicken cutlets, bottled beer, pegs, claret, and champagne that each man's white-robed and turbaned *khidmutgar*, or native servant, endeavoured to force on him. After eating and drinking till we could hardly see, and telling stories of marvel and wonder till we could barely articulate, we one by one sought our respective rooms, laid down on our couches under a punkah, and slept the sleep of the wearied sportsman, until the lengthening shadows told that the sun would soon allow us to turn out to play again. Another bath, another dress, a cup of tea, or perhaps a "peg," and then we sauntered out to the stables to inspect our cattle, to "talk horse," and to show what a lot we knew about that all-engrossing subject. A few sets of lawn tennis, a scratch game of cricket, a row or sail on the river, a drive, a stroll, or a comfortable chair, with a box of cheroots and "the materials," helped to relieve the tedium of life until dinner, which was a joy for hours. A few games of billiards, a rubber of whist, or a round game wound up the evening of a well-spent day.

Mr. Webb is endeared to every one in Tirhoot by his unaffected goodness of heart, kindly ways, and devotion

to sport. He can ride about 10 st. 4 lbs., is a perfect
"pocket Hercules," and would shine across country if
he could only remember that it is not always advisable
to go full speed, and if he would sometimes exercise a
little judgment in picking out an easy place. I once
told a characteristic story of him in the columns of the
Illustrated Sporting and Dramatic News. He was out
pigsticking with a friend one day, when the boar, a large
one, being wounded and hard pressed, backed into a deep
nullah, or ravine, which was too narrow for the horses to
be ridden through. From this point of vantage he defied
his two pursuers. Charlie Webb having lost his spear
in the *mêlée* looked round for a weapon, and saw a
native a couple of hundred yards off, cultivating his
patch of ground with a *kudalee*, or short hoe. Webb
rode up to him, took the hoe, and galloped back. He
then dismounted, climbed up the side of the nullah,
and having taken the boar in flank, crept down until
he was close to his foe, who could not get up the
precipitous ascent, sprang astride on his back, and
began to belabour him with the hoe. The old grey
boar, surprised at this unexpected manœuvre, dashed
out of the nullah at full speed with Webb, and then,
making a mistake over some broken ground just in

front, gave his rider a desperate purl. He and his friend, however, slew the pig after a stubbornly fought battle.

Mr. Webb and his friends Mr. Bob Crowdy, the great steeplechase rider, Mr. Buxton, another fine horseman, who won on Sweep at Lucknow in 1876 and was on Hermit when he broke his back at Ballygunge, were dangerous men to follow, or even to sit alongside of in a dog-cart when any one of them held the reins. Bob Crowdy never hesitated at putting his racehorses and chasers into a trap without any previous training, and as he invariably used harness "as rotten as pears," and scorned to go on the high road when he could take a short cut across country, he seldom escaped without an accident or two. Although Bob would spend his last penny in buying a horse fancied, he used to think that any old tackle was good enough to serve as gear. The subject of his horses' clothing, their saddlery, and his own "get-up" furnished many a joke. I remember well, at the Lucknow Races one day, seeing an energetic steward of the meeting rush up to a pony that was meekly standing in a corner of the saddling enclosure with an old and torn blanket on his back, and indignantly order the supposed grass-cutter's *tat* out of

R. CROWDY, ESQ. ("Mr. Bob").

Page 159.

the paddock reserved for racehorses, not being aware that the meanly-clothed one was " Mr. Bob's " Maori, the best pony in India. Bob is a Colonial, stands about 6 ft. 1 in., is as "thin as a match," can ride about 9 st. 10 lbs., and is as regardless of his personal appearance in the somewhat select society of Indian military stations as he was when stock-driving in the bush. At the Calcutta Races, 1875, when all the great gentlemen riders assembled in their brightest of boots, most spotless of breeches, and newest of colours, to sport silk and satin before the Prince of Wales, " Mr. Bob," as usual, was late in getting ready. At last he found his boots, and in the hurry of dragging them on he shoved his foot right through the left one beyond all repair. As some one reminded him that he could not appear before H.R.H. bootless—it being a right-handed course, he solved the difficulty by putting the right boot on the left leg, and tied, with a piece of string, the remains of the left one on the right leg.

Poor little Maori succumbed to the fatigues and excitement of jackal *latee maroing.* One day during the hot weather, Mr. Warburton on the pony, Mr. Bob Crowdy on Sweep, and Mr. Ruxton on Deception, if I remember right, went out to ride down jackals with no other aid than that of their horses and stout walking-sticks. After some desperately hard gallops they accounted for three brushes, and then the gallant Maori, being short of work, laid down and died from congestion of the lungs. Except a wolf or black buck, I know nothing so hard to catch as the swift and wily "jack."

Bad as "Mr. Bob" was to sit alongside of, his two friends were infinitely worse, as, being short-sighted, they used to trust implicitly to the honour of their horses, which was anything but judicious on the Tirhoot roads, which are high and narrow constructions, with yawning ditches on each side. The last time I drove with Mr. Webb, we were returning to his place, about twelve o'clock on a dark night, in a curricle drawn by a couple of mules, which always insisted on running away immediately they were yoked. We got into the trap somehow, but the mules would take a straight line across country instead of keeping to the road. I held on bravely for a time, until, when passing through a wood, and not being able to see a yard in front, a branch of a tree caught me under the chin, and swept me clean out of the trap on to the ground. I luckily escaped with nothing worse than a severe shaking and a scratched face.

I got used to Tirhoot driving, although at first it tried my nerves to the utmost. Except on the line of railway, travelling from one part to another of "the three districts" is done by driving *dawks*. A man wants to go a journey of, say, fifty miles. To accomplish this he will require nine or ten *dawks ;* so he sends on two or three horses of his own for the first three or four stages, and then writes to the planters whose factories are near the road he is taking to supply the remainder. This request is acceded to with the greatest good-will, on the understanding that the traveller must accept hospitality on his way through. He has then nothing to do but to drive his dog-cart or gig, and change at each stage. The horses are generally good ones, in capital condition, and not overworked, so make very light of their five or six mile "spell." If they run away at times it doesn't very much matter, as the native carters, when they see a *sahib* coming, promptly drive their bullocks off the road, lest swift chastisement might fall on them.

I can never forget the unbounded kindness I have received from the Behar planters, and especially from my best of friends, Charlie Webb, who, the last time I stayed with him, wanted me to stop as his guest for a couple of years, make his house my home, and use his horses to race or ride just as I liked. I would have accepted his offer, as I knew it was meant, but I was broken down with intermittent fever, and had to say good-bye, with a very heavy heart, to the warmest-hearted friend and bravest sportsman I have ever met.

Second to none for hospitality and fondness for sport is Mr. H. E. Abbott, who manages the large "concern" of Jaintpore, which is about sixteen miles distant from Mozufferpore. Of the many real sportsmen I have met among Indian racing men—who, take them "all round," are an uncommonly "good sort"—Mr. Abbott is the only one who persistently studies his friends' interests rather than his own. His stable is always filled with other people's horses, which he keeps for the ridiculous sum of about a guinea a month, trains and races them generally with great success, though without pecuniary profit to himself, simply out of sheer love of sport and desire to do a good turn to his friends, among whom he counts every visitor to Tirhoot. The first time I met him was at the lotteries of a Mozufferpore meeting. "To set the ball rolling," I tossed for some tickets, lost them, and wound up by buying what I might have known was a certain loser. When the gambling was

H. E. ABBOTT, ESQ.

Page 163.

over, Mr. Abbott gave me a seat in his trap to take me home. On the way back he said that he was sorry I had been unlucky, and advised me to take a share in a horse whose chance he had purchased. Knowing Mr. Abbott by repute, I heartily thanked him, accepted the offer, and next day found my balance to be on the right side. I need hardly say that to do thus and live, Mr. Abbott has a large income from his factory. A short time ago he started a capital newspaper in the interests of indigo and sport, to which I have the honour to contribute occasionally, and which has already attained a large and well-merited circulation throughout India.

The time to see the planters in all their glory is during one of their race meetings, the chief of which is that of Sonepore, the other being Mozufferpore in Tirhoot, Mootihari in Chumparun, and Chupra, which is generally presided over by that good sportsman, Mr. Gwatkin Williams. At these fixtures each of the leading planters forms a camp, to which he invites his friends and any strangers who may happen to be near. The usual programme is four days' racing on alternate mornings, four balls on race nights, lotteries on non-ball nights, hunting and paper-chasing on non-race mornings, polo every evening, lawn tennis all day, jolly dinners, delightful parties, and occasionally a cricket match.   Each meeting lasts for about ten days. Another capital institution, though of lesser importance from a sporting point of view, is the annual "meet" and inspection of the Behar Mounted Rifles, which numbers close upon two hundred sabres, the members being all planters.   This regiment is a truly magnificent one, in the ranks of which the race-goer may see many a horse that has distinguished himself " on the flat " and " between the flags ; " for the planters pride themselves on being the best-mounted corps in the service, and with good reason too.   The different squadrons pitch their tents, during the week, so as to form separate camps, the members of which mess together, invite their friends from far and near to stay with them, and have a " real good time of it."   The gaiety and sport are similar to that of the race meetings, though on a smaller scale, while there is always a grand fancy dress ball to wind up the festivities.

Many of the planters—Jimmy Macleod, Rowley Hudson, Gilbert Nicolay, Tom Barclay, Mackintosh, C. Thomas, and Harry Crowdy, in particular—are magnificent polo players, and it is a real treat to see them on their clever ponies (12.2 and under), which are so quick and handy that the ball is always in play. Besides this, on an animal of that size, the player has far more command over the ball than on a bigger one. The question of height has little to say to the ability of carrying weight, even up to fifteen stone, for I have seen 12.2 ponies in Tirhoot, and 11 handers in Cachar, as capable of carrying that burden as any 14-hand polo pony in England. I do not for a moment deny, as I saw proved once at Allahabad, that, in a match, big ponies against small ones, the former, owing to their superior weight, would win ; but I maintain that, with the latter, the play is far better, and that the chance of accidents is reduced to a minimum. I speak without any bias, as I hardly ever played polo, for I had neither time nor ponies suitable to it while in India. I had, however, admirable opportunities of witnessing this grand game at Cachar, Calcutta, Tirhoot, and Allahabad. At many places in India, men are forced to play with ponies 13.2 high and under, as smaller ones of the requisite speed and power are only to be procured in certain districts.

Though there is keen rivalry in matters of sport between the planters of Tirhoot and Chumparun, it would be impossible for me to say which district bears the palm. The Chumparun men maintain that, as compared with the size of Tirhoot and Chupra, their district shows more sport. They were the first to introduce polo into the indigo country. Their team won the Three Districts Polo Challenge Cup in 1877, on the only occasion the match was arranged. They have grounds for this game at almost every factory, as well as in the two stations—Segowlee and Mootihari ; while in the Bettiah division they have polo regularly, once, and sometimes twice, a week, the whole year round. They play by turns at the different factories, always dining and sleeping wherever they play, and having a spin across country next morning before they separate, sometimes after a pig or wolf. The same hospitality and good fellowship which exists in Tirhoot is to be found everywhere in Chumparun. This district has brought out some grand horses, as witness, Fisherboy, Finette, Raven, Armadale, Fieldfare, Mercedes, Geraldine, Bluebell, and the chasers Delphos, Brown Duchess, and Kilmore. At the weekly polo meetings many amusing incidents occur, although it is almost impossible to give a fair idea of them by a mere written description. On one occasion, after a very jolly dinner with the 2nd Bengal Cavalry at Segowlee, one of the planters who had been playing polo, and who had driven in a tandem pair, was obliged to go home instead of sleeping in the station as usual. As the night was very dark, and the road narrow and raised, his friends tried to induce him to unharness the leader. But as he had just enough champagne to make him "contrary," the mere suggestion that he was not able to manage a tandem in the dark was sufficient to make him insist on displaying his ability to do so. A happy thought struck one of his friends, so they ceased endeavouring to persuade him, and, when the trap was announced, they had all the lights taken away from the mess verandah. They gave the syce a rupee to hold his tongue, took off the leader, and fastened both pairs of reins to the wheeler. The jovial planter climbed up, started off immensely proud of himself, and never found out his mistake until he arrived home safe and sound.

If Mr. Bob Crowdy is the best across country in Tirhoot, Mr. Macleod is undoubtedly "the pick" of Chumparun. He is one of those exceptional cases of a man who learned to ride after he was twenty years of age, attaining a high degree of proficiency as a race-rider. Great natural aptitude, incessant practice, and iron nerves, made up for early training. Although he may not have as strong a seat as Bob Crowdy, or as fine hands as Rowley Hudson, he beats them and every other G. R. I have seen in India, except poor Bill Thacker, for patience and fine judgment — qualities which render him, perhaps, better on the flat than across country. I shall never forget the patient manner in which he rode Delphos at Lucknow in the spring of 1873, when he beat Captain Franks on the lightly weighted Time. In one season he scored fifty wins out of seventy-five mounts ; and in another year, twenty-one out of twenty-six ! He is the largest owner of horses in the three districts, and has bred many good ones at his place, Lalseriah. Like a true sportsman as he is, he takes almost more pride in teaching his assistants and young friends to " harden their hearts " and ride in good form, than in training and " making " his own horses—a pleasure and duty which he reserves to himself. Like Mr. Abbott, he is always only too happy to " bring out " any likely animal which his friends may happen to send him.

Mr. Rowland Hudson, for perfection of seat, artistic style, and good hands, is the " show " gentleman rider of the indigo districts. He was bred to the sport in the county of Louth, Ireland, where his people for ages were devoted to horses. He got his first lessons in

ROWLAND HUDSON, ESQ.

Page 169.

riding from his father, who, for over five and twenty years, was one of the best men to hounds in his county. At the age of twelve Rowley Hudson was able to steer any of his father's hunters, and was constantly put up to give some of them their work over the Ardee steeple-chase course, which his father had constructed, as Mr. Hudson had generally a couple of thoroughbred ones to pick up hunt races, &c.; and thus Rowley and his brothers took to racing quite naturally. The best practice he had, and what made him the fine horseman he is, was continually riding animals of all kinds to hounds over a stiff country. When he was eighteen years of age he went to India and rode his first race there in 1871, being second on Red Gauntlet to that old Cape hero, Echo. Since then his services as a G. R. have been in great request, and he has a steady average of about thirty wins each season. During his first couple of years, he rode and won several chases, the best of which, perhaps, was at Mozufferpore in 1872, on Blackboy, an Australian horse that was taken to England, and won there two or three hunt cross-country events. Blackboy, at that time, was such a desperate puller that no one would ride him until Mr. Hudson volunteered; and after a grand race, in which his skilful handling of the uncertain and boring Waler was greatly admired, he managed to get home a length in front of Mr. Macleod on Delphos, who was supposed to be the best chaser in India. Blackboy struck the last wall, carried a considerable part of it away, "pecked" badly, and would have fallen had his rider been shifted out of his seat in the slightest. Shortly after that, a fatal accident to his brother when riding a hurdle race in Ireland put an end to Rowland Hudson's sport "between the flags." The last time I saw him riding and winning was at Mozufferpore, in 1880, on his good mare Mercedes, who won him many useful stakes. I may add that he is a brilliant pig-sticker, and has, single-handed, killed many an old grey boar off horses which few would have cared to ride.

When the Prince of Wales went on a tiger shooting expedition to Nepal while he was in India, Mr. Hudson was chosen to accompany H.R.H. Unfortunately there was little chance of showing sport on horseback, except on one occasion, when they had a chase after a wild elephant. Lord Suffield, Lord Charles Beresford, Mr. Rose of the 10th Hussars, and Mr. Hudson, had the fun all to themselves when the riding became bad and dangerous, their *rôle* being to keep the tusker in view and engaged until the fighting elephants could be brought up. It was risky work drawing charges, as they did, from the furious brute in deep ground, and sometimes in long grass. He several times got within a few yards of them, and had any of their animals fallen, he would have smashed up horse and rider in a few seconds. H.R.H "spotted" Mr. Hudson's taste for horses, and at the breaking up of the party gave him a very handsome gold-mounted riding whip as a souvenir.

In his own part of Ireland, to which he returned in 1881–82, Mr. Hudson is known as a grand man for "opening a country," as it is called, which means watching how hounds are running, keeping just near enough to them, never trying impossible places, and never turning from anything that can be jumped. In 1882 he was selected to play for Ireland in the International Polo Tournament at Hurlingham, but was obliged to decline, as he could not spare the time. He was captain of the Westmeath polo team in 1881–82. He is a capital shot both with the smooth-bore and rifle, and has played for the last two seasons in the Westmeath first cricket eleven. I think I may safely say that, as an all-round sportsman, he would take a deal of "beating" in any company.

CHAPTER XIV.

I RETURNED from Tirhoot with the Waler mare Rebecca, which belonged to Mr. Edward Studd. She was a light little mare which had run unsuccessfully up Chumparun way in some selling races, and had a great reputation for being able to jump anything—a stick held up by two men, for instance—in cold blood. Though, to the casual observer, she might not have looked capable of performing under more than 9 st., still I did not mind that, for she had lots of quality, was very true-shaped, "well let down," and had extraordinary large, well-formed hocks. "No 'ocks no 'unter," as the immortal Mr. Jorrocks used to say.

I found that Rebecca required a great deal of schooling to make her take her fences in steeplechase form, for she had a nasty habit of dragging her hind legs after her when jumping a wall or timber. She liked fencing so much, and was so tractable, that I was able to school her on a small course Major Roberts (Bombay Artillery), who commanded the battery at Cawnpore, allowed me to make on the ground occupied by the Artillery riding school. I had an Irish double and a few walls of loose bricks, which I found the best kind of obstacle for teaching horses to jump walls cleverly without risking one's neck too much in the tuition. I kept Rebecca so quiet that only my own immediate friends knew anything about her real good chasing form. On one occasion, I took her across the river on the Oudh side to our regular steeplechase course, and sent her over a few of the big jumps, which she negotiated with great ease and precision. But judge of my dismay at seeing Mr. Germany, on another part of the course, practising his strangely named cross-country horse, Poor Cripple, who was clever enough, though too slow, to distinguish himself over a country. Mr. Germany rode up to me and asked me the name of the extraordinary good jumper I was riding. I was fortunately able to put him "off" with an evasive answer. I schooled her, on that day, over some water, and then, to test her staunchness, I raced her at a few deep circular water holes made by buffaloes for wallowing in. She neither turned to the right nor to the left, but jumped them in her stride, as if she thoroughly enjoyed the fun. She was a brilliant exception to Whyte Melville's rule, that horses do not like jumping.

As Rebecca, being a maiden, had a light weight to carry in the Lucknow steeplechase, I asked Mr. Baker, of the Horse Artillery, to ride her. I had seen him ride an excellent chase at a previous meeting, over the Meryaon course, on the grey Arab Galloway Sekunder, who was beaten for speed by Magdala with Captain Papillon up. Mr. Baker won a good race for me on Rebecca, beating a fair field, with Mr. Short, an indifferent second, on Don Juan.

On the following week we had a meeting at Cawnpore. Remembering how the Lucknow people had treated me with that 4 ft. 9 in. wall, I determined to show them that Rebecca could beat all comers for cleverness, as she had already done for speed ; so I made a stiff course, the *pièce de résistance* being a very high bank with deep drains on both sides, and a straight-cut watercourse about 14 ft. wide, running diagonally in front of it, with an interval of 20 ft. or 30 ft. A rider approaching this double obstacle, had either to take the water diagonally and then go straight at the bank, or he could

go direct at the brook and then turn short at the high
fence. So, anyhow, it would take some "doing." The
second jump was an ordinary Irish double in front of
the impromptu stand, on which had assembled all the
rank and beauty of Cawnpore to view the chase. As I
felt certain I could win, I made the conditions of the
race so that Rebecca should run on equal terms with
the platers, although she was a maiden of the season.
This, on my part, looked well, and prevented her from
being made a warm favourite. Mr. Short on Don Juan,
Mr. Hartwell on Marquis, Mr. Germany on Poor Cripple,
faced the starter. Mr. Short, who had helped me in
making the course, and Mr. Germany jumped off in
front the moment the flag fell. I kept just behind,
while Mr. Hartwell was outpaced. The two leaders, on
getting over the first fence, raced at the Irish double, Mr.
Short being a couple of lengths ahead. Don Juan was
going so fast that he could not collect himself, so struck
the bank, rolled over, and fell on his rider, breaking his
collar bone and most of his ribs on one side. Poor
Cripple topped the double cleverly, and then, seeing Mr.
Short and Don Juan lying on the ground, "threw such a
lep" that he jumped Mr. Germany out of the saddle and
then stood still. Dignum being at hand, and having

backed Don Juan, entreated Jack Irving, who was standing near, to mount him, but Jack curtly replied, "Ride him yourself, I won't," and Don Juan was sent back to his stable. In the meantime I cantered Rebecca, who fenced in grand form, round the remainder of the course, and left Mr. Hartwell and Marquis perched on the top of the big double, off which, so high was it, the country-bred was afraid to jump for some time.

Being impressed with the evil effect the practice of allowing honorary secretaries of race-meetings to make what kind of steeplechase jumps they saw fit had on sport, I wrote several letters on the subject, under the *nom de plume* of "Glenbrook," in the *Pioneer*, and advocated certain limits as to height and length. I am glad to say my teaching was taken to heart. The Meerut course was reconstructed on the model I had sketched out, and the authorities of several other fixtures followed suit.

After the Cawnpore Meeting, Mr. Studd wrote to me to sell Rebecca, as he had purchased the well-known chaser, Jovial. I sold Rebecca to Captain Grant for Rs. 1000, which was fully her value, as her fore legs were too light to stand the weights she would have to carry as a plater, and was Rs. 200 more than Mr. Studd had paid for her. The terms on which I had taken the mare were, that Mr. Studd and I were to share all expenses and divide all winnings in stakes, lotteries, and bets. In fact, he provided the mare and I the training. These were the terms on which I always took horses. Mr. Studd seemed very much pleased at having got such a good horse as Jovial out of Rebecca's winnings. He wrote and told me that I was to enter Jovial for the Allahabad and Umballa chases, and that I was to ride her myself. As I had to get down a lot of weight, I "put the muzzle on," and by long walks and starving I found that I was light enough and very "fit," when I arrived at Allahabad. But no Jovial turned up. I at last learned, just before the races, that Mr. Studd had exchanged Jovial for a useless and untried animal called Prodigal, and that my wasting and trouble had been all in vain. After this Rebecca won two chases, one at Umballa and another at Lucknow.

The next horse Mr. Studd sent me was a fine weight-carrying hunter style of horse, called Cæsar, who was far too slow for any one in his senses to take the trouble of wasting and getting fit. I put up a lad who rode him very well at Allahabad, but fell off towards the end of the run, on Cæsar making a mistake and pecking badly.

The race being such a foregone conclusion, I took so little interest in it that I forget who won.

All this time I have left Mr. Short lying on the ground at Cawnpore. I took him home with me to our mess-house, where I had quarters. The poor fellow had a very bad time of it, but his brave spirit kept him from uttering a murmur or giving a sign of the pain that was racking him, on account of one of the fractured ribs pressing against his lungs. While we were watching over him one night, some one whispered sadly to another: "Poor fellow; I don't think he will pull through." "I'll bet you a hundred rupees I do," gasped the undaunted Bertie. In a month he was nearly all right again, and then went up to Dehra Doon.

At the end of this year (1874), Captain Papillon, who was one of the hardest men to beat I have ever met, left India and quitted the saddling enclosure for ever. A mutual friend was travelling in the far north of Scotland with a resident of those parts, in February, 1881, during the time that great fall of snow covered Great Britain, and even suspended the railway traffic on the Great Western, so we may imagine what it must have been in the Highlands. The two companions, after a terrible climb up the side of a mountain, gained its top, and then saw in front of them a valley entirely blocked up with snow, with nothing to break the white surface except a couple of chimney pots, from which curled blue wreaths of smoke. "I wonder who lives there," remarked my friend. "Captain Papillon," answered the resident, who explained that the great "David" had married and settled down, on condition that he should race no more.

CHAPTER XV.

GENERAL "MONTY" TURNBULL.

EARLY in 1875 Colonel Turnbull, having served the allotted time for his colonel's allowances, relinquished his appointment on attaining the rank of Lieutenant-General, and left India for ever. He was one of those rare combinations of brave soldier, good sportsman, and true friend, which are seen, perhaps, less frequently now-a-days than formerly : not because our British Isles do not breed the material, but present times seldom furnish the opportunity for its development.

He was, in his younger days, a fine horseman, and won many races on the flat. He owned, from time to time, a number of good horses, to which I shall allude further on. He was an excellent trainer and judge, in which capacity he was always at the service of his many friends, to their gain, though sometimes to his own loss, for he was generous to a fault. During his long stay in

Page 181.

the Hermitage—called after his favourite horse—at Alipore, near Calcutta, he did yeoman service, in the true interests of racing as a steward of the Calcutta Turf Club, and as one of the Editors of the *Oriental Sporting Magazine*, the other two being Lord Ulick Browne and Colonel W. Nassau Lees, LL.D.

As a writer he was fond of a joke, and often enlivened "The Month" of his paper by a droll tale. "Arab merchants," he relates in one of the numbers, "are apt to be too fond of trials, and so much does the term work on their imagination, that one of them was heard to apply it to a loving couple riding round the racecourse. When it was suggested that it would result in a match, the immediate answer was, "Nahiir, Sahib, we khalee try kurteṅ haiṅ." (No, sir, they are only running a trial!)

What a fine old Indian flavour there is about the following story, which a correspondent to the magazine tells as having happened in Calcutta. "One of the Southern Confederates bet two noble and gallant sportsmen a dozen of champagne that he would carry each of them one hundred yards on his back, in front of the stand, on a race morning between the races, in fourteen seconds. 'Done,' and 'done' was said. Down goes the Confederate, down go the Northerners accompanied by a small crowd, while the whole stand is radiantly expectant. The Confederate doffs his coat and girds up his loins. The gallant and noble No. 1 comes up to mount. 'Take off your coat,' says the Confederate. It is done. 'Your waistcoat.' It is removed. 'Your collar.' 'Well, I don't see the use of that,' replies the other. 'Then book up,' retorts the Confederate. 'Carry me first, if you can,' insists No. 1, whose friend with the best of stop watches is standing gravely by. 'Not a bit of it,' replies the Southerner. 'I backed myself to carry you, but not one stitch of your clothes ; and here I am waiting to do it.' And amid a roar of laughter the Confederate opened the champagne *pro bono publico*. It may be an old sell, but it was new to us."

Colonel Turnbull's father was in the Bengal Civil Service, and rose to be the judge of the High Court. Four of his sons went to India, and became brilliant representatives of the Civil Service, Artillery, Engineers, and Cavalry. The Engineer brother died at his post from fever contracted on duty on the Jumna Canal. The brave Gunner was killed in the Indian Mutiny, and Colonel Turnbull and his brother the judge returned to England together, after, respectively, thirty-nine and thirty-six years of honourable and faithful service. My friend and his wife often think of the stirring scenes they passed through, and the happy days they spent in India. Mrs. Turnbull rides still the handsome Arab horse, Cuckoo, she brought back with her from Calcutta, and has many a feathered pet in her aviary to remind her of the glorious East. They call their pretty place, which is hard by the green of a lovely, old-fashioned village in Sussex, the " Hermitage," in memory of their gallant Arab, and of the old bungalow at Alipore.

When speaking of my friend, I use the rank by which he was known to us all in India, rather than the more distinguished one he now holds.

He joined the 7th Bengal Light Cavalry in 1837, and soon obtained the adjutancy of that regiment. He served through the Sindh campaign under Sir Charles Napier in 1844 and 1845 ; and acted as Quartermaster-General to Sir H. Wheeler's force through the Punjab War, in which he gallantly saved the famous Hodson's life. This great cavalry leader, as Lord Ulick Browne describes, " had flogged some camp followers of a sepoy regiment, nearly a whole company of which rushed with fixed bayonets on five or six of his troopers, killed them, and then pursued Hodson with the loudly avowed object of taking his life also. At this juncture, Colonel Turnbull, supported by a single Native Infantry officer, interposed in a gateway between the sepoys and Hodson, checking the former, while loudly calling a bugler to sound the 'assembly,' and thus saved Hodson's life, as his relation, Mr. Thomason, Lieutenant-Governor of the North-West Provinces, observed in a letter of thanks to Colonel Turnbull. There was no Victoria Cross in those days, but it has seldom been conferred for a more courageous act."

He married the daughter of Mr. Apperley, the celebrated "Nimrod" of the *Quarterly Review*. She was quite as fond of horses and as devoted to training and racing as her husband, although they were not agreed on all points of work and stable management, as " Moss Trooper" (Sam Wanchope), writing in the *Oriental Sporting Magazine*, humorously described in his skit, "My First Race Meeting." He tells us how, when the Turnbulls' horse, which was favourite for the chief event, went lame, Mrs. Turnbull insisted on icing the affected limb, while, the moment her back was turned, the Colonel slipped out to the stable, on pretence of smoking a cheroot, to parboil it.

She was one of the most accomplished horsewomen we have ever had in the East. Her brilliant riding stood her in good stead through the many dangers she passed through by her husband's side, and which would have crushed a less dauntless spirit. Although she was everything that was soft, winning, and womanly, her heart knew no fear. During the time of the Sindh Mutiny she rode along with her husband at the head of his regiment, which was disaffected, 129 marches from Umballa to Shikarpore, where the mutiny burst out. They were encamped in the month of July under canvas at Roree on the Indus, with the thermometer ranging from 127° to 130° F. daily in the shade. Strange to say, during that heat they had only one man sick in hospital, although after they reached their head-quarters at Shikarpore, only Colonel Turnbull and eleven of his men remained fit for duty. On their long march from Shikarpore to Muttra, they rode over the late battlefield of Ferozeshah to reach their camp. When proceeding with the Bombay column from Sukkur *en route* for Mooltan, before the surrender of that fort, Sir Charles Napier stopped the regiment, at the head of which was the Colonel and his wife, to compliment her on the example she had set during her two years' stay in Sindh. Sir Charles and his staff often drank a toast after dinner to "The Star of the Desert," as they used to call her.

She was present with her husband at Shikarpore during
the Sindh Mutiny, when that wily old General, George
Hunter, induced a Native Infantry regiment to proceed
to Sukkur to have their supposed grievances inquired
into, and then trapped them on arrival by a wing of the
13th Light Infantry and a masked battery of European
artillery. This *ruse* resulted in about sixty of the
mutinous ringleaders being given up on threat of the
regiment being annihilated. Fifty were transported for
life, and eight were hanged on one gallows. Seven of
the latter spared all trouble to the executioner by
jumping off the platform, and thereby strangling themselves ; while the eighth continued to call on his
regiment to come to his rescue until the bolt was drawn.

Out of many hair-breadth escapes, three of the closest
which Colonel Turnbull had were when he escaped the
Cabul massacre in the first Afghan war by being suddenly transferred from the 5th to the 7th Light Cavalry ;
when, at Wuzeerabad, the massive court-house, which
was built on sand-brick pillars, came down with a run
during a storm, and buried the table which Colonel
Turnbull had just quitted to avoid the wind ; and when
on a night alarm during the Sikh war, as he was riding
full gallop to the main-guard to turn the regiment out,

his Arab charger suddenly stopped, and then made a desperate bound forward, but only far enough to land with his fore-legs on the edge of a large masonry well of great depth, while his hind-legs were hanging over the edge. The gallant horse, by a supreme effort, worked himself forward with his fore-legs, struggled on to the bank, and saved himself and his rider from certain death. In those old days Indian officers had quite enough hardship and danger to give zest to their luxuries and pleasures.

The following is a brief description of a few of the best horses which Colonel Turnbull owned from time to time.

Hermit was a flea-bitten grey Arab. He stood close on 15 hands, had immense bone and substance, and was full of "quality." His knees and hocks were well let down, and he looked a racehorse all over. Although he won thirty-four races at all weights and distances during the six years he was in training, he never showed even a wind-gall on any of his legs. He was purchased at Bombay, in 1857, for "Mr. Pitt" (Colonel W. P. Robbins), and was sent for sale to Calcutta for Rs. 1200, but no one would buy him as his feet had got bad from mismanagement. Colonel Turnbull took him on racing terms, and finally bought him.   After nearly two years' trouble he got him sound and entered him for the Calcutta Derby—a race for maiden Arabs, 2 miles. For this event his owner stood to win over £3000 on him, but the grey could only run second to Rocket. Six days after that Hermit had his revenge by defeating his former conqueror, after a dead heat with him in the Great Welter.   This was the commencement of a long series of victories with but few reverses.   Some of the ablest judges who knew him have always maintained that he was the best Arab they have ever seen in India, as we may well believe from his giving Ellerton, a good Waler, 7 lbs. and a beating for the Calcutta Stakes, 2 miles in 3 min. 51 secs.   Probably his best performance was that for the Trades Cup, 2 miles, 13th February, 1862, when he ran a desperate race with the English mare Voltige, and was beaten by two lengths in the extraordinary time of 3 min. 46 secs.   Mr. Chaplin, who was in India at the time and saw this race, declared that it was, on the part of the Arab, the gamest struggle he had ever witnessed, and that he would call a colt after him.   The name of the Derby winner of 1868, and sire of Shotover, Peter, Thebais, and many others, was the result of this promise.

BILL BREWTY.

Page 189.

Hermit was defeated at Mysore by Dr. Campbell's Grey Leg, who was one of the best Arabs that ever ran on the Bombay side. He was ridden by Jack Irving, and Grey Leg by Bill Brewty, who used to own that pretty house on the Old Sandpit Lane in Newmarket, now occupied by Jeffries. The result was so astounding to the Calcutta people that they looked askance on Jack when he returned from his trip. But I believe the truth is that Hermit was not "fit." He had been sent in charge of a man who knew little about race-horses, and who did not attend to his training. As I am writing I have before me a letter from Brewty, who has returned to India, telling me that, on his honour, the race was a fair and square one. Irving, too, whom I have known for several years, has often spoken to me about it, and has assured me, with almost tears in his eyes, that this defeat was the bitterest he had ever experienced, both for his own sake and that of Colonel Turnbull's grand horse, for he and Brewty were the two great rival jockeys of that time.

The Arab Opal, so called from his colour, belonged to Mrs. Turnbull, and was taken by her to England, where he won first prize in the Arab Class at the Islington Show in 1862. On one occasion, when

Colonel Turnbull's Engineer brother was staying with the Turnbulls at Calcutta, he said to them that he wanted the handsomest horse they could get for money to take up country, and requested them to effect the purchase for him. These two ardent lovers of the horse were delighted with the commission, and made many enjoyable tours to the different stables, the proprietors of which were only too glad to trot out their best for the inspection of two such good paying visitors. At last they saw the desire of their eyes in the shape of a grey Arab belonging to old Sheikh Ibrahim, and purchased him for Rs. 2500. On their return to Alipore they delightedly showed him to their brother, who, casually remarking that he must get a side-saddle for him, sent him off to the saddlers. When the horse came back with his new gear on, his owner gracefully presented him, fully caparisoned, to Mrs. Turnbull.

Mangosteen, who was afterwards called Starlight, was a celebrated Arab racehorse. Colonel Turnbull won him in a raffle got up by Sheikh Ibrahim. The old Arab dealer, being in need of money, raffled off three of his horses, a grey, bay, and chesnut, for Rs. 6000 —three throws with three dice. Colonel Turnbull, to a number corresponding to his own age, threw 49, but being beaten by two Arab dealers with 50 and 53, he obtained only third choice. The first Arab merchant took the grey, which he sold shortly afterwards for Rs. 2000 ; the second chose the chesnut, who in his day was the invincible Shah-in-Shah ; while the bay fell to Colonel Turnbull's lot. Either of the two last-mentioned horses was worth more than the whole amount Sheikh Ibrahim obtained for the three. Before the raffle came off, the old dealer was accused in some of the Calcutta daily papers of attempting, by its means, to " palm " off a trio of worthless screws on the public. The evident moral of this is, never abuse an Arab or his horse until you have tried them.

Dirk Hatterick, who won the Colonials in the good time of 3 min. 18½ secs., was bought by Colonel Turnbull from Jim Collins, the owner of Vanderdecken, and was afterwards sold to go to Madras for the big race at that meeting, which he won and got back his purchase money.

Maperoni, the Colonel's charger, was a very fair race-horse. In one event, when ridden by Fendell Thompson, of the Bengal Civil Service, the girth broke in the middle of the race. Finding the saddle shifting back towards the horse's tail, this fine horseman worked himself forward, got hold of the saddle in one hand, rode in and won the race barebacked amidst great cheering.

On leaving India, Colonel Turnbull took three horses with him to breed from in England. They were Cuckoo, a very handsome, high caste Arab; a son of Hermit, Hermes, for whom he had been offered £500 at Ceylon, and who had taken first prize at the Calcutta Horse Show; and Hebe's daughter, a country-bred. Hermes died of sunstroke in the Red Sea, the mare proved barren, while Cuckoo disdained to fulfil his duties. This was cruel bad luck for one who was so fond of horses as my gallant friend.

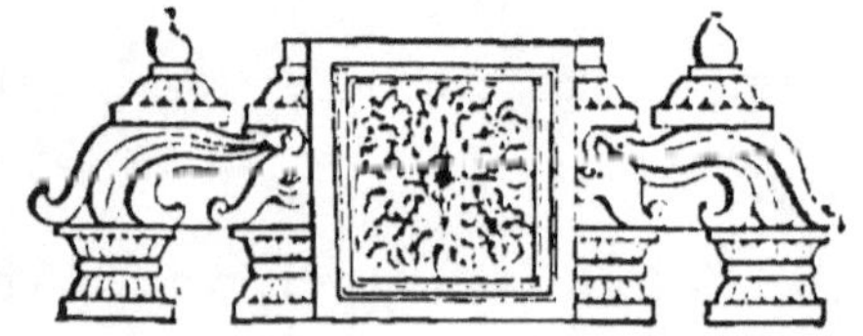

LORD ULICK BROWNE.

Page 193.

CHAPTER XVI.

LORD ULICK BROWNE.

THESE pages would be incomplete indeed were I to abstain from mentioning the name of Lord Ulick Browne, who has been for years the lawgiver of the Calcutta Turf Club, and is regarded and honoured throughout the empire as our Indian Admiral Rous. Before he took the matter in hand, the racing rules of that country presented many anomalies which involved injustice to owners and horses. Lord Ulick brought to bear on this intricate subject the experience of a thorough sportsman, and a mind trained to decide judicial questions, as an Indian Civil servant of high standing. I may here appropriately sketch his career in connection with sport, as he was joint editor and proprietor of the *Oriental Sporting Magazine*, as I have before mentioned, with Colonels Turnbull and Nassau Lees.

Lord Ulick was, so to speak, bred to the Turf, as his father was a real sportsman, who kept a racing stable and bred thoroughbred stock for many years, without ever betting a sovereign. The Irish Racing Calendars for the early part of this century record how seldom, during a series of years, there was a day's racing at the Curragh without a horse of Lord Sligo's starting. Like many other Irish gentlemen of that time, his chief ambition was, however, to win the Doncaster St. Leger. Although he did not quite succeed in doing so, still he ran second twice: once with Canteen in Jerry's year; and again with Bran, who was good enough to have won this race in most years, but had to succumb to Touchstone. His horses ran with success at other meetings, both in Yorkshire and elsewhere. Some of his best were Waxy Pope, Langar (sire of Orlando's dam), Starch, Fang, Miss Staveley, and Oiseau; while the last of the Westport Stud was Wolfdog, who was running as top weight in the principal handicaps in 1847 and 1848, after having beaten, as a three-year old, the great mare Alice Hawthorn in a race for a Queen's plate on the Curragh.

Lord Sligo bred most of the horses he ran, and did much for thoroughbred stock. More than fifty years ago he recognized the excellence of the Waxy blood. In a series of papers on horsebreeding in Ireland which appeared, a few years ago, in *The Sporting Gazette,* now *The County Gentleman,* there were long lists of the produce of the Westport Stud and their performances; while a saying of his, " You cannot have too much Waxy," was quoted as having been borne out by the fact that there are very few good horses running at present who are without that strain in them. Waxy Pope and Wire were the principal son and daughter of Waxy through whom Lord Sligo carried out his theory.

Lord Ulick arrived in India in September, 1851, and first appeared on the Turf at Calcutta, on the last day of the race meeting of the following December, when he rode his black Australian mare Jessie (well known with the Calcutta Turf Club), second to the famous half-miler, Edward Morgan, then the property of Mr. E. (" Salamander ") Studd, of Seryah factory, in Tirhoot, and afterwards owned by Mr. H. B. Simson. The next Calcutta meeting was wound up by two hack races; one for all horses, to be entered and ridden by jockeys for their own benefit, and the other for Arabs, G. Rs. Hartley won the first with Jessie, while Lord Ulick secured the latter with The Shah, an old grey Arab hack and buggy horse, formerly known up country as Revenge. He then bought Firefly, who had won The Colonials four years previously, and took him and the other two to Berhampore in 1852, where he won the hack race with Firefly, but was unsuccessful with the others. At this meeting he rode in the Arab Welter, which was carried off by a horse steered by General Parrot, who, I am glad to hear, has been breeding lately some very good stock in India. In 1852 Lord Ulick rode, at Sonepore, Mr. Kenneth Macleod's horses, then trained at Chuprah by Mr. Hewitt, in two welter races; in one of which he beat the English horse Bedford, late Festus, by a neck, with the Australian gelding Emperor. So inferior were the Walers at that time, that the latter running the mile in 1 min. 55 secs. with 11 st. up, was considered to be a remarkable performance. During the next cold weather at Calcutta he won a couple of races. After that he went to Tirhoot, where he re-established the Mozufferpore races, which had been discontinued about six years previously, but have been carried on most successfully ever since. It was at this meeting that the famous 12.2 country-bred pony, Jenab-i-Ali, made his first appearance. A week before the races, Lord Ulick and five of his friends agreed to buy, out of the bazaar (part of the town occupied by native shops), ponies that had never been ridden by Europeans, and to run and ride them in a race of quarter-mile heats, without dismounting: weight for inches. Jenab, who had been just cured of his habit of starting off at an amble, and taught to pull against a plain snaffle, won the race, and was afterwards never beaten in a long career of pony racing at Mozufferpore, Sonepore, Bhaugulpore, and other places. In 1854 he brought out two indifferently bred Walers, and secured, at Sonepore, a maiden race with one, and beat Edward Morgan with the other. He then set up a racing stable with Mr. F. A. Vincent, of Barh, the principal horses being the Australians Beeswing and Boomerang, and had a successful season; but as he got married the next year, he sold off his stud.

In 1859, being transferred to Calcutta, he took up the two important questions of Racing Rules and Racing Weights in India. As regards the former, there were then about ten rules in force at all meetings, with one providing that all other points should be governed by the Newmarket rules, which were seldom to be had on Indian racecourses.   Lord Ulick, after stirring up the Calcutta Turf Club into active existence again, drew out a regular code of rules, embodying those of the English Jockey Club with the special local ones, though departing from the former on a few points : such as providing that the progress of a horse must be actually impeded to establish a cross ; not disqualifying an animal on account of the death of his nominator, &c.   These rules were adopted by the Calcutta Turf Club in the beginning of 1861, and have, with but few alterations, remained in force ever since throughout India.   The Madras and Bombay Turf Clubs were not long in following suit.

When Lord Ulick took up the question of weights, the state of things was as follows.   There was everywhere in India a single scale of weight for age for all distances and all classes of horses, regardless of the different times of foaling of the various classes ; although in the Colonies and at the Cape horses take their age from the 1st August.   Here is the old Calcutta scale :—

		st.	lbs.
3 years	... ...	7	4
4 ,,	... ...	8	4
5 ,,	... ...	8	12
6 ,, and aged	... ...	9	3

The Bombay scale, which was as follows, was a peculiar one, for by it a 6-year old gave a 5-year old only 1 lb. less than a 4-year old gave a 3-year old, over two miles, for instance!

							st.	lbs.
3 years	...	...	...	...	...	...	7	4
4 „	...	...	...	...	...	...	7	12
5 „	...	...	...	...	...	...	8	5
6 „	...	...	...	...	...	...	8	12
Aged	...	...	...	...	...	...	9	0

These scales being taken as a basis for calculation, English horses (when different classes ran together) were required to carry 1 st. extra, country-breds were allowed 7 lbs. or 1 st., and Arabs 1 st. or 21 lbs. ; while Walers ran according to the scale. Finally, all classes of horses took their age from 1st May, which was a great hardship to the Australians and Capes, whose time of foaling is from August to November, inclusive. The other classes always got the benefit of the doubt even if there was good reason for believing that they had been dropped between January and May. Incredible as it may appear, it is a fact that no one in the then Turf Club, nor any steward of a Race Meeting in India, knew the meaning of the rule, that "horses shall take their age from 1st May" (or any other date), viz : that a horse is one year old on the 1st May succeeding the date of his birth. When the actual date of foaling was known, it was the custom to count the period between that and the 1st of May for nothing in the case of English horses and country-breds, although it was reckoned as a full twelvemonth against the unfortunate Colonials. This confusion of ideas was owing to the fact that the two dates in the former case were in the same calendar year, while in the latter they were in different ones.

To remedy these incongruities, Lord Ulick drew up, on the English principle, an admirably constructed table of weights for age and class, which were soon adopted throughout India with general satisfaction. The weights were varied according to the distances, so that the longer the journey, the lighter was the burden on the young ones ; and also for the different months, so that the allowance to a colt diminished as he gradually approached his next birthday. The age allowances which are in force in England, Australia, and the Cape respectively, were adopted for the horses of those countries ; while the English scale was modified to suit Arabs and country-breds, who are more backward when young than our own animals. The allowance for class, after different changes, stood for a long time as follows :—English horses to give Walers 7 lbs., Capes 21 lbs., Country-breds 2 st. 7 lbs., and Arabs 3 st. 7 lbs. The improvement made by Australians has been so great, that the 7 lbs. conceded to them by English horses has recently been abolished.

Another reform Lord Ulick effected was the substitution of class handicaps for winners' and losers' handicaps. It had previously been the practice to have on the last day of a race meeting, a forced handicap for all winners of every class ; thus giving the stewards the absurd task of bringing a good English or Australian horse with a winner of a maiden race for Arabs, and again of trying to adjust the weights among the losers of these classes. One of the last instances of the old style of winners' handicap was at Sonepore in 1867, when Colonel Robart's Rocket was weighted at 12 st. 7 lbs., and an Arab winner at 6 st. 7 lbs. !

CHAPTER XVII.

IN 1875 I again went to Tirhoot, and returned with the
Walers, Red Gauntlet and Piccadilly, who belonged to
Mr. Gilbert Nicolay. Old Pic had chronic fever in the
feet, so I could do nothing with him. I put the other
into training for the Trial Stakes at the Lucknow Monsoon Meeting, and my country-bred Fairymount for the
Maiden Arab and Country-bred Race, for which I gave
the surplus accruing from the Cawnpore Derby Sweep
I had organized, and, of course, was anxious to win it
myself. I was also training Mr. Paul Bird's bay Waler,
Freetrader, for the Lucknow chases. This animal was
a bold and clever fencer, fairly fast, but had a doubtful
fore-leg, having sprained the check ligament before he

came to India. He was no boy's horse, but one that required a man to ride him. Through that excellent trial horse, Red Gauntlet, I found that Mr. Elphick's cast off Fairymount, was a very smart animal. About ten days before the Lucknow meeting, I was down early one morning with my country-bred and Red Gauntlet on the Cawnpore racecourse. As I happened to have only one boy to ride, I asked Mr. Germany to get on Mr. Nicolay's horse, and gave directions for a steady gallop. Whether Mr. Germany had but vague notions of what half-speed meant, or whether Red Gauntlet ran away—he could pull tons—I know not, but the moment they started, Mr. Germany rushed to the front and went along as hard as he could split. To my horror I saw a cowherd driving some bullocks across the course about a couple of hundred yards in front of the flying pair. I held my breath and thought it hours as bullock by bullock crossed at a slow trot, and nearer and nearer Mr. Germany and Red Gauntlet drew on them. The last humped brute had plenty of time to get beyond the galloping track, but, with all the perversity of his race, he broke into a walk and then stopped. The brave Germany, scorning to be shoved off the course by even the object of Hindu worship, charged the bullock, with the firm impression that Red Gauntlet would take the animal in his stride, but the Waler "chanced" him, and then I saw a bullock rolling on the ground like a huge football, a horse and man turning a somersault in the air, and a cloud of dust.   When the dust had cleared I perceived Red Gauntlet and the bullock lying on the ground looking at each other, and the cowherd, pursued by Mr. Germany, running madly across the plain.   I gazed till my aching eyes lost them in the distance.   I do not think the horse got over his "cropper" by the time he ran at Lucknow, for he was easily beaten by Necromancer, well ridden by Captain Maunsell of the 13th Hussars, who once could hold his own in any company across country.   As to that cowherd, I believe Mr. Germany, to use Tommy Atkins's expression, " made away with him :" he certainly did not " lose him through neglect."   Morning after morning, as I sent the horses their gallops on the racecourse, I used to look out for that Hindu, but although the cause of all the evil with his bovine companions came to eat the young grass on my carefully tended galloping track, the cowherd never appeared again.   I trust that in his next birth the name of "Germany" shall not be written in his fate.

Mr. Anderson had entered a very fast country-bred called Pole Star in the race for which Fairymount was to run. Before it came off we gave them a "rough-up" together, and Pole Star won very easily. Of course we bought him in the lottery, and let Major Hastings, if I remember right, have Fairymount. At the last moment I took a small share, an eighth or a quarter of my horse, merely to show his buyer that, however the money went, I meant to give him every chance. Blackburn rode Pole Star and got cleverly beaten by my stable lad, Oodit, on Fairymount. So much for trials!

I had bad luck with Freetrader. In the first chase at Lucknow the jockey who rode him appeared afraid to let him go out of a canter. In the next one, Mr. Gartside Tipping was not able to hold him at the start, and let him bolt away in the wrong direction. Both races were won by Dignum on Highflyer, who beat Jerry, ridden by Mr. Germany, in the second event, after an exciting contest.

As I had nothing better to do during the hot weather of 1875, I went down to Calcutta to read with the well-known and talented *munshi*, Adalut Khan, for the High Proficiency in Urdu. I was, luckily, successful, and after giving my Bengalee friend Rs. 300 for his trouble, returned with Rs. 1200 for the next racing campaign.

About that time my regiment was ordered to Cachar. As I did not relish being exiled for three years in the utmost limits of Eastern Bengal, I applied for two years' furlough, got it, and went to Dehra Doon with Freetrader, Fairymount, and Jovial, who belonged to Mr. George Thomas, a gentleman well known in Calcutta as a good sportsman.

I was sorry to leave Cawnpore, where I had spent a very enjoyable four years. I had there every facility for training my horses. As the parade ground was close to the racecourse, I was able, the moment I had dressed (by candle-light) and got into uniform, to mount my charger and ride down with the horses to the course, and after they had walked or trotted enough, to send them their gallops and see how they had borne their work before I had to " fall in " with the regiment. The galloping track was always in excellent order, thanks to the litter I was able to get from the Artillery lines and the tan from Colonel Stewart's leather establishment, which turns out as good harness as many London shops. The residents were a sporting lot, very hospitable, and had a most comfortable little club. There was capital ground for riding and schooling on the other side of the river, and lots of pigsticking. Although I did not take a very active part in the pigsticks myself, for I had no suitable cattle to ride after the wily boar, I enjoyed going out to the meets, where I was always certain to be in the best of company — to wit, Messrs. Maxwell, Dunbar, Chapman, Carr, poor Bonner-Maurice, Leach, Preston, Cruickshank, Fishbourne, and others—and have a jolly dinner after the long ride out, yarns over the camp fire, a sound sleep in the tent, and, instead of parade next morning, a ride and lots of fun.

We had, while there, several sky-meetings, which showed good sport. I remember on one occasion riding Mr. Leach's b.w.m. Lady Jane for the Cawnpore Tent Club Cup. This mare was a very hard puller, and had, as the expression goes, only one side to her mouth. I rode her in a snaffle, as her owner thought that was the best bit for her. Her only opponent was Mr. Maxwell's Waler mare Vesper, ridden by Mr. Martin Gubbins. The steeplechase came off on the Oudh side of the river over a fair hunting line of country. As soon as we started, I found it impossible to keep Lady Jane straight at her fences, if I went at all fast, as I had no power over her in the plain snaffle. I was obliged to pull her into a canter on coming to an obstacle, and then make up the lost ground between the fences. As Mr. Gubbins knew that I had the speed of him, he used to get alongside me when coming up to a fence, and then make Vesper refuse in front of Lady Jane, who, on that provocation, used to "run out" and carry me away for some distance, before I could get her round again and over, while Mr. Gubbins used to turn Vesper, who was a very handy mare, sharp round, take the fence, and go away as hard as he could. When I caught him up he used to try on the same game. About a mile from home I slipped him and got away in front. When I was fairly in the straight, and had only one hurdle, which was a couple of hundred yards distant, to clear, we were joined by all the serjeants and corporals of Mr. Leach's Battery, who were mounted on their troopers, and had come out to see their young officer's mare win. The sight of her companions and the clatter around her was too much for her excitable nerves, so she tore away, and I never got a pull at her until she had gone about three miles off in the direction of Lucknow, which was at about an angle of forty-five degrees to the line of the flags. "Give me a bit and a bridoon," as Captain Papillon used to say.

Before I left Cawnpore poor old Caliph was raffled for the second time, and went up to the Punjab—for stud purposes, I hope.

The Dehra Doon Meeting of October, 1875, was well attended, and I had a great chance of winning a large stake in the steeplechase, for which there were many entries, including Ring, Daybreak, Clarion, Shanbally, Red Eagle, Gaylad, and others. I had tried Freetrader to be better than Jovial at even weights; although, being a maiden, he would have to get a lot of weight from Mr. Thomas's horse, who was good enough to win, heavily penalized as he was.

Some days before the steeplechase came off, Freetrader broke away from my riding boy and hurt his bad leg. He managed, however, to run a fair second to Mr. F. Johnson's Ring, and would, I have no doubt, actually have won, had not Mr. Short made too much use of him up the hill immediately on starting. I was to blame for this, as I had given him orders to make the running, because the owner had told me that staying was his *forte.* I, foolishly, believed my sanguine friend and never asked the horse the question, as I ought to have done. The shifty and unschooled Clarion, late Hunting Horn, admirably ridden by Lord William

Beresford, finished a fair third. Three finer horsemen that day than Mr. Johnson, Mr. Short, and Lord William, it would have been hard to find.

Mr. Johnson's luck, I am sorry to say, came somewhat late. When he first arrived in England from Canada he was an extraordinary good "sprinter ;" but the big Sheffield handicap, which was to have made his fortune, never came "off." He enlisted, and was sent to the Canterbury Riding establishment, where he was known as the smartest non-commissioned officer in the service. In a short time he got his commission in the 11th Hussars, who had reason to be proud of their young subaltern, for he was good-looking, "the best of company," and one of the sweetest singers ever heard on or off the stage, besides being one of the best "drills" that ever handled a regiment on parade. But he would back his luck, whether in or out of it. At first the jade favoured him, and then she deserted him. On one occasion, at Umballa, he stood to win a great stake on his horse, April Fool, in the big steeplechase, and when he had his field settled, and had only to canter home, poor April Fool broke a hind leg, and the chance was gone. Again, on the same course, Teddy O'Neil, late Barrister, carrying Mr. Johnson and a pile of money, fell when it was 100

BERTIE SHORT, ESQ.

Page 211.

to 1 on him. A third time he got a chance in the chase with Ring at Dehra, but his colonel would not give him leave. He took it, however, and had to "send in his papers." Then Fortune, with her usual irony, smiled once more on him, and loaded him with her favours for a whole year, but to break him at the big Umballa Meeting of 1877, at which there was heavier and more reckless gambling than was ever known before or since in India.

At the time Mr. Short met with his accident at Cawnpore, he was absent without leave from the police service, in which he was acting as District Superintendent. Routine work, especially at an out-of-the-way station, no more suited the somewhat volatile "Bertie" than the unutterable weariness of going to parade twice a week did that *beau sabreur*, Frank Johnson. The Hussar, though a fine rider, was not within measurable distance of Bertie across country on a difficult horse. Short was one of the very few men I have ever met who knew no fear. The faster his horse went, the harder he pulled, and the bigger the country, the more did the brave Peeler like the fun. His only fault in steeplechase riding was that he was rather too fond of making the running. On the flat he was as good as most professionals. Shortly after throwing up his appointment he met with a far more serious accident than that which he had at Cawnpore. Riding down from Mussoorie to Dehra one afternoon, he wished to pass, on his way home, a small watercourse, at which his pony jibbed. He stretched his right hand, in which he was holding the reins, forward on its neck, and shook the reins to make it go on. The vicious brute caught his hand between its teeth, pulled him down to the ground, and then "savaged" him. When poor Bertie at last tore himself free, his hand was a shapeless mass, and had to be amputated.

Some time before this terrible occurrence, Mr. Short and I had a rather heated newspaper correspondence about the construction of steeplechase courses. A few days after his accident I received from him a letter with the following lines scrawled with his left hand: " Dear Horace—Forgive the words I used against you, for the hand that wrote them is now no more. Yours ever, Bertie Short." Dear old boy!

Three or four days after my arrival at Dehra, I happened to go into my stable about one o'clock at night, and found Jovial shivering with cold and without his clothing, which the syce had appropriated for his own use, although I had given to each of my native grooms a couple of blankets before starting from Cawnpore. The swift and sharp chastisement which fell on the syce was unable to avert the ill effects of the chill from the horse, who, next morning, on coming out of his stall, was hardly able to move out of a walk, and presented all the symptoms of congestion of the liver— a disease which is peculiarly rife during the autumn in those parts of India where the days are hot and the nights bitterly cold. Of course it would hardly ever occur were the stables free from draughts, though well ventilated, the horses comfortably bedded down, and warmly clothed with a body-piece and a good English rug, or two country-made ones. I would advise that no hoods or "nightcaps" be used. The former are very inconvenient for employment at night, for if they be tied to the roller or body-piece they will prevent a horse getting his head down ; while if they be unattached, they will, when the animal lowers his head, fall over his ears. I have always found that the use of "nightcaps" is very apt to give horses that wear them coughs or colds. My experience on this subject is corroborated by that of Mr. J. H. Moore, who has abolished them from his stable on that account. If horses do not require any head-covering during the bitter winter nights in England and Ireland, they can hardly be a necessity in the milder climate of India. I think it would be desirable to do away with clothing for horses in stables, were it possible, during cold weather, and to substitute for it some arti·ficial means of warming the stalls, such as properly arranged fires, which would not interfere with the purity of the air inside the stable, but would, on the contrary, promote it. Horses which have lived any length of time in a warm relaxing climate, such as that of Bengal, particularly if they have been highly fed and but lightly worked, are very prone to attacks of liver disease on being brought up to the North-West or Punjab during the autumn or cold weather. They ought, before tra-velling, to be "cooled down" by bran mashes, green meat, and a little relaxing physic.

I had a bad meeting at Dehra. I was not able to run Fairymount; Jovial went amiss; Freetrader got beaten; and I lost the first part of a double event bet of Rs. 2,500 to Rs. 100 which I laid Mr. Johnson that he would not win both the Dehra and Umballa Steeple-chases. Though I sought counsel from many veterinary surgeons, Jovial remained very ill.

I arrived with the horses at Umballa in the worst of

spirits, for I did not see my way to win a race or get the wherewithal to pay stable bill and my expenses to England, where I wanted to go at the end of the season to write a book, that, in time, developed itself into "Veterinary Notes for Horse Owners." Fairymount, after showing good form for half the journey in the country-bred race, got beaten, from want of condition, by Lord Evergreen, who was trained by Bowen. I backed Mr. Johnson's Chang for the big chase, so got something back from my double event folly, as the big horse won very easily, at the end, from Dignum, who rode a very fine race on Spec. As Captain Franks had sent me, some time previously, the grey Arab Sikundur to run for the Arab and country-bred, and Galloway chases I had at last something to do me credit. I brought the little Arab out as well as work, care, and corn could make him, and it was with no small pride that I looked at him taking his preliminary canter with his coat shining like burnished silver and that dauntless rider, Mr. Short, up. He was opposed by Shanbally and the pony Robin Hood. On coming over the water-jump in front of the stand, Sikundur and the country-bred jumped a part at which the ground on the landing-side was knee deep, on account of the water having filtered through, and came down. Before the riders could re-mount, Mr. Webb on Robin Hood got such a long lead that he was never caught. I did not mind this defeat, as I had a little on the winner, and felt confident that I should have my revenge in the Give-and-Take chase, for which Sikundur with Mr. Short up, Mr. Webb on Robin Hood, Crossbie with Mr. Maitland in the saddle, the Clown with Mr. Irving from Madras to steer him, Ginger, The Jackal, and Alonzo, also started. Mr. Short dropped his hands on Sikundur, let him "rip," and had his field settled in the first mile. This win brought my balance round to the right side of the ledger.

During this meeting I saw a good deal of my friend Captain (now Major) Kinchant, of the 11th Hussars, who generally owned a useful horse or two, was always ready to lend a hand to promote sport, and, as honorary secretary of the Umballa races, lavished time, money, and trouble in raising that fixture from being a third-class affair to be one of the most important in India. We who are acquainted with him know him as a cheery companion and staunch friend.

Before the Umballa Meeting I sold Fairymount for Rs. 1,200, on condition that I should run him there ; so at the conclusion of the races I sent him off to his new

MAJOR KINCHANT, 11th Hussars.

Page 217.

owner, who took him down to Secunderabad and won a mile and a half race against Arabs with him, then ran him in a handicap with eleven stone up, with the result that the colt dropped dead.

From the effects of the Umballa Chase, Freetrader went lame in one of his fore-legs, which had for some years before been "dicky," so I sent him back to Calcutta.

Taking the meetings one after another, I went to Meerut with Jovial on the sick list and Sikundur in rare trim. As the latter did not belong to me, and as there was no betting on his race, I did not feel justified in paying Mr. Short Rs. 200 for a winning or Rs. 100 for a losing mount, so put up Mr. "Tim" Baker of the Royal Scots, whom I told to let the Arab have his head, and not to touch the plain snaffle which I had put into his mouth. Mr. Baker having had a previous "school" on Sikundur, was quite willing, at first, to follow my instructions, but was over-persuaded by some would-be good advisers to demand from me a snaffle in which to ride him. I begged that the gear might remain as it was; but a lady, who is the finest horsewoman I have ever seen in India, came up while the discussion was going on, and begged that I might not sacrifice Tim's life for a "fad" of my own. To prove my point, I wrongly yielded, for I knew that, straight rider as Mr. Baker was, still he had not good enough "hands" to ride the impetuous Sikundur in a bit and bridoon without touching the curb. I changed the snaffle for a double bridle, and the Arab and Tim went to the post. When the flag was dropped, away went Sikundur, and up went his head in the air the moment Mr. Baker snatched at the curb reins, as amateurs will do. The first being a bush fence the Arab carried it away with his knees, but the next being a stiff mud wall, he struck it full with his chest, turned over in the air, smashed my saddle into small pieces, and gave Mr. Baker a shake which he did not get over for many days. So much for men with bad "hands" riding impetuous horses, who have light mouths, with a bit and bridoon!

At Meerut I had the good luck to meet Mr. Kettlewell, the well-known stud veterinary surgeon. He advised me to give Jovial two drachms of ipecacuanha twice a day in a ball for the attack of liver from which he was suffering. I did so with the happiest results, for after a week of this treatment his eyes and gums lost their yellow appearance, his mouth its foul smell, and his general health improved so much that I was able to put him into work.

I had the opportunity of utilizing the valuable "tip" I got from Mr. Kettlewell for the treatment of congestion or inflammation of the liver; for while I was staying at Allahabad, Mr. Farrell, the veterinary surgeon, came to me and asked my advice about two horses belonging to the Prince of Wales—Coomassie, H.R.H.'s favourite riding horse, and another—which he was treating for that disease without any good effect. The English attendant, not knowing that *gram* is almost identical in composition with beans, and is, consequently, very "heating," gave each of the very lightly worked animals 18 lbs. of it daily, with the result that their systems got into a state most prone to inflammation. This tendency to disease was doubtless heightened by the practice, so common among syces during the cold weather, of removing the horses' clothing for their own use. The chill thus received, especially in the case of predisposed animals, causes congestion of blood in the internal organs, of which the previously overtaxed one will be, naturally, the first to suffer. I strongly recommended Mr. Kettlewell's course of treatment, which was adopted by Mr. Farrell, with the result that both horses recovered within a week. The Prince's stud groom was so delighted with the success of my advice that, when I met him a year after that at the Windsor races, he came up, thanked me again, and asked me to come and inspect H.R.H.'s stables whenever I wished ; an offer I have not had the opportunity of availing myself of, I am sorry to say.

The Allahabad Autumn Meeting of 1875, for which I waited, was well attended. Mr. Bob Crowdy brought Hermit, who won the Maiden Chase, defeating Ring ; and Rival, who, the day before the races, broke away from his syce and lamed himself. Mr. Johnson had Chang and Ring ; while Mr. Edward Studd appeared with the well-known Australian hurdle-racer W. F. and Not On, both of whom were imported, two or three months before that, by Mr. Baldock, and were in charge of the colonial riding lad, Kain. W. F., who was ridden by " Mr. Bob " in the big chase, before he had gone a mile overreached himself badly on the back tendons of one fore-leg from sheer distress, as he was unfit and had become touched in his wind. Instead of keeping W. F. in a shed on the course, and having had him treated there, his owner had him walked for about three miles to the Artillery Infirmary, where he got tetanus. The veterinary surgeon put him into slings which were rotten or badly fixed, for they gave way and let the horse fall down. W. F. died in a few days.

I went down to Calcutta early in January, 1876, to run Jovial at the Ballygunge Steeplechase Meeting, as the old horse was recovering his form a little and as Mr. George Thomas, his owner, ardently wished to win the Merchants' Cup, value Rs. 1,000—a handicap for all horses belonging to members of the Ballygunge Steeple-chase Association. This meeting was the best one I have ever seen, over a "flagged course," in India. The Ballygunge Cup was won by Mr. Studd's Not On, well ridden by Mr. Johnson, with Lord William Beresford a good second on Mr. Macleod's Gameboy, a recent importation from Ireland, where he had won some small events. Jovial, with Mr. Short up, also ran, but led his field at such a clinking pace that he was "done with" after the first couple of miles. Mr. Hardy, of the Rifle Brigade, was a bad third on our cast-off Rebecca. Charlton, Princess, and Prizefighter were unplaced. "Mr. Bob" won the Open Steeplechase on old Star of the South, who, years before that, had been bought out of a circus, and then commenced a long and successful career on the flat and across country. The Suburban Cup was won by Mr. Johnson on Mr. Hill's Batchelor, beating Rival, ridden by "Mr. Bob," and five others. This was a fine race all the way between the first and second, and would have had a different result had not Rival's bad leg given way. "Mr. Bob," on Viceroy, made amends for this defeat by winning the Trial Chase from a field of six maidens; and also the Merchants' Cup, on Jovial, who just managed to defeat Gameboy, ridden by Kain, after a punishing race. This, the big event of the meeting, was an immensely popular win with all the Calcutta people, with whom the brothers John, William, and George Thomas are great favourites; and quite right too, as they encourage every form of sport, especially racing and polo, have their house always full of visitors, and provide an excellent tiffen every day at 8, Mission Row, to which they expect their friends to drop in whenever they are not otherwise engaged.

This meeting was wound up by Mr. Short winning, in his old go-ahead style, the open handicap chase on Red Eagle, defeating Colonist with Kain up, the Sweep with "Mr. Bob" in the saddle, Ring, Hermit, Jolly Boy, and Prizefighter. Mr. Ruxton, who had not been round the course, and, besides that, is very short-sighted, took Hermit to the front when the horses had gone about half their journey, and, getting out of the proper line, raced him at a blind ditch, into which Hermit galloped fell, and broke his back. This was a heavy blow to his owner, " Mr. Bob," for Hermit was undoubtedly the best chaser of his time in India ; his form was comparatively unexposed, and, but for his fatal mishap, he could have won this event by a distance.

Sad to relate, it subsequently turned out that Not On was not the *bona fide* property of Mr. Studd, but that Mr. Baldock, his importer, had more or less an interest in him, so the Ballygunge Cup, which was strictly limited to members of the Association, was given to Mr. Macleod, the owner of Gameboy. I believe the fact of Mr. Studd not absolutely concluding his bargain with Mr. Baldock was a pure oversight.

I returned to Allahabad from Calcutta with Jovial and Mr. John Thomas's Raven, who had, in the previous December, won the valuable Merchants' Cup at the Calcutta races with the flattering burden of 6 st. 12 lbs., beating R. Y., Askin, Satellite, Confusion, and Lord Clifden, who were giving him "lumps" of weight. He was the extreme outsider of the party.

While at Allahabad I stayed with my friend Mr. Darley, the adjutant of the 5th Fusiliers, of the Mess of which regiment I was an honorary member. As I was a steward of the spring meeting, I was fully engaged in helping Dr. Tippetts, the honorary secretary in looking after the course, and in getting the horses fit. I had a pleasant ride on Jovial in the steeplechase, and had little difficulty in winning from Daybreak, with Dignum up. As the Lucknow meeting came off shortly afterwards, I sent Jovial over to the capital of Oudh without removing the light shoes I had run him in. The jockey in whose charge I had despatched him, gave him a severe gallop on the course, which that year was as hard as a turnpike road, with the result that both fore feet were badly bruised ; in fact, he had "corns" all round, underneath the "bearing" of the fore shoes, so I could not run him. Seeing the nature of the ground, I should of course have at once put on him comparatively stout shoes.

Raven won for us the one mile handicap, in which he was top weight, beating Jessie, Necromancer, and Yanathon ; but, being crushed with 10 st. 7 lbs., he was defeated by Thisbe, to whom he was giving 23 lbs.

Those good sportsmen and fine indigo planters, the Crowdys, had at this meeting the great country-bred mare Deception, the Waler pony Maori, and the steeple-chasers The Sweep and Viceroy. Mr. Ruxton rode the Sweep in the first chase. As it came on to rain just before the start, Mr. Johnson, who was riding Van Amburgh, late Not On, to our great amusement, insisted on making a delay, in order, as he said, that Mr. Ruxton's spectacles should get wet, so that he might not be able to see. It did not matter, for the brave rider of Sweep rushed to the front, and, favoured by his light weight, won easily. He had a narrow escape, however, at the double, for he made the pace so fast, and the ground was so slippery, that the Sweep could not take off properly, so slid over the broad bank on his belly, landing, luckily, all right on the other side. That grand Waler pony Maori, with Mr. Ruxton up, won the Galloway steeplechase; but lost the half-mile pony race in an absurd manner, for his rider could not get him down to the starting-post in time. The little rogue would not be ridden down, and he refused to be led in the ordinary manner. Had Mr. Ruxton only taken the reins over his head, he would have followed him down to the post like a dog. So much for knowing the peculiarities of horses. While the races were going on, the Crowdys received a telegram saying that rain had fallen in their district, and that they must return at once to prepare for sowing indigo, so they departed to Tirhoot and left the horses with me. Deception, ridden by Mr. Short, won the Arab and country-bred handicap, and Sweep, steered by that same fine horseman, secured the steeple-chase handicap.   As I had the money principally on Viceroy, and as I was in want of a rider, I put up Captain Atkinson of the 85th, who had ridden some steeplechases in England very fairly.   Unfortunately I put a snaffle instead of a double bridle in Viceroy's mouth, as "Mr. Bob" used to ride him in it.   The little horse was a hard puller and inclined to refuse timber if he was given the chance, which, I need hardly say, he never got from "Mr. Bob."   As Captain Atkinson was somewhat out of condition, he was too much "blown," after they had gone a mile, to keep Viceroy straight at the posts and rails, and allowed him to "run out."   Mr. Short and Mr. Johnson rode a grand race against each other in this chase.   As the former had the speed of his opponent, he managed to lead him up to each fence by about half a length, until they came, after they had gone a mile and three-quarters, to a small obstacle, which Van Amburgh caught with his hind legs on account of jumping too soon, fell, and broke his back.   This accident was a sad illustration of the danger to a rider, when going fast, of keeping half a length or so behind another horse racing alongside him at a fence ; for his horse, watching the one in front, will be inclined to go stride for stride, and take off at the same moment as his opponent does.

Mr. Edward Studd's speculation with Mr. Baldock was an unlucky one. Both the horses, Not On and W. F., died, as I have described, from injuries received in steeplechases during their first season in India; while poor Kain, the riding boy who brought them over, was killed at the Barrackpore Steeplechase, about five weeks before Not On's fatal accident, on Prizefighter, whom various good riders had, unsuccessfully, attempted to get over a "flagged course." Perhaps it was not the poor horse's fault, for he had corns—a fact which was subsequently found out—and, consequently, would not jump; but as Kain was one of the brave sort who brook no refusal, Prizefighter fell over one of the fences and killed him.

After Lucknow, I sent Jovial and Raven back to the Thomases, and then went to Tirhoot to settle up, with the Crowdys, the Lucknow accounts, which showed a good balance in our favour, and to have a few days' sport with "Mr. Bob" and Mr. Webb. Shortly after that I left for England. I spent the most of my stay at the New Veterinary College, Edinburgh, learning as much as I could about horses, working up material for a book I wanted to write on the treatment of the diseases of horses from an owner's point of view. The Professors of the College readily accorded me all the assistance in their power, and I produced my "Veterinary Notes for Horse Owners," which was very favourably received by the Press and the public, and is now well on into its second edition.

CHAPTER XVIII.

CACHAR — TEA PLANTERS — HORSES IN EASTERN BENGAL — EXILE OF ERIN — MUNIPURI POLO PLAYERS—NAGAS—INDIAN JAILS.

I RETURNED to India in the autumn of 1877, and landed in Bombay, after a tedious voyage of thirty-five days *via* the Suez Canal. On my way through, I stayed a day at Lucknow, and was surprised to meet my former servant, Meer Khan, coming from the 13th Hussar mess. The moment he saw me he rushed up to me and asked where I was going to and when I was leaving. I told him that I was on my way to Cachar, which was about 1200 miles distant, and that I intended to depart by the evening train. This lad, whom I had brought up from his childhood in my service, looked quite pleased at hearing this news, gave his head a toss to one side, uttered his usual " bahut achcha " (very good), and without even making a *salam*, ran off as fast as his long legs could carry him. I was so disgusted with this unceremonious treatment from this saucy, good-looking boy, whom I really liked, that I could relieve my mind only by cursing his ingratitude. My feelings, however, were quickly changed, when, on driving up to the railway station in order to continue my journey, I saw Meer Khan waiting for me with an enormous bag on his back containing his portable property, a thick stick in his hand, and a turban tightly wound round his head, ready for the march. I inquired from him if he had got leave from his master. "No," he laughed, "I just came along." So off we started together. I stayed for about a week in Tirhoot with my friends Charlie Webb and Bob Crowdy, and then went to Calcutta to find how I could proceed to Cachar, where my regiment was stationed. The only particulars of my route which I could learn there were that I had to go to Dacca, and make further inquiries in that ancient Mahomedan stronghold, which is on the banks of the Megna. At Dacca I found that the only way I could get to my destination was to hire a native boat and to travel in it across country through the network of rivers, streams, and lagoons which intersect Eastern Bengal. The after-part of the craft I engaged was covered in with thin matting and bamboo framework, so as to form a rude cabin for me to sleep in ; while the crew of ten men slept, cooked, and worked their ship for'ad. As we went against stream, the boatmen had to tow us almost the entire way. Contrary to the custom in European countries, each Indian *Manjee* on the bank uses a thin, light tow-line attached to the mast of his boat, so, in our case, we were hauled along by three or four lines. This method is admirably suited to the broken ground over which these native towers have to travel, and obviates the necessity of stopping the way of the craft in the event, as often happens, of one or two of the lines getting " fouled" by trees, or passing boats. As I had overstayed my furlough, and could draw no pay until I rejoined my regiment, I stimulated my crew so well by promises of " bukhsheesh " that they accomplished the distance of 260 miles in eight days, which I may claim for them to be a " best on record."

The station of Cachar consists of a church, native mud-built " lines " (barracks), hospital, mess-house, and nine or ten " dab and wattle " houses, situated around a level grass field of thirty or forty acres in extent. This minature plain serves as a racecourse, polo field, and parade ground ; while, in the season, it is a certain "find" for snipe. The river Berak flows behind the station. A considerable portion of the surrounding country is low-lying, and is occupied by rice fields ; while the higher ground is taken up with tea gardens, the planters of which are a pleasant, hospitable set of men, though unfortunately they lack the good-fellowship of their Tirhoot and Wynaad brethren, the reason being that they are split up into various cliques : in fact, there are actually three clubs of fifteen or twenty members each at Cachar, or rather at Silchar, which is the correct name of the station, although both designations are used indiscriminately for it. One institution is sacred to the use of proprietors and managers, who are far too august to " mix " with their assistants. The " collar club," as it is called, " draws the line " at ruling that its members must wear linen, cotton, paper or celluloid round their necks. The third and more democratic society " careth for none of these things." Instead of having one good club like the indigo *sahibs* possess at Mozufferpore, or the jovial coffee planters boast of at Manantoddi, where one can get a good dinner, game of billiards, and rubber of whist, the tea growers in this district are restricted to three miserable little shanties which can produce nothing in the way of amusement beyond a bottle of beer or a brandy and soda. This absence of friendly cohesion is perhaps owing to the fact of the society having a leavening of the artisan class. Owners of tea gardens have found, to their cost, that gentlemen's sons are not always skilled in the production of good "leaf;" hence they tried, successfully in most cases, I believe, the experiment of importing Scotch gardeners who are thoroughly versed in the conditions favourable to plant life. These sons of toil do not, as might have been expected, amalgamate well, as a rule, with their more aristocratic companions, who, perhaps, resent their superior knowledge more than their lack of social polish. Of course, the ideas of the two classes clash ; as happened on one occasion at the annual race meeting, when it was proposed to give a subscription ball, and that, as usual, all expenses as to band, room, refreshments and supper, should be equally divided. To this, a fresh importation, in the form of a Scotch gardener, strongly objected ; "for," urged he, "if I dance with a young lady, and afterwards ask her to have some champagne, it will be no compliment to her unless I can treat her to a bottle and pay for it then and there!" Although the canny Scot did not carry his point, he, in my poor opinion, was not the fool his conservative associates deemed him to be.

Owing to the frequency of earthquakes at Silchar, the majority of the houses are made of a simple framework of wood surrounded by bamboo screens, plastered over to render them impervious to the weather, the whole being covered by a thatch roof. Such a construction of half a dozen rooms will cost, perhaps, £100. As there is nothing to pay for the ground on which the bungalows stand, I need hardly say that rent there forms but a trifling item in one's expenditure. Beer, wines, and oilman's stores, or "Europe stores" as they are called in India, are very expensive, as they have to be brought all the way from Calcutta, which is distant about a fortnight's journey; while the mutton has to be imported, often, from places still further away. Beef is hard to get there, and when procurable is of inferior quality. Our mess, as is the usual custom in India, used to keep at Cachar a flock of about one hundred grain-fed sheep to supply our requirements. I was told, however, that we should have no mutton to eat after the spring, as at that time the sheep used to sicken and die. As I was fresh from veterinary practice, I determined to investigate the cause of this mortality, and found that, owing to the nature of the herbage during that season, these small ruminants were very liable to get inflammation of the true stomach, which complaint had been, almost invariably, attended with fatal consequences. I tried the effect of a draught, composed of 3 or 4 drachms of oil of turpentine and 4 oz. of linseed oil, with the result that we lost no more sheep, and had our mutton as usual. Turpentine is, probably, the most generally useful medicine that is to be found in the veterinary pharmacopœia.

The scientific knowledge I had acquired at Edinburgh enabled me to grapple with the important subject of feeding horses in Cachar, where the only grain the natives give their ponies is *paddy* (unhusked rice), which, being indigenous, is very cheap. The European residents generally used *gram*, a kind of pea, which was about twice as dear as the rice; while a few who did a little racing, actually had oats imported at about double the price of gram. I may remark in passing that rice is very rich in starch, but poor in nitrogenous matter, or flesh formers, to use the old-fashioned term; while the very opposite is the case with gram. Oats hold an intermediate position in the scale of foods. I found that my horses could not do hard work on rice;

that gram, like beans, was too "heating;" while oats were too dear. Hence, I resolved to make a mixture of three parts of rice and one of gram, which would be, approximately, similar in composition to oats, and at about one-third of the price. The experiment was entirely successful. Although the art of combining grains so as to form a suitable food for horses is not of very special use in England, where oats, beans, and hay are the staple forage, still it is of great importance to those who may have to travel in foreign lands, where, singly, none of the indigenous grains may form an appropriate food, although a judicious mixture of two or more of them would make an excellent article of diet. I have treated this subject fully in my work on "Training and Horse Management in India."

I got up at daybreak on my first morning in Cachar and strolled on to the racecourse, where I saw our adjutant, Captain Goodridge, and Mr. Daly, a police officer, giving a couple of 12-hand ponies their gallops— if the tardy pace at which these diminutive animals progressed might be so designated. As the annual race-meeting was to come off in about two months' time, these gentlemen were much interested in the condition of their ponies, and eagerly asked my opinion and advice. I candidly told them that I did not think much of their "gees," and, after a talk about the "form" of the ponies which were coming to run—for nothing over 13.2 was allowed to compete—I went off to the telegraph station, and "wired" to my friend Bob Crowdy to buy a speedy pony called Exile of Erin, belonging to Mr. Edward Studd, and that we should "go halves." "Mr. Bob" effected the purchase for Rs. 500, and sent the pony up to me. Exile arrived in capital condition, and as he was fast enough to win pony races even in England, I looked forward with satisfaction to the coming events, in which I intended to show the planters the way. About ten days before the meeting I was ordered to Gauhati, a station which is on the Brahmaputra in Assam, in order to act as interpreter on a general court martial. So much for making oneself proficient in the native languages! By great good luck this tribunal closed its proceedings in time to allow me to get a lift on the mail-cart for about fifty miles to the pretty hill station of Shillong, where I arrived very late at night, and managed to get a couple of hours' sleep at the house of a friend, who lent me his pony to ride a few miles on my way. I started at four o'clock in a dense fog, with my friend's syce behind me.   This native, being new to the country, put me on the wrong road.   We wandered aimlessly through the mist for about two hours, and then I found that we had returned to the station.   Fortunately I got men to show me the way, so I dismounted, as the pony and syce were tired, and walked on through the whole of that day and following night, with a few halts, arriving at Jynteea, a distance of 70 miles in 23 hours.   As the entire journey was across the hills, I was terribly tired, and fell two or three times during the last mile, from my legs "giving way."   A cup of tea and a bath at a hospitable planter's bungalow put me to rights, and by means of relays of ponies, which had previously been posted on the road for me, I rode the remaining 40 miles in time to have lunch at Cachar, and to see Exile, who was looking the picture of good condition.   I paid the penalty of the night's walk through the deadly jungles, for, after dinner, I felt cold and ill, went to bed and raved all night in high fever.   Next morning as I was lying down, feeling very weak and ill, Mr. Daly came to me and explained that he wanted to buy Exile of Erin from me in order to win, for the final time, the Cachar thousand rupee challenge cup.   I said that I would sell him for Rs. 1000 and half his winnings, which, as subsequently turned out, amounted to a like sum, so that Mr. Crowdy and I, after paying all expenses, had Rs. 1200 or Rs. 1300 to divide between us.

The four days' racing was capital fun, although, personally, I was too ill to take much interest in the sport. The bulk of the animals were sturdy, 11 or 12 hand Munipuri ponies, who resemble closely those of Burmah, and whose *forte* is "staying." Hence the majority of the races were for a mile and over. It was a treat to see these miniature weight carriers struggle through from end to end, and answer every call of their riders with unflinching gameness. Mr. Daly won four races on Exile in good form; while my old Tirhoot friend, "Farmer" Pearce, son of "Idstone" of *The Field*, gave the Cachar men a taste of his quality by pulling off two events with his smart ponies, Rochester and Templar.

While at Cachar, I saw many cases of what was called Munipuri horse disease, which in almost all cases terminated fatally in from twelve to thirty-six hours. Soon after being attacked by the malady, the animal's head and neck begin to swell, great debility ensues, and the breathing increases more and more in quickness, until at last the animal dies from suffocation. In the

native state of Munipur, which is between Cachar and
Burmah, thousands of ponies have been reported to have
died of this malady during different seasons.   When
I was in Cachar, the people there had no idea as to the
nature of this disease ; in fact they considered it peculiar
to Eastern Bengal and Munipur, although it is identical
with Loodianah fever, and, I believe, with the South
African horse plague.   The disease is due to a micro-
scopic vegetable parasite which is found on the herbage
of certain pastures.   By means of the infected grass,
these organisms gain entrance into the animals' blood,
and, multiplying there with great rapidity, they block up
the minute blood vessels of the lungs, and thus cause
death.   The appropriate treatment is, of course, to give
some medicine, that, on becoming absorbed in the blood,
will be inimical to vegetable life.   Carbolic acid admirably
fulfils this condition.   It is given in doses of 2 or 3
drachms in half a pint of linseed oil.   One attack of
this disease, like small-pox, generally confers immunity
to subsequent ones ; hence the tenfold value, in the
infected districts of the Cape Colony, of a "salted"
horse—as one which has had the disease and recovered
from it is termed.   Taken in time and properly treated,
at least 50 per cent. of the cases ought to be saved.

M. Pasteur, the great French physiologist, has lately perfected a most successful method of vaccination (if I may use the term) for anthrax. If any Cape Colonist chooses to take my advice and go in for "salting" horses *à la* Pasteur, he may realise an enormous fortune in a very short time. This hint I believe to be quite original.

When in Cachar, I saw among ponies several cases of that strange disease, *osteo porosis*, or "big head," as it is called in America. It is a spongy condition of the bones, which, in the course of a few months, enlarge in size, become brittle and very porous, so that they are unable to afford firm attachment for the ligaments and tendons; the result being that these tissues become gradually detached, and the animal dies at length of paralysis. The bones of the face are generally the first to become affected; hence the name "big head." We have good reason to believe that this disease is due to improper conditions of food and health. It is sometimes met with among ponies which are used in English mines; while recoveries not unfrequently occur by the simple means of bringing the animal to the surface and feeding him liberally. I saw a pony in Cachar which had got over this complaint, with the exception that the bones of its face were swollen to such a degree as almost to give it the appearance of that of a hippopotamus, while the animal became a confirmed roarer from contortion of the nasal passages.

The natives of Cachar are a weakly, pusillanimous set of Bengalees who are devoid of every manly attribute. There are, however, among the population, a considerable sprinkling of Munipuri emigrants, who are fine, plucky fellows, and devoted to a man to ponies and polo. In fact, so enthusiastic are they about it, that even their small boys of eight or nine play it on foot among themselves in preference to all other games, and eagerly look forward to the time when they will be promoted to the dignity of a pony. In the native state of Munipur, polo is adopted as a regular profession by numbers of men, the most skilful of whom are specially retained by the Rajah. The skill of the best players is something marvellous. A favourite stroke of theirs, when running with a ball at full speed, is to strike it up in the air before them, and then let go the reins, seize the stick in both hands, stand in the stirrups, and, as the ball is descending, hit it forward with all their force.

Another favourite stroke, when a player desires to hit a ball at right angles to the direction his pony is galloping, is, instead of hitting it from in front of the animal's legs, to pass the ball on their near side, and to strike it a swinging, backhanded blow the moment the pony's hind legs have cleared it. This can, of course, only be done when the player wishes to drive the ball to his left. Mr. Daly, who was the finest European polo player in Eastern Bengal, could do this stroke with telling effect, especially when he was racing with an opponent on his near side, whom he wished to shove out. When he used to play against the Munipuris, they always paid him the not very agreeable compliment of telling off a couple of their men to hamper and impede him in his play.

As their ponies are so small—11.2 being the limit— and so clever, they have no restrictions as to playing. I may add that accidents are almost unknown. The ball is made of bamboo root, and is consequently light and tough. The goals are placed about 80 yds. apart, and the ground is about 200 yds. long. The great distance between the goals certainly favours free play and hard hitting. A good Munipuri polo pony will fetch from £50 to £60, and even more.

Munipuris present us with the somewhat exceptional instance of an entire nation having been converted to Hinduism. Although such cases have occurred before, still no caste of Hindus ever admits within its. pale any outsider. Many years ago, a *rishi*, or saint, appeared in Munipuri and announced that he had a mission from his god to turn the tribe into Hindus. They were only too delighted, and received the sacred thread, or *jenco*, from the impostor, and have worn it ever since, although, of course, no true Hindus will acknowledge them as " twice-born."

The Bengalee inhabitants regard polo as an invention of Satan, and will have nothing to say to it. I remember once hearing, on the Cachar ground, a friend of mine ask a strapping young Bengalee, who was looking on at some Munipuris playing, why he did not join in the fun. " God forbid," he exclaimed ; " if I were to go near them, some one very terrible fellow would knock against me ; then I should fall down and get killed, for I very coward man." These sleek wretches are the only people who pride themselves on being utterly devoid of pluck. A Bengalee assistant-surgeon who was attached, some years ago, to a regiment that went on an expedition against one of the Hill tribes, bolted right away the moment he got into the enemy's country. When tried for this offence, he triumphantly pleaded that Bengalees are a nation of cowards, and thus saved his commission, although he was never again sent on military duty.

Besides Bengalees and Munipuris, Cachar has occasional visitors in the form of Lushais, Cossyahs, Kookees, Nagas, and other Hillmen, who, with perhaps the exception of a few Cossyahs, who are becoming partly civilized, are unmitigated savages. It is no uncommon thing in Silchar to see a nine-tenth naked Naga or Kookee passing through on the prowl to pick up stray dogs, which appear to be his favourite article of diet. If he cannot catch them alive, he endeavours to stalk them down and spear them. I have on different occasions met these fellows returning from a successful foray, with two or three dead dogs over their shoulders, while they led on foot a couple of live ones captive. The natives say—with what amount of truth I cannot tell—that as soon as one of these Hillmen comes into a village, all the bow-wows clear out, as if by one consent, and escape across the river as fast as their legs can carry them. The follow-ing recipe for preparing *chien farci* was given to me by a tame Naga, whose friendship I had won by half a bottle of rum. Select a young dog; keep him tied up and feed him well until he is sufficiently fat; then give him nothing to eat or drink for three days; after that, supply him with as much rice boiled in milk as he can possibly eat. When he can devour no more, kill and roast him, and finally eat him with the rice stuffing. He assured me that nothing can equal in deliciousness this dish, which is one I do not intend to try.

Nothing surprised me so much in Silchar as the arrangements of the gaol, which is a bamboo construction, out of which any old man or woman might break with the greatest ease. Among the Cacharees such a thing is unknown, for even if one of the prisoners belonging to the district did effect his escape, he would have no where to go to, as his home and relations are known to the authorities. The case is of course different with strangers. While I was at Silchar, one of our sepoys, a North-West man, got a long term of imprisonment for attempted murder. He was put into the bamboo gaol; and as soon as evening came on, he walked out of his cell, clambered over the 8-foot fence, and has not been since heard of. All the steady old prisoners were indignant at this outrage. They had all been accustomed to regard the *darogah* or keeper as their *ma-bap* (father and mother). He treated them kindly, and they did his bidding. My friend Dr. Warburton, looked after their general health, and saw that they were properly fed. They had no insatiable *mahajun* (money-lender) or scolding wife to bother them, so could not understand the motive the young soldier had for quitting their society.

The strong love of kindred and home possessed by natives of India has solved the poor law question in that country, and also renders escapes from prison of rare occurrence. I knew a doctor who was the governor of a native gaol, the inmates of which were always distinguished by their exemplary conduct. On one occasion, not being able to sleep, he got up very early in the morning and went for a ride. By chance he happened to pass by his gaol, when, to his surprise, he saw a number of men sitting outside the gate, which was locked. He asked them who they were? " We are prisoners," they replied, "and we are waiting for the *darogah* to get up and let us in." It turned out that this worthy official used to allow the men under his charge who had houses in the town close by, to go home at night and sleep in the bosom of their families.

CHAPTER XIX.

DEHRA IN 1878—ALLAHABAD—"ROARING"—THE 22ND
REGIMENT—VESPER—DOLLY VARDEN—SHOEING—
LUCKNOW IN 1879—FISHERMAN—THE STAFF CORPS.

AFTER staying nine or ten months at Cachar, I left it,
on two months' leave, to go to Dehra Doon, in high
spirits at escaping from the dull monotony of this out-
of-the-way station. I had a pleasant trip of a few days
down the river to Dacca, and then went on to Tirhoot
to stay with Mr. Webb at Birowlee. As Mr. Studd, the
owner of the factory, had ordered my friend to give up
racing, probably on account of his own not altogether
satisfactory connection with it, Mr. Webb was obliged to
console himself by riding his clever country-bred mare
Vesper, once a day, around a stiff steeplechase course he
had constructed near his house. He was delighted to
allow me to take the mare up to Dehra Doon, on
condition that I should run her under my own name.

LORD WILLIAM BERESFORD.

Page 249.

I got Mr. Bob Crowdy to come up with me. We had good sport together, although we did not do much more than pay our expenses. Vesper won the Arab and Country-bred Steeplechase, on which, however, there was no speculation, as it was deemed to be a certainty for her. Lord William Beresford, who was staying at Dehra, won the Maiden Steeplechase in brilliant form on his chesnut Waler Telegram, and the Grand Annual Steeplechase on that accomplished fencer, Stanley. Lord William is a fine horseman, and no pace is too hot, and no country too big for him. He has won, on different occasions, all the big chases and hurdle races on the Bengal side of India ; namely, at Calcutta (the Grand Annual hurdle race on Palmerston), Ballygunge, Dum Dum, Umballa, Meerut, and Dehra. At the last-mentioned meeting, he won in October, 1882, the maiden chase on Mr. Macleod's Doleful, and was beaten by half a length in the Grand Annual by Grey Friar. In this race, poor Jack Irving had a terrible fall at the stone wall, and remained insensible for a week after. Lord William is one of the best and most enthusiastic sportsmen we have ever had in India.

We had a big gamble over a half-mile match between Dr. Thorburn's Ooloo and Mr. Shearburn's Griff, two

Galloways that had met on the first day in a mile race, which was won by the former, ridden by the jockey Cozens, although the latter led a long way for half the journey. Griff's owner, whom many of the English fielders remember as a fearless plunger, was persuaded by his jockey and trainer that his Galloway was the better of the two for four furlongs. After the lotteries, the night before the match, Mr. Shearburn, who belonged to the 9th Lancers, sat on a table in the lottery-room, pulled out his betting-book, and cheerily called out, "I'll bet against Ooloo till to-morrow morning, so who's on?" Opinions about the result being pretty evenly divided, some brisk wagering took place. Cozens, who had invested over a thousand rupees on his mount, came to me and advised me to back it. "I need hardly tell you," said he, "that mile races are not usually won at the half-mile post." This argument being unanswerable, I accepted Mr. Shearburn's offer for a couple of ponies. The result justified Cozen's confidence, for Ooloo won in a canter.

Captain John Humfrey, author of a capital little book on Indian steeplechasing, and formerly a grand man across country, furnished the surprise of the meeting by beating Mr. Maitland's celebrated Australian horse

Kingcraft, 10 st. 3 lbs., with Nimrod, 8 st., 11 lbs., who had in the Colonies shown excellent form, particularly in the race for the Melbourne Cup. Nimrod also won the handicap on the last day.

Dehra Doon is a favourite resort during the hot weather, as it is within nine miles of the hill station of Mussoorie, which is from 7000 feet to 8000 feet above the level of the sea, and as it has a capital racecourse, with, on the inside, an admirable line of fences, the majority of which are "bushed" with wild rose trees. During the season of which I am writing, the station was favoured with the presence of those thorough good sportsmen, Lord William Beresford, who had a large stable of horses, and a house full of friends of the right sort; poor D'Arcy Thuillier and Mr. Hadow, both of the Viceroy's Body Guard; Mr. Shearburn; Mr. Vere, of the 60th Rifles, who owned Nimblefoot and those great ponies Banker and Clinkerina; Mr. Muir, who had the speedy Sylph; and that most obliging of honorary secretaries, Mr. Holmes, of the Bengal Civil Service, who, without a thought of profit for himself, was always indefatigable in the promotion of sport.

Having spent my two months' leave at Dehra, I went to Allahabad about the middle of October, with Vesper, to rejoin my regiment, which had in the meantime left Cachar in course of relief, and had proceeded to the capital of the North-West. As the Allahabad meeting, for which I was honorary secretary and a steward, was to come off at the end of the following month, my stable soon began to fill. Mr. Anderson sent me Yanathon and Sprite to train, and Dr. Thorburn, Ooloo and Crossbee; while Mr. Lawrence Crowdy consigned the English mare Dolly Varden, by Claret, out of Surprise, to my care, to prepare for the Calcutta December meeting. Before leaving Cachar, I sold to a gentleman residing in Dacca my black Waler charger, Mediterranean, late Pirate, who was a useful horse for selling races, though rather a difficult one to ride, as he was inclined to buck-jump when at all "fresh." Unfortunately for the poor horse, he got drowned on his way down the river Megna by steamer; although, perhaps, the first loss would have been the least to his new owner had he arrived safely. As I wanted a horse to ride on parade at Allahabad, with the off chance of winning a race, I bought the brown Waler Reformation, from Mr. Elphick, veterinary surgeon Royal Artillery, brother of that fine rider George Elphick. This horse had run with bad luck in first-class company in the Colonies, although he had managed to win one or two big handicaps there. On his voyage to India he took cold and turned roarer. He stood about 15.2, was possessed of immense bone and substance, and showed a good deal of quality. I bought him for, if I remember right, only Rs.400, as he was suffering at the time from a severe attack of catarrh. I had a couple of other horses to ride with my regiment while Reformation was on the sick list. One was a three-year-old colt by a thoroughbred English horse out of a well-bred Australian mare that was a roarer. The first time I gave this colt a gallop as a two-year-old, he made a noise which one could hear a couple of hundred yards off. I had him blistered between the jaws two or three times, and kept on soft food, such as linseed mashes, carrots, and grass. By degrees the infirmity wore off, so that by the end of twelve months he was perfectly clear in his wind. He turned out no good, as he had "a pain in his temper." A short time before these Allahabad races, Mr. Bob Crowdy came to stay with me. He and I soon put the flat and flagged courses in capital order. As the former was very hard, we had it lightly hoed over and then covered with stable litter. I was doubly zealous in this work, as Dolly Varden was a terrible cripple.

Colonel Glass and the officers of the 22nd Regiment, which was stationed at that time at Allahabad, did everything in their power to render the race week enjoyable to the other residents, and to the many visitors who came to join in the fun, by giving garden-parties and dances, and having their Mess always crowded with guests, whom they treated with all the hospitality for which their fine corps has been so long distinguished. Captain Butlin, Mr. Bromfield, and two or three of their brother officers, backed up my efforts to promote sport. I was happy to be able to make some return for their kindness, though in a very small way, by running Vesper for Mrs. Bromfield in the race for the Ladies' Bracelet, a very handsome work of art, presented by Mr. R. Kelly Maitland, who, by the bye, felt confident of winning it himself for a lady in my regiment, on his Arab, Corone, that had won the Calcutta Derby, and accordingly backed it himself. The race was one of quarter mile heats, catch weights, without dismounting. Vesper was an extraordinary speedy mare for three furlongs, but although she could not " get " quite half a mile, could " stay " three miles of a steeplechase course very fairly, if allowed to keep a " little in hand ; " besides that, she was " as clever as a cat." In the first heat, Bob Crowdy, on my mare, jumped off with the lead, and won easily. In the next, which fell to Corone, he merely trotted in with the ruck. In the deciding one, for which I had a plunge on Vesper, who was the non-favourite, the mare came away and won hands down. Despite this reverse, Mr. Maitland, who was on a visit with me at the time, was one of the chief winners of the meeting by means of Corone and Fleur de Lis.

Yanathon won both races for which he started, namely, the mile handicap and the hurdle-race. In the former he beat Necromancer, to whom he was giving 5 lbs., and against whom I had backed him, apart from the lotteries, for £50 with Mr. Garratt, of the 13th Hussars. In the latter he defeated the Waler, Asmodeus, who had been a great horse in the Colonies, and Mr. Macleod's Game-boy, the Irish chaser. This last-mentioned animal was not given a chance, as his ignorant jockey rode him in such a short running martingale that he was afraid to jump, for the pressure of the snaffle fell directly on the bars of his lower jaw. I may remark that, for cross-country work, the martingale should be well lengthened out, so that when the rider takes up the reins it should be quite loose. Its use should be restricted to keeping the horse straight, and preventing him from "yawing" about ; while the hands alone should be employed to keep his head down. For this race, Yanathon was the least fancied of the three, as no one except Mr. Crowdy and myself believed he would jump, on account of his bad running the previous day in the steeplechase, for which Gameboy, Mr. Garratt's Mickey Free, and Vesper had also contended. The first fence in this event was a broad " Irish double," which was the exact kind of obstacle I knew, from experience, Yanathon would not jump under any amount of persuasion. I gave the mount on him to a young indigo-planter, from whom I took both spurs and whip, as I did not want the horse to be "knocked about ; " and when my jockey asked for orders, I replied, " Just sail away," which he accordingly did when the flag fell, but refused, as I had expected, at the double, and could not be induced even to attempt it. Gameboy, having the same old martingale on, also refused. Unfortunately, Mickey Free was steered by Harry Crowdy, whose taste for riding my friend Bob, brother-like, used to endeavour to repress on all occasions. A mile and a half from home Bob ranged alongside Harry, and, as he had the race in hand whenever he chose to come away and win it, he commenced to chaff and " bustle " the young one, who gave back quite as much as he got, till, at the last fence, which was a simple three-foot rise on to higher ground, the mare made a stumble, and Bob, who was riding very carelessly, rolled off, thereby losing us a couple of hundred pounds, and punishing me for the Yanathon business. A sort of fatality nearly always attends deep-laid schemes at racing. On the following day, however, Vesper got some of the money back for us by winning the Arab and Country-bred Chase. After this meeting I bought the mare from Mr. Webb for Rs. 800.

The English mare, Dolly Varden, whom I was train-ing, had in the early part of the year broken down so badly, that the fetlock pad of one fore-leg had actually come down on the ground. When I agreed to take her over, her owner, Mr. Laurence Crowdy, did not think that I could by any possibility bring her out fit to run again. When she walked, the fetlock of her bad leg descended at each step much lower than that of the sound one, so it seemed almost hopeless to patch her up. I tried the effect of continued pressure, carefully applied, for three or four months, by means of long elastic bandages, made from the same material as the webbing of side-spring boots. After a month or so of this treatment, the enlargement of the suspensory ligament, due to violent sprain, began to decrease. I gave her gentle exercise, walking and trotting in a light gig; while as soon as I found she could stand it, I used to send her two or three times a week a couple of steady canters, a quarter or a third of a mile each, on the racecourse. At last I ventured to let her have a half-mile spin with Yanathon, to whom she gave a lot of weight and a very easy beating. This was so satisfactory that I entered her at Calcutta for the Stand Plate, selling race, three-quarters of a mile, for which Lord William Beresford's Hunter, Jaffir's Thisbe, and a mare belonging to Weeks the dealer were running. We had some brisk wagering on this event. I backed Dolly with Weeks for Rs. 500 against Thisbe, and also purchased her in the lottery. On the fall of the flag, Hunter and our mare jumped off in front and raced together to the distance, when Dolly drew clear and won somewhat easily by a length. When she was put up to auction, as Mr. Crowdy did not wish to buy her in, Jack Wheal purchased her for Weeks to take down to the Colonies to breed from, for which purpose, to judge by her shape, racing form, and blood, she was worth a lot of money even in England. Next day, when I came up to see her before leaving Calcutta, I found Wheal showing her to an admiring stranger, whom I recognized as John Roberts, the great billiard player, who dearly loves a bit of racing. The poor mare was not destined to reach the end of her journey, as the ship which was taking her to Australia was lost.

Dolly Varden was one of the few English horses I have seen in India that had exceptionally strong feet. She had such good ones that I always worked her barefoot, although I had to use her sparingly on metalled roads during the rains. I have already remarked that the drier the climate in which horses are bred and reared, the stronger and sounder, as a rule, will be their hoofs. Horses with really good feet can be used for saddle work and in light draught, except on metalled roads, perfectly well without shoes, so long as the ground underfoot is dry; but as soon as it becomes wet, the horn of the hoofs, by absorbing moisture, gets so soft, that it becomes quickly worn down when subjected to friction against the ground. We may see numerous instances of this in the indigo districts, where, as there are few metalled roads, the planters usually ride their animals unshod for their district work, but as soon as the rains set in they are obliged to have shoes put on. Of course I am speaking in general terms, and am not alluding to cases in which the ground is very soft and the work extremely light. A great deal of nonsense is written periodically in English journals by enthusiasts who advocate the practice of using horses unshod in this country. They maintain, without a shadow of proof, that were animals thus employed their hoofs would gradually become sufficiently strong to resist the wear and tear of English roads. The frogs of their feet, from being brought down on the ground, would undoubtedly become much better developed than with shoes; but I fail to see how this practice would stimulate the growth of horn of the crust which is secreted by the coronet. They even bring in the law of " the survival of the fittest " to back up their argument, and assert that if horses were worked barefoot, their progeny would in time have such strong hoofs that we should require no more blacksmiths. This, doubtless, would turn out to be the case were breeders to devote their attention solely to the production of horn of extraordinary hardness and thickness. They, however, breed for strength, speed, soundness, stoutness, quality, gameness, and cleverness, so cannot sacrifice these all-important objects for the sake of a comparatively small benefit. Inexperienced persons have no idea of the immense amount of wear entailed on the shoes of a hard-worked horse on English roads, and may be surprised at my informing them that a cart-horse often wears out a pair of fore-shoes, each weighing over 4 lbs., in a month. If we take for granted that such shoes are one-third of an inch thick, how then, may I ask, could such an animal do his work unshod, when the ordinary growth of horn per month is actually less than that?

After Calcutta, Mr. Crowdy and I went to the Lucknow races with Vesper, who, carrying top weight, won the Arab and Country-bred Steeplechase, after a severe finish with Spectre, while Jowaki and Gold Dust were a long way behind. In the pony race, my friend very nearly got killed on Blueskin from riding with too short a martingale. At this meeting Mr. MacDougall, of the 13th Hussars, for the first time came prominently into notice as a cross-country rider, and soon established his reputation as one of the best men in India. He won the Hurdle Handicap, the Lucknow Grand Annual Steeplechase, and the Steeplechase Handicap, on Kilmore, belonging to my friend the Nawab Syud Ali, of Cawnpore, who is a thorough sportsman, and also secured the Pony Steeplechase Handicap and the Polo Stakes on his own pony Slipper. Mr. Maitland won a good race on

Yanathon, beating Thisbe and the English horse Choris-ter, who was the hero of Mauritius some years ago, when he belonged to poor Charlie Bradshaw.

When I returned to Allahabad to do some duty with my regiment, I found the local sportsmen clamouring for pony races, so I organized a sky meeting ; and then promptly wrote to Captain Cracroft, of the 3rd Madras Cavalry, whom I knew long ago at Kamptee, in the Central Provinces, to send me up Fisherman, a 12.2 pony he had for sale, Mr. Elphick having previously informed me that this little animal was a wonder to "stay" and gallop.   I gave, if I remember right, Rs. 400 for him.   When he arrived I found him somewhat cow-hocked, flat-sided, slightly calf-kneed, and with a decidedly fiddle-head ; yet for all that I was delighted with him, as he was just the sort which would not attract attention, and possessed many racing points.   He had a lean, long, well-put-on neck, oblique muscular shoulders, long powerful forearm, short canon bone, very powerful loins, immense gaskins, clean, large hocks, and hind-legs well under his body ; while he was essentially "short above and long below,"—in other words, although his back appeared short on account of the obliquity of his shoulders, he was, from the same reason, and on account of the length of his pelvis, very long from his chest to the furthest part of his thighs. As I knew I could not get any fair "price" about him if I ran him in my own name, I allowed Captain Goodridge, who was adjutant of our regiment, to take that honour and to ride him. He won the two principal races on the same day in a common canter, and recouped me his purchase money with very liberal interest. I sold him afterwards for Rs. 600 to go to Sylhet, which is in Eastern Bengal, where I believe he won some races. He was certainly the best of his height, for a distance, I have ever seen.

I liked living in Allahabad, as it contained a large number of civilians and men in the service who were always ready to support any amusement that might be got up. It has a large and excellent club, at which I have had many a brave gamble at that best of all games, "poker," with several kindred spirits. At this station is issued that very able Indian newspaper, *The Pioneer*, of which I was a correspondent for some years, though of late I have written chiefly for the Calcutta *Englishman*. The sporting letters from England of "Asmodeus" form one of the most attractive features of *The Pioneer;* and so closely has this gifted writer placed himself *en rapport* with his readers, that he is regarded by the bulk of old Indians as a personal friend, even by those who know only his *nom de plume*, the identity of the owner of which frequently forms a fertile subject for conjecture. With full permission from my friend Mr. T. Comyns Cole, to whom I have the honour to dedicate this work, I have great pleasure in introducing him to my Indian readers as the gentleman who has done so much, by his delightful sketches of passing events in the English world of sport, to wile away the tedium of many hours they might have wearily spent under the punkah but for him. When stationed at Cawnpore I frequently went to Allahabad, and stayed, on different occasions, with Mr. Tyrrell, of the Bengal Civil Service, with whom Mr. Phil. Robinson, the well-known writer and correspondent of *The Daily Telegraph*, lived. These two gentlemen, Mr. Robinson's father, and Mr. Cole, were, each in their way, the four ablest contributors to *The Pioneer*. Mr. Tyrrell, who shone in his own private circle by his wit and ready humour, was generally credited with the authorship of the many short, sparkling paragraphs which appeared in that paper from Phil. Robinson's pen. Strange to say, Mr. Tyrrell confined his attention to writing elaborate leading articles on grave and weighty matters. I knew Mr. Douglas Straight, who was a general favourite, and well remember a very pleasant evening I spent with him, Colonel Glass, and others, a few days before I left for England.

CHAPTER XX.

IN the spring of 1879 I effected an exchange from the
Bengal Staff Corps into "The Buffs," as I wanted to
leave the service and return to England, as I was losing
my health in India, and could not afford to live comfortably in the service in the "old country." As I had
spent so much of my time on leave and furlough, I
should not have got, had I remained in the Staff Corps,
a captain's pension for many years; though, by exchang-
ing back again into the Home Service, I was enabled to
obtain a good bonus on retiring. In doing this I
certainly "scored off" Government, which soon afterwards issued orders that exchanges were not to be
permitted between Captains of the Staff Corps and
Home Service.

I was sorry to say good-bye to my old brother officers, as they were kind-hearted, generous fellows, and were very good to me. I liked them "all round," although they did not get on over well together ; but that was less their fault than of the wretched system of the Staff Corps, which decrees that a large portion of a regimental officer's pay is dependent on the nature of the appointment he holds. Hence, if the adjutant dies, is cashiered, or invalided, the quarter-master may probably console himself by the prospect of becoming the Colonel's *factotum*, and of receiving an extra ten shillings a day—and so on throughout the entire regiment. It is not "human nature" for men whose only "line" is soldiering, to live together in perfect harmony under such a vicious system.

I joined my new regiment at Meerut, and was received with the greatest kindness by Colonel Morley and the other officers, who vied with each other in making me thoroughly at home. I look back on the year I spent with them as one of the happiest of my life. The Colonel, though a strict disciplinarian, was so fond of horses that he could not resist showing some partiality—so long as it did not interfere with duty—to those who shared his own tastes. Whenever the hounds met, one could always get leave off parade by merely telling the adjutant that one was going out with them. "The Duke," as we familiarly called him, was sharp enough to see that no unfair advantage was taken of his kindness. He was a fine soldier and good sportsman. He, Captain Hickson, Captain Harley, Mr. Kekewich, Mr. Hinde, myself, and others had many a pleasant scurry across country with his "bobbery" pack in the evenings after jackals, and also with the hounds which Mr. Skoulding, V.S. of the Horse Artillery, hunted, aided by Mr. Allsop, son of the brewer, as whip. Besides my own horse, Colonel Couper, Superintendent of the Remount Department, gave me the use of a high caste, powerful young Arab, which I subsequently bought for Rs. 1000, and called Bismillah. Colonel Morley had, in the bay Australian horse Partisan, the handsomest and most showy charger in India. This animal, who formerly belonged to Mr. Bradshaw, after winning all the races he started for in Mauritius, where they add £500 to the chief event, was brought over to Calcutta, and won there the Governor-General's Cup, beating the English horses, Castle Hill, Miss Trelawny, and Bridesmaid, the Walers, Satellite, Karpos, The Fawn, and North Australian, and the Cape horse Merryman, after a sensational race, as he was the extreme outsider of a large field, as far as public favouritism went. The last time I met Partisan was in 1880, when I went down to my old brother officers at Shorncliffe to help to celebrate the 307th anniversary of the regiment : he was looking then as fresh and well as when I saw him, eight years previously, win his big race.

I have never been in any Indian station I liked so much as Meerut. The duration of the hot weather there is singularly short for the plains, as the excessive heat seldom lasts more than two months ; while at Cawnpore and Allahabad it is usually double, and at Meean Meer treble, that extent. The station itself is really pretty, and is well wooded. The bungalows are picturesquely and centrally arranged, and the roads are broad and well shaded with trees. The presence of a Horse Artillery battery, an English and a Native Cavalry regiment, and a Line and a Native Infantry regiment, with various staff officers and civilians, provides abundance of pleasant society. There is an admirably-managed club, where whist, billiards, good dinners, and the best of liquor can be obtained ; although, unlike similar institutions at Allahabad, Lucknow, and Cawnpore, the Wheeler Club does not extend its hospitality to ladies by giving them a room to themselves and their friends. There are several lawn tennis grounds, swimming baths, cricket fields, and a racquet court. Close to the station there is a perfectly level racecourse, a little over 1 mile and 5 furlongs round, with light sandy "going," and having a large and handsomely-built grand stand, which was constructed by that indefatigable promoter of sport, Captain Charsley Thomas. Outside the flat track there is a carefully-arranged steeplechase course, the fences on which, without being in the slightest degree unfair, require some "doing." As the greater part of the country round Meerut is light, sandy soil, covered by that finest of all grass, "doob," and as there is no law of trespass in India, the trainer has the fullest opportunities for exercising his cattle; while there are numerous banks and watercourses to delight the heart of a cross-country rider. The Meerut hounds generally show good sport; there is capital pig-sticking not far away, and abundance of antelope and small game shooting within easy reach. Above all things, the hills are so close, that if one starts from Meerut in the evening, one can easily breakfast at an early hour in Mussoorie, where the climate during the hot weather surpasses in excellence the finest South of England summer.

CAPTAIN CHARSLEY THOMAS.

Page 271.

I was not long in Meerut when we got up a small meeting, which was chiefly patronized by stations near at hand. Mr. Sandeman, of the Carabiniers, and Captain Cook, of the 14th Sikhs, came to stay with me, and to run a Galloway called Twin, who had the strange habit of speedy-cutting himself behind, as well as before. As Mr. Sandeman was very keen to ride, I gave him the mounts on Vesper and Reformation. Some time previous to this, Mr. Thuillier had sent me the country-bred Jowaki to prepare for this meeting. When I used to send him and my pair gallops together, I always found that both he and the mare could "lose" Reformation at any weights and at any distance. I was so puzzled at this utter reversal of all form—for the old horse was fairly fit, although he "made a noise"—that I began to suspect he had been changed during his voyage from the Colonies to India, or that Mr. Elphick had made some mistake and sold me the wrong animal. The mischief, however, was done, as I had no time to get another horse to run against the moderate Walers I expected would oppose him. I was chagrined at this disappointment, as I had looked forward to these races as a small benefit for the brown horse, with whom I had taken infinite trouble to get "fit."

As Reformation had to meet in his first race—which was for half a mile—a smart mare called Polly, that belonged to Mr. Thuillier and had won for him a lot of money at the Umballa meeting of the previous year, I backed him for a little in the lotteries with extreme reluctance, and gave my jockey a leg-up with the sad feelings of a man who is forced to support sport, much against his will, at the expense of his pocket. I was surprised beyond measure to see him collar the mare fifty yards from home, and then win as he liked by a couple of lengths. On the second day, as he had something better to meet, and as the distance was two furlongs more, I was still more despondent, as I never believed the old roarer could "get" three-quarters of a mile. I was wrong again, for he repeated his performance of the previous day, only winning still more easily. An hour after that he came out to run for the half-mile handicap, in which he carried the steadying weight of 11 st., against Polly, Lady Ald, Empress, and Vesta. As I walked down to start the horses, I determined that Reformation should not be first away, for independently of his being my property, I almost resented his "kidding" me in the disgraceful manner he had done. As the other horses walked up and got into line, with

Reformation a couple of lengths behind, showing a bit of temper, and as I at that moment lowered the flag, the old horse stopped, made a half rear, and finally got off at least 30 yards behind his field. I walked back to the stand quite happy, as I felt certain that the speedy Lady Ald, who belonged to the jockey Cozens, and who had been given a great chance in the handicap, must have won; for I knew that Cozens was at the time badly in want of a turn of luck. When I arrived near the enclosure, a friend ran out to meet and congratulate me on my horse winning. Reformation, he said, was several lengths behind everything half-way up the distance, where he made his effort, and rushed through his horses as if they were standing still. Mr. Sandeman assured me that the old brown ran each of his races according to his own ideas; made his effort when he thought fit; and would take no suggestion from his rider as to altering his tactics. I would not have described these small events at such length did they not disclose to me, at least, a very interesting phase of equine intelligence. As I had given Reformation the most of his previous work on the racecourse, I presume that he was well aware of the exact position of the winning-post; and, further, that he was sensible enough to distinguish the difference between a real race and an exercise gallop. I may mention that during his training I gave him a good deal of linseed and carrots, and restricted his work to short spins, with plenty of walking and trotting exercise, as I had found that such food and treatment act well, as a rule, with roarers.

My Carabinier friend won the steeplechase in good style on Vesper, who was the perfection of a safe conveyance across country ; but, I regret to say, he " cut a voluntary," as many another good man has done before, on Mr. Vere's Clinkerina, whom he was riding, making a mistake in the Pony Handicap Chase. Jowaki, whom I was training, won the Galloway Steeplechase, and also the Sensation Handicap. Captain Calvert secured a good stake with Sans Culotte in the pony flat race. Although this meeting was only a local affair, I won about fifteen hundred rupees, with but trifling risk. There is a great deal of truth in the old proverb that " little fish are sweet."

After this meeting I sold Reformation for Rs. 800 to Captain Cook, who did no good with him, as he tried to make a steeplechaser out of the old roarer, who, if he objected to one thing more than another, it was jumping, as it seemed to knock the little wind he had out of him. Captain and Mrs. Cook so dearly love a spin across country, that they are never happy, if they have a horse in their stable, until they have tried if he can "throw a lep." Before I sold Reformation, I went with them, Captain Hickson, of my regiment, and Captain Charsley Thomas, on a week's leave into the Kadur country, which is the great pig-sticking ground near Meerut, to ride and shoot. We saw no pig, as the season was too late; we shot only about a black buck each and a few partridges; but we had rare good fun schooling the horses over every difficult bit of country we met in our morning and evening rides, while we thoroughly enjoyed ourselves in the evening "talking horse" and spinning yarns. As Captain Thomas had charge of the commissariat and transport departments, we fared luxuriously. I generally lent Vesper to Mrs. Cook to ride, and am certain that they would never have bought Reformation had not I been, on nearly every occasion, ignominiously "pounded" on him by my own mare. While we were out, we caught, for their plumage, several peacocks, by the simple and very easy method of riding them down. These birds, when fresh, are not able to fly more than 500 or 600 yards; so their capture furnishes no sport.

During the hot weather I went up to the hill station of Mussoorie, on two months' leave, with Vesper, Lady Ald, whom I had bought from Cozens, and Bismillah. As I knew that the last-mentioned was an extraordinary good Galloway, but that he required work and time to develop his powers, I got up a series of *gymkhanah* pony races on the small course round the polo ground in the Happy Valley, in order to provide funds for the improvement of the track, which, by dint of blasting away many tons of rock, I rendered fairly serviceable in a short time. I lent Lady Ald to Mr. MacDougall, who was also up on leave. I remember on one occasion, when he and I went to stay for a day with Mr. Thuillier at Dehra, that we rode down to the steeple-chase course, over which, for a lark, Mr. MacDougall determined to try over the jump Lady Ald, who was a nervous, weedy, country-bred mare, and the most unlikely-looking animal to make a fencer one could imagine. She safely negociated the post and rails and banks at a slow pace, after a great deal of necessary "ramming" at them; but when she came within a hundred yards of the brook which is in front of the stand, and which is no mere "water-splash," but on the contrary, an honest 16-foot expanse that will bring

D. MacDOUGALL, ESQ, 13th Hussars.

Page 277.

a horse down if he chances it, Mr. MacDougall caught her by the head and raced her at it full speed. The pace carried her over, but she was not able to keep her feet, so landed on her head. Her rider, who had not stirred an inch out of his saddle, pulled her together, gave her a dig of the spurs, got her on her legs again, and went gaily on at the next obstacle as if nothing had occurred! This was one of the finest performances of horsemanship I have ever witnessed.

Before leaving Mussoorie, I sold Vesper to go to Central India, where she won two or three good races, ridden by Captain Humfrey. Soon after my return to Meerut, I took Bismillah to Lucknow to run for the Arab and Country-bred Steeplechase, which he could have won in a trot had not he been seriously lamed, in the early part of the race, by a large thorn which penetrated one of his knees; as the foolish people who looked after the course had strengthened some of the fences with bushes that bore prickles as sharp and strong as darning-needles. As the thorn, after penetrating deeply, broke short off, thus preventing its extraction by any instrument, I applied a smart blister over the knee, and had the satisfaction of seeing the offending body work itself out in a few days. This treatment, in such cases, is far better than the usual one by poultices and warm fomentations, which encourage suppuration, and may possibly give rise to open joint: an eventuality for which the other is the best preventative, as the swollen condition of the part causes closure of the orifice. The blister, by determining blood to the vicinity of the wound, hastens the natural reparative action.

At this meeting, Mr. MacDougall commenced proceedings by winning the hurdle-race on his black Waler, Pistol, but lost the big steeplechase on the same animal by the silly mistake of going the wrong side of a flag—on his own course, too, which he knew as well as the regimental riding-school! Mr. Anderson's Dwarroon, who had been a few months before imported from the Colonies, where he was considered to be about the second or third best horse "between the flags" in Australia, was entered for this chase. On quitting the starter, Dwarroon, who was a very hot favourite, rushed to the front, and, racing over the fences in grand style, was leading about 100 yards in the first mile. He had, however, gone the wrong side of a post, and was followed in the excitement of the moment by Mr. MacDougall; while the jockey Stratford on the despised Nimblefoot took the right course. Long before the end of the journey, Dwarroon began to roll about from distress, though jumping as cleverly as ever, and soon subsided into a slow canter, leaving Pistol to come in first by a long way. About ten minues after, Stratford arrived at the winning-post, claimed and obtained the race. Want of condition was alleged to be the cause of the once mighty Dwarroon's poor display. The fickle goddess, who seldom forgives the mortal that has once slighted her favours, dealt the 13th Hussar man a crushing blow; for, in the Steeplechase Handicap Pistol jumped slovenly, on account of Mr. MacDougall keeping alongside his two very moderate opponents in order to make a race of it, caught his hind-leg in the fence, and broke the limb a little above the hock. As it was a compound fracture, he had to be destroyed. It not unfrequently happens that this bone (the *tibia*), which lies between the hock and the stifle, gets fractured, without displacement, from kicks or other blows, and unites again without any bad consequences except temporary lameness, as the covering membrane (the *periosteum*) of this bone is extremely thick and strong, and often keeps the broken ends in apposition without any other aid. Many authenticated cases are on record of horses breaking this bone by a fall in draught, or from a kick by a companion, and actually doing work with a fractured leg, but without evincing any sign of the mishap, until, by some sudden jerk, undue weight is thrown on the limb, which causes rupture of the periosteum and complete displacement of the bone: an accident that admits sometimes of successful treatment.

Mr. Anderson made up for his disappointment with Dwarroon by winning a couple of pony races with his handsome little Arab, North Star, and another one with the country-bred pony, Nadir Khan.

About six weeks after my return to Meerut from Lucknow, and a little before the Dehra races, Mr. Anderson was ordered to join the Cabul expedition. Not knowing how else to dispose of his horses, he put them into the train and sent them off to me, with the usual " Do the best you can for me, old fellow." There was the superb fencer, Dwarroon, whom I viewed with more than suspicion, despite Mr. Anderson's assurance that he could not lose the Dehra Grand Annual Steeple-chase unless he had a fit, or fell down at least five times. Then came Young Snowden, a magnificently " topped " chesnut Waler, but as he had a much enlarged suspensory ligament I put him aside as useless. Mr.

Anderson's native jockey, Jutton, next paraded before me the thoroughbred Waler Speechless, who had run well the year before in Australia. He was covered all over with deep, suppurating ulcers, for he had, as I before remarked, a bad attack of that Indian skin disease, *bursatee*. Of course, I was not able to do anything with him for the time being. The worst of it was, that these horses were engaged all over the country, without the slightest chance of paying their hay and corn bill, let alone their forfeits. I placed Nadir Khan under the standard, and found him to be well over pony height, so promptly sold him for Rs. 400 to pay expenses ; as I did not want to spend time and trouble in getting him " fit," and then to have him disqualified at the first race-meeting I might take him to for being too big, for I could not count on always meeting stewards as lenient as those of Lucknow. The young Waler mare, Czarina, was all right and in good condition, but her body was so heavy compared to her lightness of bone below the knee, while her " form " was only moderate, that I could not expect she would do more than pay her own way. Although North Star was a " flyer " for half a mile, his capabilities were thoroughly exposed.

Besides my own horses, I had another to fall back on

in Substitute, a grey Waler gelding belonging to Mr. McDonnell, of the Horse Artillery. He was a fine up-standing horse, with weak hocks, and an unfortunate habit of brushing and speedy-cutting himself on both fore-legs when he got tired in his gallop. As ordinary boots were not sufficient to prevent him hurting himself, I devised the expedient of placing on the inside of each fore-leg, from knee to fetlock, a strip of thick felt, covered with a bandage to keep it in position. To prevent the felt working loose, I had it made long, so that the part which reached six or seven inches above the knee might be folded down and kept secure by a few extra turns of the bandage. Substitute had, at the previous Meerut Sky Meeting, run against Reformation, but made no show against the brown Waler. He had, however, well ridden by his owner, won the Meerut Tent Club Steeplechase, in which I rode a mare belonging to Colonel Couper. When I arrived at Dehra, I gave Dwarroon and Substitute a gallop together, and found that the former, after going a mile, roared so badly that he was quite useless. Strange to say, he did not exhibit this musical tendency until he had gone about that distance at a fast pace. Substitute was defeated in the Maiden Steeplechase by Hector, steered by his owner,

Mr. Williams, of the 8th Hussars, who is an uncommonly patient and bold rider across country. Mr. MacDougall and the grey Waler had their revenge by winning the Dehra Grand Annual Steeplechase, after a very close finish. I quite forget who won "the odd trick" the last day in the Handicap Steeplechase. Bismillah, in the Galloway Steeplechase, being run into by Crossbie at a fence, "over-reached" himself badly on the back tendons of one fore-leg; so I left him at Dehra in charge of my native jockey, Oodit, to whom I gave strict orders that the Arab was not to leave his stable until all heat had disappeared out of the leg. Anxious to get back to his friends at Meerut, he disregarded my instructions, and started on his journey with the Galloway about ten days after I had left. Bismillah arrived at my stable on three legs, with the fourth one terribly swollen and inflamed. Had he been given three months' rest at Dehra he would have come out next season as sound as ever. The march down had, however, rendered him, to all appearance, a hopeless cripple. I sold him for a mere trifle to Mr. Baker, of the Bengal Civil Service, who, much to my astonishment when I read of the performance in the papers, won a good race with him at Lucknow a year and a half after his accident. Had Bismillah kept all

right, I believe he would have developed into a second
Caliph. His mishap was all my fault, for I ought not
to have allowed such a valuable horse to run the risks
of a steeplechase.

Having sold Vesper, Bismillah, and Nadir Khan, and
sent back Dwarroon and Young Snowden to Lucknow,
I devoted my attention to Speechless, Substitute, Lady
Ald, Czarina, and North Star. The first named, who
was entered for several down-country races, had, shortly
after his arrival in India, contracted a severe form of
indigestion; probably on account of having been put too
soon on "hard food." I may say, in passing, that when
the mucous membrane—or internal skin, if I may use
the expression—of the intestinal canal gets out of order,
the outer skin, hair, and hoofs of horses and other
animals are very liable to participate in the disturbance,
owing to the parts which secrete these structures being
continuous with each other. Thus we find that a large
dose of aloes may bring on fever in the feet, and cause
the hair of the mane and tail to fall off. Even in our
own cases some trifling error of diet may cause a rash
on the skin. The indigestion from which Speechless
suffered made the condition of his skin so irritable that
the slightest rub caused an ugly sore. This rendered

him predisposed to *bursatee*, a skin disease which appears to be due to a fungus that is prevalent during certain seasons in the plains in India. This parasite, if we admit it to be such, seems to attack abraded surfaces with great facility, unless such parts be kept covered with some dressing which, like carbolized oil, stops vegetable growth. The treatment which is clearly indicated, and which has been successful in the many cases I have seen, is the application of some strong caustic, such as pure carbolic acid, to the surface of the sore, so as to destroy the fungus, and then to prevent the attacks of fresh parasites by using a suitable antiseptic dressing. As I have discussed this disease fully in my "Veterinary Notes for Horse Owners," I need not dwell on it here. As soon as I got Speechless well enough to give him slow work, he sprung a sand-crack, as the horn of his hoofs which had been formed while he was suffering from indigestion, was weak and brittle, for the reasons I have just described. I could do nothing with him that season, for although he recovered his health, and his feet regained their former soundness, there was no time to train him.

As my application to retire from the service was not granted before "The Buffs" left Meerut *en route* for

England, I was obliged to leave the horses behind, and proceed with the regiment down country. I was relieved, however, in a couple of days, and bade a hearty and, I may confess, sad farewell to my brother officers, from whom I was very sorry to part. I hastened back to find that everything had gone wrong in the stable during my short absence. Lady Ald, whom I had kept " dark," in order to affect a surprise at this Meerut Meeting, was so favourably treated in the Arab and Country-bred Handicap that it seemed impossible for her to lose. Just before marching out of the station with my regiment, a few hours before she was to run, I ordered the syce to take her to the stable of a friend, who had also backed her, and had promised to look after her and see to her saddling. The syce, when taking her through the native part of the town, could not resist the attractions of a liquor-shop, and stopped to drink good luck to the mare, with the result that she broke away from him and galloped wildly about the place for a couple of hours. She was caught just in time to have the saddle put on her; and, of course, finished absolutely last, thereby losing me a couple of hundred pounds. She was such an impetuous mare that I knew this knocking about would " throw her back " for some months, so I sold her to Mr. Maitland, who won a good race with her the succeeding spring. Substitute, who ought to have won the steeplechase—as he was, had he kept right, certain to have run far better over the level ground at Meerut than over the hilly course at Dehra—went lame in some unaccountable manner, and also "dropped" our money. I sent him back to his sporting owner, with sincere regret that I had not been able to have won a good stake with him for Mr. McDonnell.

After that I went to the Allahabad Autumn Meeting, but could not get a chance, as the handicappers overrated the form of Czarina and North Star; so I was at my wits' end to think of some means to get back a part of the money I had been out of pocket on account of Mr. Anderson's horses, for the dangers and anxieties of the campaign seemed to have prevented my friend "Joe" answering my letters, let alone sending a cheque for expenses. Luckily, I saw the advertisement of a week's racing which was to be held at Rampore Beauleah, a place far away in the silk districts on the other side of the Ganges, where it was most unlikely that I would find anything good to oppose us. I put the three horses into the train and started off with them, Donaldson the jockey, and the native boy Jutton. After a wearisome journey of over 500 miles we left the railway, as it went no further. Having inquired our way and started our baggage carts and servants, the three of us mounted the horses and pushed forward to the Ganges, which was thirty miles distant, on the chance of obtaining shelter somewhere. Towards evening we arrived in sight of the river, and were rejoiced to see on the bank a large indigo factory. As I rode up to the verandah in front of the door, I was delighted to see Mr. Pope, an old Tirhoot acquaintance of mine, in an easy-chair on the lawn, having his evening pipe and " peg." He gave me a cordial invitation to stay with him, which I accepted with great pleasure. After a day or two's rest, Mr. Pope took my party and the horses in his boat to our destination, which was within a couple of hours' sail.

Rampore Beauleah is the civil station of an extensive district in which there are many silk and indigo factories. It is close to the Ganges, and consists of about a dozen large, solidly-built houses, with a magnificent old mansion which formed the government residency during the Dutch occupation many years ago. The station is delightfully green, and pleasantly wooded. As a large portion of the travelling in the district, especially during

H. H. COOMAR INDRA SINGH, of Paiktara.

the rains, has to be done by water, many of the planters come to this meeting, which is the great annual festival, in their large sailing boats, and sleep in them at night ; while others pitch their tents, or stay with the residents of the station. A considerable number, as well as strangers and chance visitors, stay in the residency, in which there would be ample accommodation for an entire regiment. The general rule is that the married people and ladies live upstairs, and the bachelors and grass widowers on the ground-floor ; though all breakfast, lunch, and dine together at an admirably-arranged mess in the spacious hall. The amateur management is so perfect that I found my mess bill at the end of the week to be but a mere trifle, although we had lavish supplies of all sorts of good things. About sixty gentlemen and twenty ladies generally sat down to table. As we were all met to enjoy ourselves, the time passed but too rapidly away, and the only wonder was that we were able to crowd into the ten days so much sport, dancing, theatricals, eating, drinking, and general jollity.

At first, the local talent were anything but pleased at seeing me appear on the scene with Czarina and North Star, but their fears were allayed and harmony restored on the first day, by the fact of their own crack defeating our mare who was a bit "off" on account of her journey. As I did not back her, this reverse did not affect me much, especially as she came out on the second day and won the principal event of the meeting, and also the handicap. To make things "smooth," I gave her winning mounts to a young planter, Mr. Dickson, who rode her in very good style indeed ; and I presented a piece of jewellery for a quarter of a mile race open to horses nominated by ladies. Of course I allowed Czarina to run, but as she was a slow starter I backed old Nimrod—who, having turned a very bad roarer, had come down to be a hack—as I knew that his shortness of breath could not stop him in two furlongs. He fully justified my confidence, and so pleased was everybody with the sport shown, that no one would bid for the mare when she was put up to auction ; for it was a condition of the meeting that all winners should be sold to the highest bidder over Rs. 1200. North Star also paid his way by winning the two pony races.

After the meeting was over, I stayed with Mr. Gordon, who is the chief silk planter in the district, for a few days at his beautiful place at Surdah, and then sailed down the river towards Calcutta on my way to England, after saying "good-bye" to my many new friends, who had treated me with the warm-hearted hospitality which is always to be found among planters. Had I accepted all the pressing invitations to come and stay that were given to me, I believe I should be in the Beauleah district at the present moment.

This was the last race-meeting in India at which I ran horses.

UNWIN BROTHERS,
PRINTERS,
CHILWORTH AND LONDON.

LIST OF

ILLUSTRATED PUBLICATIONS

BY

W. THACKER & CO.,

87, *NEWGATE STREET, LONDON.*

INDIAN HOUSES:

THACKER, SPINK & CO., CALCUTTA.
THACKER & CO., LIMITED, BOMBAY.

Second Edition, Elegantly Printed and Bound, 16mo.   10s. 6d.

RIDING:
ON THE FLAT AND ACROSS COUNTRY.

A Guide to Practical Horsemanship.

BY CAPT. M. HORACE HAYES.   *With 52 Illustrations.*

REVIEWS OF CAPT. HAYES'
RIDING: ON THE FLAT AND ACROSS COUNTRY.
A Guide to Practical Horsemanship.

Illustrated Sporting and Dramatic News.—"The book is one that no man who has ever sat in a saddle can fail to read with interest."

The Field.—"The general directions are in most cases in accordance with our own opinions ; and Mr. Hayes has supplemented his own experience of race-riding by resorting to Tom Cannon, Fordham, and other well-known jockeys for illustration. 'The Guide' is, on the whole, thoroughly reliable ; and both the illustrations and the printing do credit to the publishers."

The Sporting Life.—"It has, however, been reserved for Captain Hayes to write what in our opinion will be generally accepted as the most comprehensive, enlightened, and 'all round' work on riding, bringing to bear as he does not only his own great experience, but the advice and practice of many of the best recognized horsemen of the period."

Athenæum.—"Is an eminently sensible and useful manual. . . . Is in all respects satisfactory."

Scotsman.—"A thoroughly practical treatise."

Graphic.—"Is as practical as Captain Horace Hayes' 'Veterinary Notes' and 'Guide to Horse Management in India.' Greater praise than this it is impossible to give."

Vanity Fair.—"Three-fourths of those who indulge in what they call riding in Hyde Park would do well to learn this book by heart."

The Queen.—"The chapter devoted to 'ladies' riding' calls for notice in these columns, as in it will be found information of a kind which is frequently asked for, while it is not always easy to point out to the enquirer a trustworthy source from which it may be obtained."

Society.—"The whole book is written in a style eminently suited to the subject."

Bell's Life.—"There is left nothing unsaid in the present publication to ensure a thorough acquaintance with the subject."

Sporting Times.—"'Riding,' we may venture to say, will take its place as a manual for equestrians, and will be equally appreciated by the boy with his first Shetland pony and the practised sportsman of the shires. . . . It is written in an easy, pleasant style ; not too elaborate for the youthful rider, and sufficiently instructive for the practical horseman. We heartily commend it to our readers."

The Standard.—"Captain Hayes having written an able work on the horse and how to treat him, goes on by a course of natural progress to describe how to ride him, and displays in his last book the ability which characterised his previous effort. To possess knowledge and to succeed in imparting it are two different things ; but Captain Hayes is not only master of his subject, but he knows how to aid others in gaining such a mastery as may be obtained by the study of a book."

W. THACKER & CO., LONDON.

Second Edition, in Crown 8vo, Illustrated, 10s. 6d.

VETERINARY NOTES FOR HORSE-OWNERS.

AN EVERY-DAY HORSE BOOK.

By CAPT. M. HORACE HAYES.

OPINIONS OF THE PRESS.

Saturday Review.—"The work is written in a clear and practical way."

The Field.—"Of the many popular veterinary books which have come under our notice, this is certainly one of the most scientific and reliable. The author tells us, in the preface to the first edition, that any merit which the book may

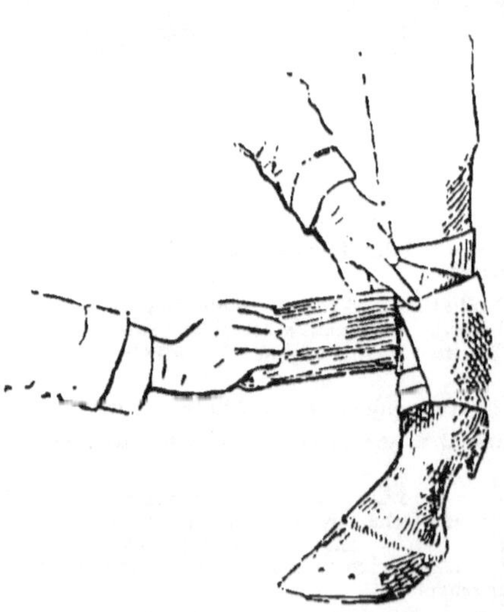

possess is to be ascribed to the teaching of the Principal and Professors of the New Veterinary College at Edinburgh, where he studied. It is much to be desired that every student would make so much use of his opportunities as Capt. Hayes has done.

"Some notice is accorded to nearly all the diseases which are common to horses in this country, and the writer takes advantage of his Indian experience to touch upon several maladies of horses in that country, where veterinary surgeons are few and far between. The description of symptoms and the directions for the application of remedies are given in perfectly plain terms, which the tyro will find no difficulty in comprehending : and, for the purpose of further smoothing his path, a chapter is given on veterinary medicines, their actions, uses, and doses. This information will be most acceptable to the majority of horse-owners, and may be invaluable on an emergency when no advice better than that of the village cow doctor can be obtained."

The Veterinary Journal.—"A handy little book for the use of horse-owners, which may prove of much service to them when they cannot obtain the assistance of a veterinary surgeon, as well as afford them some notion of many of the ailments to which the horse is exposed, and the manner in which they may be best treated."

The Sporting Times.—"It is what it professes to be—a clear and comprehensive manual for all horse-owners, and, without trenching too much

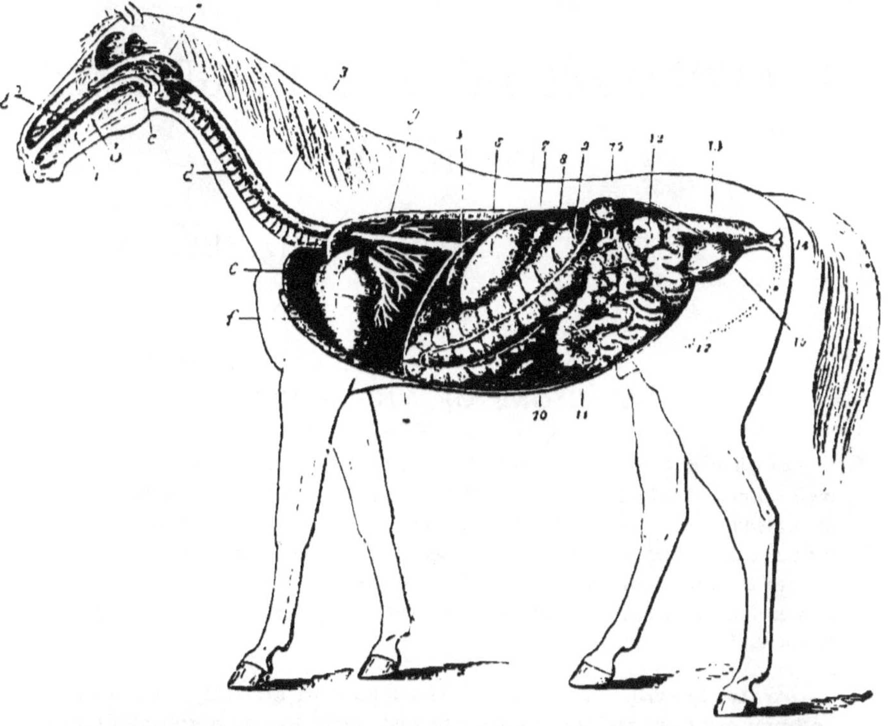

upon the almost sacred mysteries of the veterinary art, it places a valuable weapon of defence in the hands of those who may be out of the reach of professional assistance, and we should be glad to see it as a part of the 'properties' wherever a horse is kept."

Illustrated Sporting and Dramatic News.—"Simplicity is one of the most commendable features in the book. What Captain Hayes has to say he says in plain terms, and the book is a very useful one for everybody who is concerned with horses."

The Sporting Life.—"We heartily welcome the second edition of this exceedingly useful book. The first edition was brought out about two years since, but the work now under notice is fully double the size of its predecessor, and as a matter of course contains more information. Captain Hayes, the author, is not only a practical man in all things connected with the horse, but has also studied his subject from a scientific point of view."

W. THACKER & CO., LONDON.

New Edition. Crown 8vo, price 7s. 6d.

A GUIDE TO

TRAINING AND HORSE MANAGEMENT

IN INDIA.

BY CAPT. M. HORACE HAYES.

OPINIONS OF THE PRESS.

The Pioneer (Allahabad).—"The merits of Captain Hayes' book are so well known to all Anglo-Indians that it would be idle to go over old ground in praising the sound practical knowledge shown by the author in all he writes concerning race-horses. The new edition, however, goes even farther than this, for the subject of horse management is no longer made subservient to training, but is dealt with fully and clearly in separate chapters."

Oriental Sporting Magazine.—"His intentions are truly sportsmanlike and praiseworthy, and if carefully followed ought to ensure the attainment of a portion of that success in training which the author himself has been renowned for."

Englishman (Calcutta).—"It is the practical part of the book with reference to the more ordinary matters connected with horses that makes it so useful."

The Veterinary Journal.—"We entertain a very high opinion of Captain Hayes' book on 'Horse Training and Management in India,' and are of opinion that no better guide could be placed in the hands of either amateur horseman or veterinary surgeon newly arrived in that important division of our empire. We had not the opportunity of seeing the first edition, but from a careful perusal of the present it appears to contain everything pertaining to training and managing horses. The author proves himself to be not only well-informed theoretically and practically, as to preparing horses for racing in that hot climate, as well as to their equipment and handling for ordinary work, but he also shows that he is possessed of no mean amount of that knowledge which is derived from the study of veterinary medicine. His remarks on shoeing are most judicious and sensible, and if his recommendations were adopted and carried into effect, the pernicious farriery of the native shoeing-smiths would be replaced by a method which would greatly benefit horses and their owners.

" Everything relating to racing in India, and the rules of the turf in that country, is embodied in Captain Hayes' book, and not the least valuable portion of it is the Hindustanee vocabulary, containing vernacular terms referring to all matters relating to the horse, as well as diseases, medicine, etc. This alone should make the guide valuable to the young veterinary surgeon, who finds himself compelled to pick up, as best he can, the rudiments of a strange language when he commences his tour of professional duty."

Saturday Review.—" Captain Hayes has brought out a second edition of his work on the training and management of horses in India. It is, of course, specially adapted to the circumstances of that country ; but the general instructions which it contains, and which are of a shrewd and practical character, render it a useful guide in regard to horses anywhere."

Bombay Gazette.—" We have to acknowledge with thanks the receipt of the new edition, re-arranged and much enlarged, of Captain Hayes' very valuable handbook on the above subject. Captain Hayes, by his 'Veterinary Notes for Horse-owners,' as well as the former edition of the work we are now noticing, has already made his name pretty familiar to the lovers of horseflesh in India, and it would therefore be quite superfluous for us to say that he is an authority to whom the horse-owner may safely turn for advice and assistance on every kind of subject connected with the horse and his use.

" Throughout the whole of this valuable contribution to the literature of the horse and his management the author has said his say in a plain, practical manner, yet with a graphic fluency of diction which renders the book quite pleasant reading in comparison to many others of the treatises which have appeared on the same subject."

CAPT. HAYES'
HORSEMAN'S KNIFE.
(REGISTERED.)

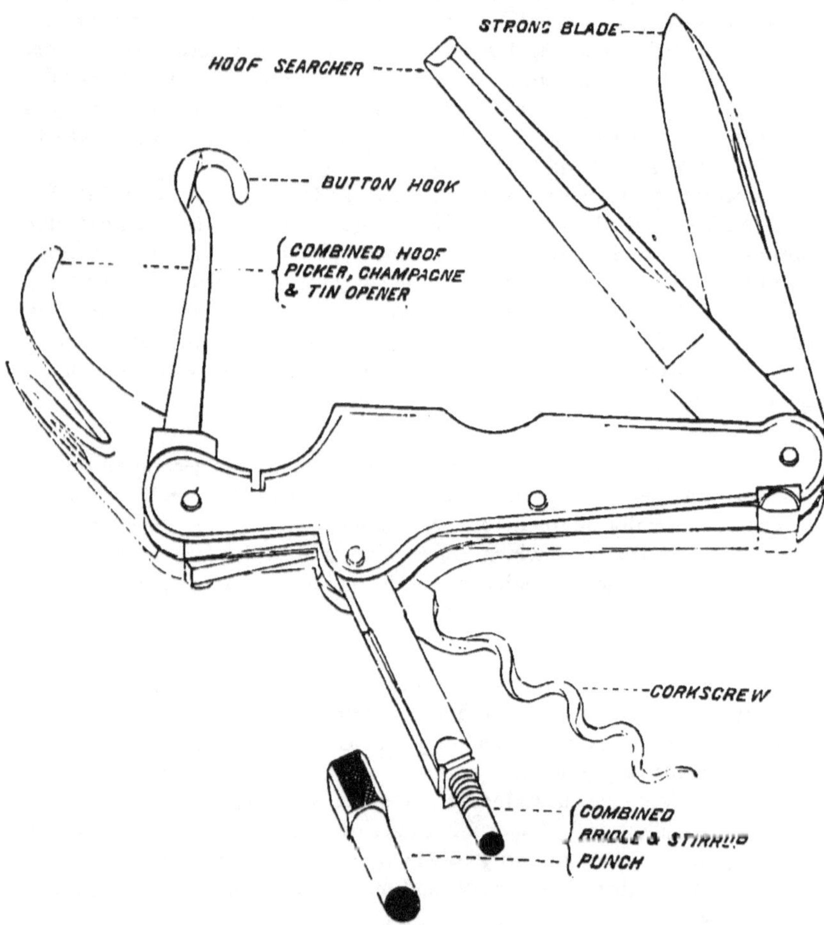

Illustrated Sporting and Dramatic News. — "Unquestionably the most perfect Horseman's Knife ever turned out. To describe all the useful articles which are most conveniently packed away in this ingenious instrument, would be to occupy more space than can be spared."

The Sporting Times. — "The best knife we ever saw."

The World. — "Well deserving of attention."

Baily's Magazine. — "We can speak of it with high praise."

The Knife will be sent post-free on receipt of P.O.O. for £1 by the Manufacturer, Mr. ARCHIBALD YOUNG, 58, North Bridge, Edinburgh, N.B. ; in India, by Messrs. THACKER, SPINK & Co., Calcutta, and Messrs. THACKER & Co., Bombay; at Indian rates.

IN PREPARATION.

Uniform with "Lays of Ind," "Riding," "Hindu Mythology,"
"Handbook of Indian Ferns," &c.

A NATURAL HISTORY

OF THE

MAMMALIA OF INDIA.

BY

R. A. STERNDALE,

AUTHOR OF

"Seonee, or Camp Life on the Satpura Range," "The Denizens of
the Jungles," "The Afghan Knife," &c.

Copiously Illustrated from Original Drawings by the Author and others.

Uniform with " Riding," " Hindu Mythology," &c.

LAYS OF IND. By ALIPH CHEEM.

COMIC, SATIRICAL, AND DESCRIPTIVE

Poems Illustrative of Anglo-Indian Life.

Seventh Edition. Enlarged, 10s. 6d.

REVIEWS OF PREVIOUS EDITIONS.

"This is a remarkably bright little book. 'Aliph Cheem,' supposed to be the *nom de plume* of an officer in the 18th Hussars, is, after his fashion, an Indian Bon Gaultier. In a few of the poems the jokes, turning on local names and customs, are somewhat esoteric; but, taken throughout, the verses are characterized by high animal spirits, great cleverness, and most excellent fooling."—*The World.*

"Aliph Cheem presents us in this volume with some highly amusing ballads and songs, which have already in a former edition warmed the hearts and cheered the lonely hours of many an Anglo-Indian, the pictures being chiefly those of Indian Life. There is no mistaking the humour, and at times, indeed, the fun is both 'fast and furious.' Many portions remind us of the ' Bab Ballads.' One can readily imagine the merriment created round the camp fire by the recitation of ' The Two Thumpers,' which is irresistibly droll. . . . The edition before us is enlarged, and contains illustrations by the author, in addition to which it is beautifully printed and handsomely got up, all which recommendations are sure to make the name of Aliph Cheem more popular in India than ever."—*Liverpool Mercury.*

REVIEWS OF "LAYS OF IND."

"The 'Lays' are not only Anglo-Indian in origin, but out-and-out Anglo-Indian in subject and colour. To one who knows something of life at an Indian 'station' they will be especially amusing. Their exuberant fun at the same time may well attract the attention of the ill-defined individual known as 'the general reader.'"—*Scotsman.*

"To many Anglo-Indians the lively verses of 'Aliph Cheem' must be very well known, while to those who have not yet become acquainted with them we can only say, read them on the first opportunity. To those not familiar with Indian life they may be specially commended for the picture which they give of many of its lighter incidents and conditions, and of several of its ordinary personages. . . . We have read the volume with real pleasure, and we have only to add that it is nicely printed and elegantly finished, and that it has several charming wood-cuts, of which some are by the author, whom Indian gossip, by the way, has identified with Captain Yeldham, of the 18th Hussars."—*Bath Chronicle.*

"Satire of the most amusing and inoffensive kind, humour the most genuine, and pathos the most touching pervade these 'Lays of Ind.' . . . From Indian friends we have heard of the popularity these 'Lays' have obtained in the land where they were written, and we predict for them a popularity equally great at home."—*Monthly Homœopathic Review.*

"Former editions of this entertaining book having been received with great favour by the public and by the press, a new edition has been issued in elegant type and binding. The author, although assuming a *non de plume*, is recognized as a distinguished cavalry officer, possessed of a vivid imagination and a sense of humour amounting sometimes to rollicking and contagious fun. Many of his 'Lays' suggest recollections of some of the best pieces in the 'Ingoldsby Legends,' or in the 'Biglow Papers' of Russell Lowell, while revealing a character of their own. Anglo-Indian terms and usages are skilfully employed, and even what appears to some the uneventful life of a secluded station is made to yield incidents for humorous description."—*Capital and Labour.*

W. THACKER & CO., LONDON.

Uniform with "Riding," "Lays of Ind," &c.

A HANDBOOK TO HINDU MYTHOLOGY:
VEDIC AND PURANIC. By the Rev. W. J. WILKINS, Calcutta. Illustrated with Ninety-seven Engravings from Drawings by Native Artists and others. 10s. 6d.

Double Volume.

A HANDBOOK TO THE FERNS OF BRITISH
INDIA, BURMA, AND THE MALAY ARCHIPELAGO. By Col. R. H. BEDDOME. With 300 Illustrations.

Specially written to meet the wants of non-scientific readers, and to assist visitors to the numerous hill stations of India in the selection and gathering of Ferns.

Fcap. 8vo. Cloth. (Rs. 1-8.)

INDIAN NOTES ABOUT DOGS; THEIR
DISEASES AND TREATMENT. Compiled by Major C———, Author of "Horse Notes."

In Crown 8vo.

MANUAL OF AGRICULTURE FOR INDIA.
By Lieut. F. POGSON, Author of "The Indian Gardener," &c.

"It is written in the form of a Catechism by Mr. Pogson, whose practical knowledge of this subject is a sufficient guarantee for the solid value of his work, while his clear, concise diction and orderly method seem specially fitted for the purpose he has in view."—*Home News.*

In the Press.

TEA PLANTER'S LIFE IN ASSAM. A Description of the Country, European Life in the District, Particulars of Tea Manufacture, &c., &c.

www.ingramcontent.com/pod-product-compliance
Lightning Source LLC
Chambersburg PA
CBHW021727110726
47902CB00005B/1381